COME SEE
THE
FAIR

Also by Gavriel Savit

ANNA AND THE SWALLOW MAN

THE WAY BACK

COME SEE

THE

FAIR

GAVRIEL SAVIT

Alfred A. Knopf

New York

THIS IS A BORZOI BOOK PUBLISHED BY ALFRED A. KNOPF

Visit us on the Web! rhcbooks.com

Educators and librarians, for a variety of teaching tools, visit us at RHTeachersLibrarians.com

Library of Congress Cataloging-in-Publication Data
Names: Savit, Gavriel, author.
Title: Come see the fair / Gavriel Savit.
Description: First edition. | New York : Alfred A. Knopf, 2023. | Audience: Ages 10 and up. | Summary: Twelve-year-old orphan Eva Root travels to the great World's Fair in Chicago where she discovers her magical abilities and becomes entangled in a sinister plan.
Identifiers: LCCN 2022022053 (print) | LCCN 2022022054 (ebook) | ISBN 978-0-593-37866-3 (hardcover) | ISBN 978-0-593-37867-0 (library binding) | ISBN 978-0-593-37868-7 (ebook)
Subjects: CYAC: Orphans—Fiction. | Mediums—Fiction. | Magic—Fiction. | World's Columbian Exposition (1893 : Chicago, Ill.)—Fiction.
Classification: LCC PZ7.1.S28 Co 2023 (print) | LCC PZ7.1.S28 (ebook) | DDC [Fic]—dc23

The text of this book is set in 12.25-point Horley Old Style MT Pro.
Interior design by Jen Valero

Printed in the United States of America
10 9 8 7 6 5 4 3 2 1
First Edition

This book is for anyone
who has ever been Burned.

Strange Fire

MRS. JENNY BLODGETT
presents

THE AMAZING

Little Eva Root

Clairvoyant!

Spirit Medium!

Channeler of the Voices of the Dead!

Her Uncanny Abilities shock the senses!

She brings forth the Messages of the Departed!

Come and see!

Come and See!

COME AND SEE!

During the first week of June 1893, these handbills were unavoidable in the village of Nadab, Ohio. Mailed ahead, they were as common as coal dust by the time Mrs. Blodgett and Little Eva arrived—piled by the door at the Hofmann Emporium, boot-trodden and filthy on the floor of Wilson's Saloon—and wherever Mrs. Blodgett encountered them, she bent to add the following lines:

Wednesday at 8:00
Back room at Wilson's
35¢
Just Like Magic

It began—as everything does—with a spark.

Mrs. Blodgett had started drinking early that day, and her hands shook as she struck at the matchbox: two times, three. A puckered woman on the front bench was fanning herself against the summer heat, and Mrs. Blodgett had to turn her back to the audience for shelter from the breeze.

With a final strike, the match head burst into flame. Glaring over her shoulder, Mrs. Blodgett lit the candle.

The presence of this candle, like so much of the evening, was theatrical: it allowed Little Eva to begin the performance by lifting the light out of the room like a grand curtain.

And séances are always better in the dark.

The truth was that Eva Root had not been particularly little in quite some time. Years before, when Mrs. Blodgett had first trotted her out, the description really had been apt—a tiny seven-year-old, wide-eyed, rosy-cheeked. But she was nearly twice as old now, and the passing days had stretched and sharpened her like the fires of a forge: every day a new town, every night a new bed, and in between, train car after train car after train car. By the time they found themselves in Nadab, they'd given well over a thousand séances in the towns that had budded up from the steel boughs of the railroad—Carthage, Kansas; Finisterre, Iowa; Goshen, Nebraska—and though she no longer had the smoke screen of innocence to hide behind, Eva had learned all she needed to know about passing on the communications of the dead. Which, of course, was impossible.

But all the same—she had a way of making it seem as if it were not.

From the back of the room, Eva considered Nadab's paltry crowd. Not counting herself or Mrs. Blodgett, there were five of them there—more than had been at the smallest séance she'd given, but not by much. They were mostly old, too, which muddied things: the more one lives, the more one loses.

She took a deep breath. It wasn't her favorite trick, but there was always the war to rely on: practically everyone over forty had lost someone who'd served in blue or gray.

Cannon fire, gun smoke, *The Union forever, hurrah! boys, hurrah!* . . . It was going to be that kind of night.

She flexed her fingers.

Someone in the slack, sweating audience let out a little fart, and this seemed to deplete Mrs. Blodgett's already scarce reserves of patience.

"Fine," she said. "Ladies and gentlemen, it is my privilege to present to you Miss Eva Root, a young innocent touched with the power to channel the voices of the dead. Kindly give her your attention, and in return, she will show you things that you never thought possible."

This speech had once been considerably longer—and considerably better—but then Mrs. Blodgett had once cared.

"Eva?"

Five heads swiveled back to stare at her. She stumbled forward.

"There?" she said, blinking at the chair that had clearly been set out for her.

This performance of uncertainty generally made a better impression when Mrs. Blodgett responded in some way, but she had already begun to wobble gently around the room snuffing the gas lamps.

Swallowing, Eva slid into her seat. Soon only the flickering candlelight was left.

"It works better in the dark," she whispered. "Can I . . . ?" and she gestured to the candle.

Her eyes passed slowly over the faces before her. This was the most important part of the evening, this moment of anticipation. She could make all the right guesses, say just the right things, and still, if these people didn't *want* her to do impossible things for them, then she simply couldn't.

The lady on the front bench gave a curt nod—engaged, but not terribly enthusiastic. Three rows behind her, though, was a man with an unkempt beard who smiled kindly.

That was good: a foothold.

Eva pressed her eyes shut, leaned forward, and blew. The candle guttered and died.

Darkness.

Now she began to thicken her breathing with effort.

"I hear thunder," she said. "Men yelling. There's smoke. Fire." She went quiet for a moment. "Is it . . . a storm?"

Somewhere in the room, a chair creaked.

"But there's no rain," she said. "No, not a storm." Another little pause. "Is it thunder? Or . . . ?"

"Cannon," said an eager woman in the third row. "It's cannon."

Eva turned her head immediately. "Yes."

"Was he afraid?" said the eager woman.

To be sure, it would've been kinder to say that whoever this woman was thinking of had died without suffering. But that would've made for a rather duller séance. And besides—the more you agreed with them, Eva found, the more people began to believe you.

She nodded sadly. "There's quite a lot of fear. But gratitude, too. He wants you to know that he thought of you before the end."

"Me?" said the eager woman.

Eva chuckled. "He knew you'd be surprised."

"Oh," said the woman fondly.

Eva didn't know whom they were talking about, of course, but it didn't matter—the woman in front of her did, and her certainty filled in Eva's sketchy outline with a memory so clear it almost seemed to breathe.

That was how it worked.

Eva spent a fair amount of time on the eager woman; she was well disposed to believe, and Eva had a tendency to make her guesses work even when they were a bit wide in their aim. By the time Eva moved on, the woman was sniffling softly: a job well done.

The lady in the front row came next. She was the sort who wanted to be won over—a little reserved, a little skeptical—but Eva, as always, was patient, and mere minutes later, she was forgiving the lady for her unkindness to a niece who (Eva was almost certain) had fallen to her death in a well.

And then, in a flash, everything changed.

Eva had just turned to engage the man with the unkempt beard when, with a spark and a sputter, the dead candle at her elbow flared back to life.

She made a sound somewhere between a gasp and a yell, and was on her feet before she knew it.

"What is it?" said the woman in the front row.

The candle was burning bright, its flame tall and unwavering. Eva wasn't sure what to do. Nothing like this had ever happened before.

"Someone," she said, improvising madly. "Someone is here with us."

And this was truer than she knew.

"Who?" said the woman in the front row. "Who is it?"

Eva turned her eyes back to the audience. The candle flame gave a wobble, sending inky shadows vaulting across the expectant faces.

She still had a performance to give.

"That," said Eva, gesturing with her chin, "is a question for you."

The bearded man frowned. "Me?"

"Yes. Who is it?"

The bearded man took a deep breath and began to speak. Eva barely heard him.

Come see the Fair!

The voice in her head had spoken so loudly that the words of the bearded man had been entirely blotted out.

"What?"

"Why, I said my daddy always—"

Come see the Fair!

Eva gasped. Nearly half her life, Eva had pretended to hear messages that weren't there. Now, all of a sudden, her mind was filled to bursting with an impossible voice.

At the back of the room, Mrs. Blodgett shifted uneasily from foot to foot.

"I—I—I . . . ," Eva stammered. "Who?"

And as if in answer, a rush of sound nearer to her than anything had ever been before overcame her: the tinkle and bray of the band organ, the laughter and chat of the crowd.

An impossible voice, loud and commanding and clear:

Come see the Fair!

"I don't understand," said Eva.

The room was suddenly silent.

It was only a moment before Mrs. Blodgett swept forward, her face twisted with anger.

"I am afraid," she said, "that Little Miss Eva is tired and must withdraw."

There was a hubbub of protestation, but Mrs. Blodgett's voice cut through it sharply.

"Thank you," she said. "*Thank you.* Good night."

And taking Eva roughly by the arm, she seized the candle, blew it out, and marched swiftly from the room.

When she first met Mrs. Blodgett, Eva Root was living in an establishment in Fletcher's Gulch, Indiana, called Miss Augusta Grandage's Home for Unwanted and Destitute Girls.

She had no memory of anything before that place.

The handlers at Grandage's seemed to see themselves rather more as salespeople than caretakers: anything that bred attachment was strenuously discouraged, and the penalties for talking out of turn were severe.

But there were many worse institutions to be in. No one was violent or neglectful. Adoptions were frequent. Miss Augusta was rigorous, but generally benevolent.

When Mrs. Blodgett arrived that day, she asked that the girls be shown to her in a private room, one by one. Most of them were dismissed without a word, but those deemed promising enough to address were offered a single question:

"Do you remember me?"

Mrs. Blodgett had, of course, never before visited Fletcher's Gulch; it would've been impossible, then, for any of the girls to say yes truthfully. Nevertheless, everyone who said no was immediately dismissed.

Eva happened to be one of the last shown into the room that day, and whispered word of what went on there had made its way back to her.

When Mrs. Blodgett asked her question, Eva was prepared.

"Oh, yes," she said. "Of course I remember you."

Mrs. Blodgett's eyes narrowed, and taking sudden inspiration from a painting on the wall, Eva spouted an idyllic story about a picnic in the town square.

It was a complete fabrication—they both knew it. And this was precisely what Mrs. Blodgett had been waiting for: someone to convince her of the impossible.

The expectations were never directly articulated. Instead, Mrs. Blodgett had taken Eva to observe séance after séance, night after night, in town after town, and sometimes at the facilitation of the very same medium.

Slowly, the tricks of the trade became clear—how to sow confidence; how to make the general feel specific; how to leave room for people to fill in their own details—and an audience began to seem to Eva like a craggy rock face, here a handhold, there a ledge.

And then, one night, leaving a little theater somewhere in Pennsylvania, Mrs. Blodgett had spoken.

"He wasn't very good, was he? That medium."

The medium in question had been an old man with gigantic sideburns, and he'd been far too prone to making real, specific guesses.

"No," said Eva. "Not very good at all."

"You'll do better," said Mrs. Blodgett.

The next night, Eva gave her first séance. She, it turned out, had something of a talent, and the people crowded around, wanting, needing, begging for her impossible answers.

They were so grateful. Soon Eva felt quite fond of her audiences.

But a structure built on a lie can only stand for so long. Eva's fondness began to rot into resentment, then disdain, and before she knew it, her disdain had become a dull, tarnished pity.

It was the *need* that made her so sad, the constant need for something that simply wasn't there. And if her audiences went home with the impression that they'd gotten what they paid for, she knew it could not last; in the morning they would wake again as lonesome and grief-stricken as they ever had been.

She was sure of it. She did herself.

Because the need that the people brought to lay at her feet every night was the very same need that Eva carried from town to town, village to village, séance to séance: the need for things to be different—better, brighter— than they were.

And this was why, as Mrs. Blodgett tore her from the saloon in Nadab, Ohio, Eva caught a strange feeling blossoming in her chest—strange, and deeply concerning:

It was hope.

Eva sat in silence, her shoulders high and tight, as if she were waiting to be hit.

No one in the audience at Wilson's had been happy with the early ending of the séance, but Mrs. Blodgett had already arranged for a local drayman to cart them to their accommodations in the next town, and thankfully they were able to leave before anyone asked for their money back.

That was the greatest calamity that Mrs. Blodgett could imagine: paying refunds.

Crickets, hoofbeats, the creak of the cart; it was only once the lights of Nadab were far behind that Mrs. Blodgett took the candle from her bag.

Eva braced herself. Mrs. Blodgett didn't so much have a temper, generally, as the temper had Mrs. Blodgett.

"How did you do it?" she asked.

"I didn't."

Mrs. Blodgett narrowed her eyes. "Don't lie to me, girl."

"I *didn't*," Eva insisted. "Did you?"

"Don't be foolish," said Mrs. Blodgett.

Eva leaned in to get a better look. "Is there anything—?"

Mrs. Blodgett shoved her away. "No," she said. "It's just an ordinary candle," and she tossed it roughly into her bag.

The drayman's lantern swung gently with the gait of his horse.

"Would you care," said Mrs. Blodgett, "to explain that disgraceful display? Gasping and flopping about like a fish."

"I was thrown."

Mrs. Blodgett shook her head. "You're never thrown. What happened?"

Eva took a breath. What could she tell her? What could she say?

Usually, Eva and Mrs. Blodgett ate their supper to-gether after the séance. Tonight, though, Mrs. Blodgett ushered her into their little hotel room without so much as a crust of bread and stood there in the doorway, hands on her hips, just waiting for an objection. Eva stayed quiet—she had no interest in worsening the situation—but her silence only seemed to make Mrs. Blodgett angrier.

"I think," she sniped, "that you ought to sleep on the floor tonight."

In general, where there was only one bed, Eva and Mrs. Blodgett shared. This was no particular plea-sure, but it was certainly more tempting than the rough wooden floor.

"I—"

"Yes," said Mrs. Blodgett. "Sleep on the floor."

The door slammed shut. Eva could hear Mrs. Blodgett turning the key.

With a sigh, she took a stained pillow from the bed and set about trying to make herself comfortable. But even when she'd laid her body down, Eva couldn't seem to bring her mind to rest. How had the candle relit itself? Whose voice had spoken in her mind?

And what *Fair*?

For hours, Eva's grumbling stomach traded cho-ruses with the questions in her mind, and she tossed and turned and tossed again. She only realized that she'd begun to doze when she was woken by the sound of Mrs. Blodgett outside—stumbling drunk, cursing, trying five or six times to fit her key into the lock. Once the woman was inside, Eva heard her rifling through her carpetbag, counting, crinkling cash, and Mrs. Blodgett's footsteps paused as she caught sight of Eva there on the floor.

Hunkh. She hocked up a clod of something and then swallowed it back down. "Idiot child." And ricocheting from wall to wall, she made her way back out of the room.

Eva opened her eyes. Mrs. Blodgett had left the door ajar; a handful of crumpled bills littered the floor. The hallway outside was empty, but nonetheless, Eva crept toward the head of the staircase as softly as she could.

". . . this enough?" Mrs. Blodgett's voice, slurring, overloud, rang out from below.

Instinctively, Eva pressed herself against the wall.

There was a shushing, papery sound—the cash.

A heavy male voice spoke. "This is much less than you said."

"Don't you worry," said Mrs. Blodgett. "Hold up your end of the bargain and there'll be more. Much more."

The man sighed. "Nine o'clock tomorrow morning, then, in front of the train station?"

"Oh, I'll be there," said Mrs. Blodgett.

"And what about your girl?" said the man.

"What about her?"

"She won't come looking for you, will she?"

"Pfff," said Mrs. Blodgett. "That idiot child's never done a single thing without my help."

"And what will you tell her?"

"Tell her? Nothing."

Now there was a tight little pause.

"Don't look at me like that," said Mrs. Blodgett. "Do you keep a horse that can't pull a plow? Do you keep a cow that stops giving milk? I've got my own life to live."

"Of course," said the man. He didn't sound convinced.

"You just keep your end of the deal," said Mrs. Blodgett, "and there'll be twice that much for you when we get to San Francisco."

The sky above, strewn with stars.

The water's whisper at the prow of Eva's boat.

Lights.

Lights in the darkness.

Great white buildings, towers, domes; an unending forest of columns and archways.

Thick flocks, crowds of people, their eyes turned to heaven.

A screech, a bang: colored light drenching the shoulders of the white city.

There was fire in the sky.

She passed beneath a bridge into a wide basin wreathed with palaces and temples. In the distance, a colossal statue rose in golden robes, her head crowned in laurel; Eva could feel her gaze.

Another explosive barrage: fireflowers above.

Come see the Fair!

She leaned forward to see who had spoken, and with a lurch, Eva tumbled from her boat.

She was just about to plunge into the water when she woke.

Light gray morning skulked outside the hotel room window. Eva was on the floor.

At nine o'clock, Mrs. Blodgett intended to abandon her.

Eva had meant to stay awake, to remain vigilant so that Mrs. Blodgett couldn't sneak off in the darkness, but there seemed little danger of that now—there she was, still dressed atop the bedclothes, snoring aggressively.

Slowly, Eva rose.

It was now, she supposed, or never.

And so she shouldered the bag that held her meager

assortment of belongings, and moving as quietly as she could, Eva crossed the floor to Mrs. Blodgett's carpetbag and pulled the handles apart.

There, at the very top of the jumble, was a thick wad of cash.

Eva took a soft, shallow breath. In all their years together, Mrs. Blodgett had never—not once—given her so much as a red cent. Eva had earned that money. And now she would need it.

She was just about to close the bag up again when last night's impossible candle came peeking up out of a snarl of dirty clothes, its scorched wick coiled like a question mark.

The cash felt oddly light, insubstantial between the fingers of her left hand; the candle felt just as solid and heavy in her right.

Mrs. Blodgett snorted and rolled over. Eva's heart surged, and she was out the door before she even realized it.

That was it.

She'd done it.

She'd left.

The thrill in Eva's heart only grew as she made her way down the wooden sidewalk slats. The sun was rising, and everywhere, people were beginning their daily rituals: opening doors, stoking fires, carefully arranging their wares. Everyone else seemed bounded in, cornered by the day ahead of them.

But not Eva.

There was a train waiting when she got to the station, and a pleasant sense of industry—conductors pacing the platform, porters lifting luggage, men and women taking their leave. Only one of the ticketing windows was open at this early hour, and Eva joined the short line, day-dreaming idly of where she might like to go. She hadn't seen much of the East, and she'd spent almost no time in cities.

Boston, maybe? New York?

Eva was next in line when the sun erupted over the roof of the neighboring tavern. Warm light flooded her face, and she smiled, raising her hand to shade her eyes.

Immediately, her gut gave a sickening lurch.

There, coming around the corner, bedraggled and furious, was Mrs. Blodgett, clutching the carpetbag in her hand.

"Next, please!" sang the ticket agent, and Eva hurried to the window.

"I need a ticket," she said frantically. Mrs. Blodgett had turned toward the train station.

"Very well," said the ticket agent. "Where to?"

"All aboard!"

"Where's that train headed?" she said, pointing at the platform.

"Well," said the agent, "to Chicago. But—"

"Good. That's where I'm going."

Mrs. Blodgett was only half a block away now; she'd broken into a run.

"Are you—?" The agent meant to say *sure,* but she cut him off.

"Yes." Eva tossed far too much money onto the counter. The man's eyes widened.

"All aboard!"

"It's yours," she said, "if I'm on that train when it leaves."

The ticket agent bent swiftly to his work. Mrs. Blodgett would be there in less than a minute.

"Hurry," Eva whispered, and just as the station door swung open, the agent held out her ticket.

When it was all said and done, Eva would look back on much of what happened with a heavy heart—unsure where the sweetness ended and the bitterness began. But one memory never failed to bring a smile to her face:

Mrs. Blodgett on the platform, red-faced and ranting, as Eva slid away safe on the train.

It was almost like Magic.

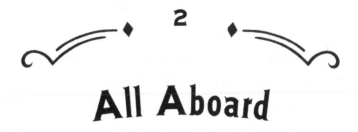

All Aboard

Time passes differently on trains. The world outside is made to stand aside safely behind wide windows; the thrum and huff of the engine is as hypnotic as rain on the roof.

Moments become minutes. Hours become days.

The train was crowded, and Eva paced up and down the aisle, carefully evaluating her seating options. Finally, she chose a place opposite a boy in white linen also traveling alone. He was busy sketching in a thick brown book, lank hair fallen in front of his eyes. He didn't look up.

Eva took him in quickly, just as she might've at a séance: a year older than she, maybe two. He drew in charcoal, his fingers absolutely thick with the stuff, but he was well practiced, his cuffs and shirtsleeves spotless. There was something extreme, almost dire, in his concentration, like there might be terrible consequences if he let his charcoal make a false mark.

The set of his lips somehow made her sad.

The train ran on; the boy continued to draw. By and by, the conductor came along to tear her ticket.

The boy spent some time searching for a particular stick of charcoal in his things and then returned to his drawing. Still, he did not look up.

The long shadow of the train shortened as the sun climbed through the sky. Noon passed. Sunlight began to shine in through the window. The drawing boy tipped his notebook to take advantage of the shifting light, and Eva's eye was pulled down onto the page in front of him.

She gasped.

Great buildings, towers, domes; an unending forest of columns and archways. It was the white city from her dream.

"That place you're drawing," said Eva. "Where is that?"

The boy looked up with a start. Slowly, as he stared, his eyes grew wide.

"What? What is it?" said Eva, patting at herself in alarm.

In answer, the boy began to flip back in his notebook.

"I drew this," he said, "about a week ago," and finding his page, he turned the sketchbook outward.

It was she. And she hadn't worn her hair that way in—well, in about a week.

Eva lifted her eyes from the notebook.

The boy stared straight back.

"Who are you?" they said, almost together.

After a long moment of wobbly silence, Eva said, "I'm Eva Root."

"And who's that?" asked the boy, as if he expected her to say something like *a fairy princess* or *the queen of England.*

Eva shrugged. "Well, who are *you?*"

"Oh," said the boy. "I'm Henry. Henry Poole."

"All right, Henry Poole," said Eva. "Why have you been drawing me?"

Henry's cheeks colored. "Well, honestly," he said, "I didn't know."

"Didn't know what?"

"That it was you."

Eva gave her head a gentle shake, trying to tumble this idea into place. "You expect me to believe that you drew that picture a week ago without even knowing that it was me?"

Henry frowned. "I don't think I expect anything. Here: Where were you last week?"

Eva scrunched up her brows and thought. "Michigan."

Henry nodded. "I was in Philadelphia. I'm almost always in Philadelphia."

Again, Eva shook her head. "But I've never been to Philadelphia."

Henry tipped his head as if to say, *You see?* He shut his notebook. "Maybe I should explain."

"Yes," said Eva. "I think you probably should."

"I'm not supposed to draw. Or, at least, not as much as I do. My father—have you heard of him?"

Eva raised her eyebrows. "I don't know."

"Oh," said Henry. "His name is Hiram? Hiram Poole?"

Eva had not heard of him.

"He's an attorney. In Philadelphia. People know him. Anyhow, he doesn't think drawing is a suitable use of a young man's time. He says art is for women and Italians."

This was ridiculous, but it didn't seem to amuse Henry one bit.

"I have to hide it," said Henry. "I can't let him see me draw. Or anyone who might talk to him. Which is a lot of people. So mostly, I draw from memory and after dark. I like to use a gas lamp because the light is steadier, but I think Father's been catching on—he's started keeping them in his study, and I have to go in and ask, and then he wants to know what I'm doing. He can always tell when I'm lying. It's no good.

"So perhaps a week and a half ago, I shut myself in my room to draw after supper. I took a candle because, well, the light isn't always steady, but it's better than nothing, and it's *certainly* better than asking my father for a lamp.

I was just about to settle in and begin drawing, but I had to use the, um . . ." Henry's cheeks grew pink again. "I had to use the necessary. And when I came back, the candle was already burning. I didn't think much of it then—maybe the chambermaid lit it—but when I sat down, the paper looked different in the candlelight."

"Different?" said Eva. "What do you mean?"

"It looked," said Henry, flipping back in his sketchbook, "like this."

He held the book up again to reveal a wide panorama.

"That was already drawn?" said Eva.

"No, no," said Henry. "I drew it after. But that night, it was like the candlelight was helping—giving me hints." Now Henry turned the book around to look at his drawing. "I never used to draw buildings. The line has to be so straight, and the perspective is so, so rigorous. . . ."

Eva cleared her throat. "And what about me?"

"Hmm?" Henry looked up. "Oh, yes. Well, it didn't stop. The next day, there was just so much more I needed to draw. Buildings, yes, but machines, too, flowers, ships, statues, guns, vases, furniture—everything. And you."

Eva's cheeks suddenly felt very warm.

"It's not like drawing from memory," said Henry. "Or even from imagination—I'm not moving things from my mind onto the paper. It's like I'm trying to pin something down that's floating between the page and me. Like it's inside the light. Do you understand?"

Eva wasn't sure.

"Anyhow, this went on and on, and eventually I couldn't take it anymore. I wanted to know what I was drawing. For a whole day, I sat looking in the library. I thought for sure it would be Europe: Venice, maybe, somewhere in Italy. I knew it must exist somewhere outside of my head, but I just couldn't find it. I was frantic. So I started showing people, asking if anyone recognized the buildings. Finally, a watch salesman out-side of McGinty's said it was the Columbian Exposi-tion."

"Columbian what?"

Henry nodded. "Exposition. But everyone I've talked to just calls it the World's Fair."

Deep in Eva's mind, something blossomed like a fire-flower.

"Fortunately," said Henry, "my aunt and uncle live out in Chicago, and when I telegraphed, they invited me to come see the Fair."

Come see the Fair.

This caught Eva's attention. "What did you say?"

"The Fair," said Henry, frowning. "The Chicago World's Fair. Are you all right? You look as if you've seen a ghost."

And she felt like it, too.

"Would you believe me," said Eva, "if I told you that the same thing had happened to me?"

Henry blinked. "What?"

He watched her carefully as she spoke—the sud-den spark of the candle, the summons in her mind. Eva could almost feel his attention: warm, like a sunny spring breeze in a room too long shut up.

What she said was true, if decidedly incomplete—she couldn't quite work out how to tell him about her séances without admitting to fraud—and now, in the little silence that settled between them, she found herself desperate for Henry to believe her.

"Yes," he said. "Yes, it *is* the same, isn't it? The candle and the Fair?"

Eva nodded eagerly.

"What do you think it means?" she said.

Henry sighed. "I don't quite know. But one thing is clear enough."

"What's that?"

"We've got to see the Fair together," said Henry. "Where will you stay in Chicago?"

Eva hadn't even considered this. "Oh," she said. "I'll find a hotel room."

"A hotel room?" said Henry. "But what about your parents? Where are they?"

Eva opened her mouth to answer and shut it again quickly. What could she say? She didn't even know enough about parents to invent a plausible lie. "I d-d-don't, uh, I d-don't . . ."

"Oh." Henry seemed to understand her stammering better than anything she could've said directly, and once more, he blushed. "I'm sorry. I didn't mean to . . . Well, if you'd like to come and stay with us, I'm sure my aunt and uncle would be happy to have you."

"Really?" This seemed incredible to Eva. She'd slept

in many, many beds in her life, but none of them had ever come free. "Are you sure?"

But Henry had no doubts. "There's always more than enough room in their house. They love to have company." He lowered his voice to a conspiratorial whisper. "And they don't have any children of their own, so they let me come and go as I please, like an adult. It's *tremendous*."

Henry's aunt, Mrs. Isabella Overstreet, was lovely. She was there, apple-cheeked and waiting on the steamy platform at Central Station, when they arrived, and she smiled with genuine warmth when Henry introduced her to Eva.

"She was going to look for a hotel room," said Henry. "But—"

"Why, of course you must stay!" said Aunt Isabella, handing Eva's small bag to her coachman. "Any friend of Henry's is a friend of ours."

Eva had never really had a friend before. The closest thing in her experience was Mrs. Blodgett.

This was so much better.

As the coach jostled south along State Street, she braced herself to dodge Aunt Isabella's polite inquiries—

where was Eva coming from? who were her parents? what had brought her to Chicago?—but they never came.

At first, Eva was surprised at this; she could see Aunt Isabella thinking, noticing, wondering. But Henry and his aunt were well-to-do, and in their circles, the proper introduction entitled a person to certain dignities and comforts. Aunt Isabella didn't want to say anything that might lead to embarrassment, and so she kept her questions to herself.

Slowly, Eva felt her graciousness descend like a warm, soft stole.

Slowly, she began to feel welcome.

Soon Henry and his aunt fell into an easy chatting rhythm, gossiping about family, sharing the news. Eva's eyes, however, were irresistibly drawn to the window: just outside the coach, the great machine of the city was champing at the bit.

"Eva," said Aunt Isabella, and Eva looked up with a start. "Have you ever been in Chicago before?"

Eva shook her head. "Never."

Aunt Isabella smiled and called out to the coachman. "Willie?" she said. "Let's take our guest through the Loop."

The Loop, Chicago's beating heart, seemed to Eva like a bird's nest built in a steam engine. She'd never seen anything like it—industry everywhere, smokestacks, workshops, gas lamps, construction, a roaring torrent of shirtwaists and dented lunch pails. Trolley cars thundered down the riven, dusty streets, coaches and drays and omnibuses on every side, and far above it all, the sun lurked, sullen and belligerent, behind a thick veil of soot.

It was filthy and rusty and thrumming and dense. It smelled like oil and hot iron. Eva could not bear to look away.

"It's s-s-so . . . ," she stammered, and Aunt Isabella smiled.

"Yes," she said, "Chicago is very different from Philadelphia, I think. We were a much younger city even before the fire, and now—"

"The fire?"

Of everything they discussed that day, this question alone seemed to leave a scuff on the surface of Aunt Isabella's good cheer. "Twenty-two years ago. Nearly destroyed the entire city. But we are resilient in Chicago—we build back again. That is why everything here is so new, so modern. And I daresay that is why the Fair is so fantastic, really—we have practice in making cities."

And what a city they had made out of the ashes of the Great Fire: buildings rose up in orderly rows on all sides, massive, almost incomprehensibly tall, like ranks of giant teeth. It was only when the traffic ground to a halt that Eva saw what had been caught between them—there, shoved off into an alleyway, was the mottled corpse of a draft horse, its skull, oddly clean and white, peering out through the open flesh of its cheek.

It was sick and it was intoxicating.

Eva needed air.

"Willie," said Aunt Isabella. "That's enough of the Loop, I think." She leaned forward and patted Eva's knee. "It can all be a bit much at first."

But Lake Michigan was only blocks away, and the water, steely blue that afternoon, stretched out as far as Eva's eye could see. Scow schooners dotted the harbor, flitting between the steamboats and freighters like white-winged doves, and the breeze blew gently, rinsing away the musty fug of the Loop.

Eva let out a sigh. She had never seen so very much water. It seemed to go on forever.

"There," said Aunt Isabella. "That's better."

Mr. and Mrs. Overstreet's Prairie Avenue home was not far south, but when they arrived, Eva felt as if they were in an entirely different world. Here, the broad street was lined with trees and stately homes, and everywhere the pace was unhurried and leisurely. Mr. Jefferson Overstreet had come home not long before them, and he laid his newspaper aside with genuine interest as his wife presented Miss Eva Root.

It was only when Uncle Jefferson finished his bright and unqualified welcome that Eva realized she'd been waiting for someone to correct the mistake: she surely did not belong here, in this gleaming mansion of marble and stained glass. Surely, someone would object.

But no one did. And soon there was no denying it: Eva was a guest of the house. The chambermaids rushed off to prepare her room, and Eva took her place upon the settee.

Henry was eager to get to the fairgrounds directly, and as soon as it was at all mannerly to do so, he asked when they might go.

"Oh goodness," said Uncle Jefferson. "Not until morning, I shouldn't think. If you went now, you'd only have to turn around and come back for supper, and I imagine you'll want as much time as you can get. It really is spectacular."

"Yes," said Aunt Isabella. "A marvel."

After a short and pleasant conversation, Eva was shown to her room, an almost implausibly large space studded with comfort: overstuffed armchairs, fat feather pillows, and a great brass bedstead that shone as if it had never been touched. Iris, the chambermaid, had hung Eva's little bag neatly from the back of a chair, and she explained that if Eva wanted to change for dinner like the others (Eva had only two dresses, one of which she was wearing and neither of which was particularly clean), then they would be happy to launder what she had on now.

Eva could hardly believe her luck.

Dinner was bright and beautiful and delicious: consommé and whitefish and roast spring lamb. Eva couldn't remember when she had ever eaten so well—or so much—and though she was full enough that she thought she might burst, she couldn't stop herself from taking a second slice of custard pie.

"I think you shall find the Fair well worth the trip from Philadelphia," said Uncle Jefferson. "If I didn't have the trouble of work to see to, I imagine I'd be out there with you myself."

Aunt Isabella nodded. "I simply can't wait to hear what you think. Willie will take you in the morning and pick you up in time for supper, but you must promise to stay together—the fairgrounds are quite large, and it would be all too easy to get lost."

"Quite right," said Uncle Jefferson. "But whatever you do, you mustn't miss the—"

With a flurry of shushing, Aunt Isabella quieted her husband. "Don't spoil it for them, now. I want to hear their honest opinions."

After they ate, Henry taught Eva a new card game on the drawing room floor, and they laughed and slapped their palms across the tricks faster and faster until it was suddenly very late.

"Dear me," said Aunt Isabella with a yawn. "You ought to be headed for bed if you want to make a good start tomorrow," and they all climbed the stairs together.

Henry's room was just down the hall from Eva's, and they paused to say goodnight outside her open door. At first, Eva was embarrassed, thinking that she'd inadvertently left the bed in an untidy state, but Henry explained that Iris had simply turned down the linen to prepare the bed for sleep.

Not twenty-four hours earlier, Eva had been huddled in a corner with a stained pillow on the hard wooden floor. Now there was a whole person whose job it was to make her comfortable.

She was searching for the words to thank Henry—for his kindness, for his trust—when she caught a strange look on his face.

"What?" she said. "What is it?"

"Your hair," said Henry, his eyes narrowing. "It's different than I thought. I have to draw you again."

Eva's cheeks were still burning when she shut her bedroom door. She was used to being looked at—every night before a paying crowd.

What she was unused to was being seen.

It was a moment, in the morning, before Eva remembered where she was. Iris had slipped in to open the drapes, and now Eva lay in the sun-warmed cloud of her bed, walking back through the previous day like a hazy dream.

All her life, she'd lived with the orphan's quiet question—what was it like to have a family? what was it like to be at home?—and in the blinking of an eye, she'd seen what the answer must look like.

It wasn't the same, of course—not the same at all. Aunt Isabella wasn't her mother, Uncle Jefferson wasn't her father, and Overstreet House wasn't her home. But if she closed her eyes and concentrated, she thought she just might begin to understand: a feeling of warmth, of care, if not quite of belonging.

Overstreet House was a tinkling tune played on the same piano as Home.

But Eva could linger only so long in this fantasy. There, just across the room, slung over the back of a chair, was her little bag, and she could tell just by looking where the candle taken from Mrs. Blodgett was nestled inside of it.

It was this candle—and its mysterious summons—that got her up out of her bed.

It didn't take long for Eva to see that Henry had woken with much the same impulse—he was up and dressed at the foot of the stairs, and there was a broad smile on his face.

"Ready?"

Eva nodded.

The carriage was waiting outside. Sadie, the cook, had prepared bacon sandwiches for them to eat on the way, and for much of the trip, Henry and Eva sat chewing in silence.

After dinner last night, there had been some conversation about where it would be best to enter the fairgrounds. Uncle Jefferson thought there was no more magnificent approach than by water, and Aunt Isabella hadn't disagreed: for splendor, there was nothing like the steamboats. But for the routing—for the best possible path—she insisted that the Sixty-Fourth Street gateway, near the Court of Honor, was superior.

It was beside this entrance, then, that Willie reined in his team.

Inside the echoing archways, the turnstiles whirred and snapped.

The World's Columbian Exposition was the greatest festival ever mounted. Covering nearly seven hundred acres on the Lake Michigan shorefront, it featured over two hundred splendid buildings that together rivaled the grandeur of any others in the world. One of these, the Manufactures and Liberal Arts Building, was the largest structure in all the world. Even the ground on which the Fair was set had been designed—drained, carved, cultivated. Months before, it had only been swamp; now there were broad lagoons and stately canals crowded thick with gondolas, passenger launches, square-rigged caravels, even a replica of a sturdy Viking longship.

And this was just the setting.

There was so much to see and do that weeklong, book-length itineraries were published touching only on the highlights of the Fair. Eighty-six countries from across the world participated, contributing over sixty-five thousand exhibits so varied and far-reaching that scarcely any aspect of human endeavor remained beyond their scope.

There were restaurants, cafés, bandstands. There were buildings representing each state and territory in America, as well as over a dozen erected to represent foreign countries.

There was a choral hall where an ensemble of twenty-five hundred singers performed; there were instruments that had belonged to Bach, Mozart, Haydn, Beethoven; there was even a life-sized sculpture of a knight on horseback made entirely out of prunes.

It was as if the whole world had been boiled down to

a rich, intoxicating concentrate, and for the price of fifty cents, Henry and Eva were allowed to drink up as much of it as they could possibly take.

Henry led the way, practically bursting through the turnstile.

"Come on," he said. "The Court of Honor should be just over here."

On their right, the Terminal Station, end point of ten, twenty, thirty-five tracks, bled more and more fairgoers into the exposition. The crowds grew thick around the ankles of the golden-domed Administration Building, and Eva felt Henry's warm fingers twine into her own, tethering them together in the press of bodies, pulling her forward.

If the Fair were a palace—which, in a certain sense, it was—then the Court of Honor would've been its great hall. If the Fair were a temple—which, in another sense, it was—then the Court of Honor would've been its altar.

Side by side, Henry and Eva stumbled to a halt.

"Oh," said Eva. "Oh my."

Great white buildings, towers, domes; an unending forest of columns and archways: the Court of Honor.

A massive basin of water stretched far off into the distance, the spotless blue sky glimmering glorious on its surface. At the far end, there was a golden colossus—the

Statue of the Republic, crowned in glory—and for just a moment, Eva thought perhaps it had smiled at her.

This place was a miracle.

Thrilling, they plunged forward. They wanted to see everything, but there was just so much, and they couldn't move nearly as quickly as they'd have liked with their heads craned back to take in all the sights. Here was the huge Agriculture Building, nearly ten acres in area, where Henry named the characters of classical myth in the statuary like relatives in a photograph: Ceres in her lion-drawn chariot; Diana the huntress, bow in hand. There was the massive Peristyle, a double rank of monumental columns pierced by a triumphal arch through which boats could pass between the Grand Basin and the lake. Far, far above, at the very height of the arch, there were letters spelling out a motto, and Eva stopped to read it aloud:

"Ye shall know the truth," she said, "and the truth shall make you free."

But Henry's head was lifted in another direction.

"Chocolate," he said. "I smell chocolate."

It was on the far side of the Grand Basin that they found the origin of this aroma: Walter Baker & Company's Cocoa and Chocolate Pavilion, a dainty construction of arcs and awnings. The drinking chocolate sold there was absolutely delicious—somehow even better than the aroma had advertised—and once they'd finished, Henry looked first to the milky brown bottom of his cup, then to Eva, as if he couldn't quite understand how it was gone. They left laughing, licking their chops; somewhere, a brass band was playing a bright march, and it quickened their step, driving them forward into the neighboring exhibition hall.

The aisles of the Manufactures and Liberal Arts Building were laid out like broad city streets and lit with ornamental streetlamps. Five enormous chandeliers, each seventy-five feet in diameter and the largest that had ever been made, hung up above, and the displays were arrayed in elaborate showcases the size of mansions—ninety and a hundred feet tall, built of wrought iron and marble and oak.

Aunt Isabella had been right. It was just like a city.

"Where do you want to go first?" said Eva, but this was like asking which part of the ocean one wanted to get wet in—all they could do was wade in.

Everything in the world seemed to be here. Henry was marveling at tiger skins and elephant tusks when Eva pulled him away to stumble through the splendid reproduction of the salon of Louis XIV. Then there were the *gugunbok*—colorful Korean military uniforms—which gave way to a display showing millions of dollars' worth of gold and jewelry. There were sacred geese of Ceylon carved in rare wood and a model of a steam locomotive made of silken thread—more and more and more and more. At the very center of the building stood a tall clock tower, and Eva heard its bells chiming several times, but she could never tell the hour inside that huge pavilion: time itself seeming to dawdle, even to stop now and again to gaze in amazement at the assembled wonders. The quiet conversation of all the gawking fairgoers floated up toward the high ceiling, and out of the swirling hubbub, Eva imagined she heard a single voice emerging.

Come, it whispered. *Come and see!*

Eva was surprised that she could not recall when she had separated from Henry, but in the moment, it seemed natural enough. After a while, there was a numbing effect to all the stuff of that great pavilion, sight after sight clamoring for her attention. She'd simply wandered on, following her interest from display to display, until she looked up—hours, perhaps days, after entering—and found herself alone.

All the same, she shivered when she realized. Aunt Isabella had said they should stay together.

"Henry?" she murmured.

Eva could hear the sounds of others high up in the

echoing air—footfalls, the occasional word—but no-where around her could anyone be seen.

Here: a narrow little alley. She could turn along it now, and it would surely lead to a larger thoroughfare or out to the edge of the building. If she could only get her bearings . . .

Eva turned.

At the alleyway's end, there was neither an open aisle nor a wall, only an empty exhibition stall flanked by a pair of copper lions, streaky and green with age: the first, on the left, tall and attentive; the second, on her right, sprawled out flat.

Between them, there was darkness.

Eva squinted, peering into the gloom. A warm breeze shifted before her, and deep in the dim, she heard a distinct rustling.

The darkness didn't seem to be empty.

"Hello?"

Eva's voice didn't behave as she expected; it disappeared from her lips without a hint of an echo.

This was strange.

What was out there, between the lions?

Softly, the memory of an impossible voice thrummed through the darkness.

Come.

Eva stepped forward.

The grass was thick here, tangled and tall, and it took real effort to raise her foot with each step. Eva found herself exhausted, footsore, her throat so parched that she thought it might simply fuse shut.

The sun blazed down from above, soaking her collar in sweat. If only she could have a reprieve from the heat . . .

In the root of Eva's mind, something rebelled. Was there supposed to be grass here? Had she been out in the sun a moment ago?

But Eva was walking toward something very powerful indeed, and as soon as these doubts arose, they curled, blackened, and blew away like dry leaves on a hot fire.

Not far across the grass, she saw a double avenue of low, stocky trees.

Shade. Blessed, blessed shade.

It was just a short trot and Eva was there, spilling herself out along the ground. The breeze stirred the branches above her, scattering the crystalline sunshine, and the sweat began to cool upon her brow.

Gently, Eva flexed and stretched her aching feet. Her mind was as hazy as the sun-scorched air—where was she going? from where had she come?—and just as she began to pick at the scabby surface of her memory, an aroma, rich and thick, reached her nose.

There were peaches above her, slung amongst the leaves—ripe, juicy peaches.

Lunging up and tugging softly, Eva pulled a peach from its place. The fruit was heavy in her hand, the color of sundown, and her teeth tore into its yielding flesh, the sweet juice filling her mouth and running down her wrist. Far, far too soon only the little pit was left in her hand.

Eva sat back and sighed. She had never tasted anything so good before, so perfectly sweet and juicy—like a star made flesh.

The breeze shifted, rustling through the bright green spearhead leaves.

Now Eva raised her eyes to the field beyond the trees, and quite by accident, she saw the great house, its roof a mountain range of steeply pitched gables. A cascade of porches clung to its side, all spindly balustrades and lacy spandrils, and a gauzy white curtain billowed from an open window.

She knew that house, didn't she? It felt terribly familiar, as if she could navigate it in her sleep, but she didn't think she'd ever seen it before: it was vast and rambling, somehow larger than her gaze could take in all at once, and when she looked away, its details seemed to slip from her mind.

She had just planted the heel of her hand in the grass

to rise and look closer when a voice came cutting through the trees.

"Eva?"

It was Henry.

He had to see this: this house—these peaches.

"Henry?"

"Eva!"

She got up and trotted back, her eyes scanning the sun-drenched grass, but the moment she passed through the last two trees—rooted in their place like a pair of copper lions—the light shifted harshly.

Suddenly, things were just as they had always been.

She was in a narrow alleyway deep in the Manufactures and Liberal Arts Building. There was no sun above her, just five enormous chandeliers.

"Eva," said Henry, ambling up the alley. "There you are."

Eva was confused. She had meant to tell Henry—to show him . . . something.

There had been Something. But now there was Not.

"I think we ought to stay together," said Henry. "The fairgrounds are so big. We might never find each other again."

Eva, distracted, gave a vague nod.

"All right," said Henry. "It's past noon. Shall we get some lunch?"

Eva agreed, and before she knew it, Henry had led her out through the northern exit into the shining summer sun.

This reminded her of something, but she couldn't quite say what.

"I'm starving," said Henry. "What do you want to eat?"

Eva shrugged and let Henry choose; she found with some surprise that she wasn't hungry at all. In fact, she was completely full.

Her fingers were sticky; she couldn't stop smiling.

And she didn't know why.

Henry spent the rest of the afternoon dashing from structure to structure, and Eva trailed behind: it was all impressive, all beautiful, without question. But it wasn't impossible.

And even the warmth of Overstreet House failed to delight her that evening: at dinner she still had no appetite, and when the flow of pleasant conversation came around to her, she didn't know what to say.

"And you, Eva?" said Uncle Jefferson. "What did you like best?"

Henry's answer to this question had been long, overflowing with passion and observation, but Eva could only think of a certain quality of sunlight, thick as honey, sweet as peach nectar.

"Oh," she said. "Oh, it was all so wonderful."

Eva didn't linger downstairs after dinner. She and Henry were planning to go back again tomorrow, and she couldn't seem to focus on the conversation: something tugged at her attention, flitting in and out of the corner of her mind's eye. Perhaps if she lay down and closed her eyes, she thought, she might be able to put her finger on it. It had the feeling of a dream, what she had seen that day.

But Eva didn't have to wait for sleep—it came tumbling out from her skirts as she prepared for bed, small and hard and tawny, all wrinkling and ribbing, clattering across the polished wooden floor.

A peach pit.

And as soon as her eyes fell upon it, she knew:

There was a place, a place behind the Fair, where, out of the tangled grass, the sweetest peaches grew. And there was a house there: a great and rambling edifice.

Tomorrow she would go to that house and she would pick another peach and she would walk the halls and eat it and see what other wonders might come sprouting up in that place.

It felt familiar: warm and strange all at once.

And she wanted to know why.

Eva found that she was on the floor. The peach pit was in her hand, and she was squeezing it tight, its mottled edges cutting into her palm. But she relished the discomfort—the assurance of what had been:

Yielding flesh; yellow, rusty red, dusky purple.

She wished she had it to eat again.

And all of a sudden, the space between her fingers began to swell and push outward. Eva's eyes were wide.

Her wish had been answered, the peach returning to its pit, growing back, ripening around the stone—hard and small and green, and then larger, softer, heavier, spreading her fingers gently until, finally, there it was, resurrected, as fresh as if it had just been plucked from the tree.

Eva lifted the peach to her nose, the fuzz on its sun-warm skin brushing against her lips.

It smelled exactly as good as she *hadn't* remembered.

Eva began to chuckle, then to laugh and weep.

No one can deny the Magic that happens in their own hand.

Root and Poole

Eva tore open her bedroom door and raced down the hall.

Henry had to see.

With trembling hands, she knocked at his door, once, twice, three times.

"Goodness," said Henry, tying up his dressing gown. "What's the matter?"

Eva chuckled and raised the peach.

Henry looked down at it and back up at her without the slightest comprehension.

It was only then that Eva realized she couldn't possibly say anything that would communicate what she had experienced. But here she was. And she had to say something.

"I just . . . ," she murmured. "I had a great time today."

"Oh," said Henry. "Oh, good. Truly. I was beginning to wonder."

Eva swallowed a grin as she played it all back in her mind: the gentle breeze in the leaves, the peach juice dripping down her wrist—*great* scarcely even touched it.

"Good night, Eva," said Henry as she turned back toward the hall.

"Good night," she answered, and almost as an afterthought, Henry's door half-shut, she added, "Henry?"

"Yes?"

"I'm going to show you something tomorrow. At the fairgrounds."

"All right."

He didn't seem to understand, and that was just as well. She couldn't imagine how he possibly could until he'd seen it for himself.

In the morning, it was Eva who waited at the foot of the stairs for Henry, Eva who led the way out the door to the carriage. When they reached the Fair, Willie stopped to double-check that they had money for lunch and admission, that they would meet him back at the gate at four o'clock as planned, but only Henry was left behind to agree; Eva was already halfway through the turnstiles.

Once they were inside, Eva drew Henry on and on, past the Terminal Station, past the Mines and Electricity Buildings, across the North Canal Bridge. Henry was talking, asking questions—where were they going? what did she want him to see?—but Eva kept her eyes fixed forward, drawing him ahead until they reached the entrance of the Manufactures and Liberal Arts Building.

"Eva," said Henry. "What's going on?"

"I told you I had something to show you."

"Yes," he said. "But can't you tell me what it is?"

Eva's cheeks ached; she'd been smiling as broadly as her muscles would allow since the fairgrounds had come into sight.

"No," she said. "I can't. Come and see."

Now Eva plunged through the southern door of Manufactures and Liberal Arts, barely waiting for Henry to keep pace. Onward she led, farther up and farther in, weaving to and fro amongst the fairgoers. She turned sharply when she reached the avenue that divided the Austrian and Japanese sections, casting an eye back as she went to be sure that Henry saw.

Yes—this was where she'd been.

Before long, she'd found the little alley, and her feet slowed as she began to approach its end.

Her heart was pounding.

"Eva!" She heard Henry panting behind her. "Eva, slow down!"

But there was something wrong.

The lions were gone.

Henry saw her expression as he drew up beside her. "What is it?" he said.

"It—it—it . . . ," stammered Eva. "It was right here. . . ."

"What was?" said Henry.

"The—the . . . ," said Eva. "I—I . . . ," and she darted forward into the empty stall.

No grass beneath her feet, no sun above her head. She went all the way in, pressing her palms against the wood paneling on the back of the neighboring showcase.

There was nothing there.

"Eva?"

What had happened? Had she imagined it all? But she knew that she hadn't—even now the impossible peach was in her bag, carefully wrapped in cotton to keep its tender flesh from bruising.

"I don't understand," said Eva. "It was right here."

Henry laid a gentle hand on her shoulder. "I'm sorry," he said. "Maybe you could just describe it? Whatever it was?"

Eva sighed. She wanted to very, very much. But she couldn't imagine how he could possibly understand until he'd seen it for himself.

Despite Eva's disappointment, Henry could scarcely have been more excited to be moving toward the pavilion he was most determined to explore that day: the Palace of Fine Arts. As they skirted the lagoon, he recited all the facts he'd learned about the palace since they'd first seen it the day before: how large the galleries were, how many nations were exhibiting artworks there. Henry said that the Palace of Fine Arts was the only solid building on the fairgrounds, and idly, Eva asked what he meant.

"Oh," said Henry. "All the other buildings are constructed of staff—a kind of artificial stone made of plaster of Paris. It holds up fairly well against the weather as long as you don't expect it to last too long, but the Palace of Fine Arts is real brick and stone. Uncle Jefferson said they couldn't get the art insured unless the building was fire resistant."

The Palace of Fine Arts, opulent though it was, contained no more Magic than had Manufactures and Liberal Arts, but Henry was entranced all the same, moving swiftly from canvas to canvas, gallery to gallery, annex to annex. Eva stood at a distance: the tangled grass, the peach trees, the rambling house—she knew that they had been there before.

Where were they now?

By the time Eva was ready to move on, Henry had been running ahead for nearly an hour, and it took her

long minutes of searching to find him—sketching away before a cast of a Gothic church doorway.

"There you are," said Eva.

Henry said nothing, his eyes leaping between the door and the page.

"Henry," said Eva. "I'm ready to go."

There was a heavy pause, and then Henry said, "Just a moment," in a way that made it clear that he would be anything but a moment.

Eva sighed and turned back to the galleries.

Situated at the northern end of the Fair's lagoon, the Palace of Fine Arts sported a great entry porch with a broad flight of steps that ran right out to the water, and it was toward this porch that Eva went now, hoping for a bit of rest. There was laughter and conversation on the other side of the door, and as Eva pushed her way through, the dazzle of the light and the sudden flow of wind made the tangled grass before her seem to ripple just like the water of the lagoon.

Sudden silence: no laughter or chat—no other fair-goers at all.

There were floorboards beneath her feet. But the portico of the Palace of Fine Arts was paved in stone.

Eva's heart surged.

The steps that descended were flanked by a pair of green copper lions, one tall and stalwart, the other languid and lazy. The aroma of fruit floated in the air, rich and thick, and in the distance, she saw no pond, no lagoon, but a double rank of wizened trees swaying in the breeze.

Eva wasn't alone.

The man was sitting in a rocking chair, gazing out

at the lawn. His hands were clothed in gloves of spotless white. His tailcoat was well cut, his bow tie perfectly straight, and the mustache on his face was as carefully cultivated as a rose garden, each waxed hair lying precisely beside its neighbor.

He turned back and smiled. "Hello," he said.

Eva stammered a greeting; the man rocked in his chair.

"You needn't worry," said the man. "You are welcome here. Come, sit," and he gestured to a small rocking chair beside his own.

Eva approached. It seemed awfully pale, that little chair, as if it were made of bleached hardwood, or even bone, but it was neither. Her chair was crafted of smooth, solid candle wax.

"Now," said the man, with a look toward Eva's bag. "I believe you have something of mine."

Eva blinked, bewildered—did he mean the candle she had taken from Mrs. Blodgett?—but the moment the bag was open on her lap, she knew precisely what he meant.

"Oh," said Eva. "Oh, of course," and reaching in, she produced her resurrected peach, still wrapped in white cotton.

The man beside her smiled and gestured with the back of his gloved hand. The fruit's wrappings gave way and unraveled, floating off like gossamer on the breeze.

"My, my," said the man. "It looks wonderful," and he held out his hand.

Gently, tentatively, Eva deposited the big round peach in the man's gloved palm. He lifted it to his nose, breathed in deeply, shut his eyes.

When he opened them again, there was a soft smile on his lips.

"I must say," declared the man in the rocking chair, "I am pleased that you managed to find your way back here, Miss . . ."

"Root," she said. "Eva Root."

The man took a large hungry bite from the peach. "Yes," he said. "Miss Root. Very pleased. Many fair-goers come once and never quite manage to return. It is only those who truly understand what they see that find the strength to seek us out again."

Eva nodded, and the tears that stung at her eyes came through a chuckle of relief. "Yes," she said. "But where were you when I looked this morning? I thought, I thought—"

"Miss Root," said the man. "The art that we practice here does not simply come when it is called. We cannot, like our friends in the Machinery Building, throw a lever or turn a crank and expect to achieve identical results each time. No, no, no—the Impossible Art must be constantly entreated, petitioned, discovered anew. It is a wild thing—not at all interested in our expectations."

Eva nodded. "I see," she said. "Only I thought . . ."

"What did you think?" said the man fondly.

"I thought I wasn't good enough," said Eva.

"Well, that," said the man, "remains to be seen. But what is clear now is that the Pavilion is interested in you."

Eva shook her head in confusion. "Interested in me?"

The man nodded. "My Pavilion shows a different face to each of its guests, and it has already begun to prepare for your visit tomorrow. I very much hope that you will come again. I should be eager indeed to see what it has in store."

The man in the rocking chair rose to his feet.

Eva's heart was racing. Tomorrow? Tomorrow seemed so far away, and she still had so many questions.

"Can I go in now?" said Eva.

"I am afraid not," said the man. "The Pavilion is not at leisure."

"But how can I get back here?"

"Simply seek," said the man, "and you shall find."

"Find what? What is this place?"

Now the man began to amble slowly across the porch, idly picking the last hunks of flesh from Eva's peach with his teeth. "I should have thought that was obvious," he said. "This house is like any of the great buildings of the Fair—Machinery, Horticulture, Electricity, Mines. Here we seek to display the greatest accomplishments of our field; to foster—amongst the select few to whom we are open—an interest in our Impossible Art; and to assure its prominence in the country's coming century." At the very threshold of the house, the man turned back to look at Eva. There was no door in the arched entryway, but rather a lazily spinning turnstile. "This place," said the man, finishing the peach, "is the Pavilion of Magic."

"And who are you?"

The man's bright smile flashed out beneath his mustache.

"I, Miss Root, am the Baron of American Magic, and I am known by many names. But perhaps it is best, for the present, if you call me Mr. Magister."

With a flick of his white-gloved hand, Mr. Magister tossed the peach pit across the broad porch. Eva scrambled to catch it, and when she looked up again, it was not at all the rambling house in the field of tangled grass that she saw—it was the play of lagoon light rippling on the shoulders of the Palace of Fine Arts.

Eva's feet pounded against the floor, sending echoes clattering off the high gallery walls. On every side, prim ladies in huge hats gave her *Slow down* glares, but she didn't care.

Henry. Where was Henry? The light around her had shifted. It was later than she'd thought.

Eva ran in and out of all the annexes, but Henry was nowhere to be seen. Finally, her excitement beginning to melt into anxiety, Eva pushed her way out of the palace's west entrance. There was no doubt in her mind: the sun had shifted.

It was late. Had four o'clock passed? Had Henry gone home without her?

Eva trotted down the western palace steps. If she was lucky, perhaps he and Willie would still be waiting at Sixty-Fourth Street.

And if it hadn't been for the brassy voice cutting through the crowd, she might've missed him entirely.

"Oh, I'm sure of it. No doubt in my mind: Jack Coagulo. It's been some time since I seen him, of course, but I never forget a face, no sir. I know he's a private fellow, now, and I won't take it hard if he don't come hisself, but if you should happen to see him again, you go on and tell him old Bill Gabbermann's staying up at Briggs House on the corner of Randolph and Fifth, and I'd be much obliged if he could send up what he owes."

There, just to Eva's left: a portly fellow in checkered pants and a dented bowler hat. He was drawling loudly at a boy seated on the edge of the Michigan Building porch: Henry.

"Here," said the fellow, seizing his notebook. "I'll write it down for you. Bill . . . Gabbermann . . . Briggs . . . House . . . Randolph . . . Fifth . . . There. You just tell him, see!"

And the man strode off quickly, heading toward Fifty-Seventh Street.

"Henry!"

He looked up sharply, scanning the crowd for the source of the call, and Eva charged forward across the lawn.

"Oh," said Henry. "Hello, Eva."

"What was that?" said Eva, raising her eyebrows in the direction of the departing man.

Henry shrugged. "No idea," he said. "He insisted he knew the fellow I'm drawing, but I don't see how he possibly could."

"Why not?"

"Well, because I'm making him up as I go."

Eva couldn't help a chuckle, but Henry's face stayed still.

"Henry," said Eva, lowering her voice. "Henry, I have something to tell you."

Henry had gone back to his drawing, and he didn't look up from the page. "Where did you go today, Eva? I thought we said we'd stay together."

Eva took a deep breath and sat down beside him. "But that's just what I want to tell you," she said, and she was on the brink of explaining when she realized that she didn't know how she possibly could: there were images in her mind, memories that she thought she might just describe, but she couldn't seem to string together the words.

One place and then another. Fruit trees in the sun. Tangled grass. A pair of clean white gloves. A Pavilion of—what was the word? Majesty? Magnetism? Margarine?

The long silence stretched on between them, and soon Henry gave an impatient sigh, his sketchbook flopping forward on his knees.

"This thing you want to tell me," he said. "Is it like the thing you wanted to show me this morning? Or does it really exist?"

This was unkind, and Eva was about to protest, but at that very moment, her eyes fell on the sketchbook, and for the first time, she saw the man that Henry had been drawing.

She began to laugh.

"What?" said Henry.

"You said you were making up that drawing as you went."

Henry nodded. "I am."

But the portrait was unmistakable: the man called Mr. Magister.

"What?" said Henry again. "What is it?"

Eva cast about for some way to explain.

The peach—she still held its pit in her hand. And if she couldn't explain to Henry, then perhaps she could demonstrate.

"Here," said Eva with a broad smile, tossing and catching the pit lightly. "Are you hungry?"

Henry's eyebrows fell. "Yes," he said. "Actually, I am."

Eva nodded. "Good. Hold out your hand."

In later days, Eva would find herself astonished at the confidence with which she acted then—laying the pit in Henry's palm without a second thought, closing his hand around it with both of her own.

Eva shut her eyes and thought back as clearly as she could: warm, tender flesh; the sweet, sweet scent; the tickle of the grass.

It was all so close.

Come back, she thought, *come back,* and in the little basket of their fifteen fingers, something began to grow.

Henry looked up with wide, wondering eyes; Eva smiled.

No one can deny the Magic that happens in their own hand.

"Eva," said Henry, breathless behind her. "Eva, where are we going?"

"Just trust me."

Eva was on fire with urgency, scouring each structure they passed for any hint that it might provide a way back—the double towers of Colorado, the Spanish *misión* of California, Illinois's towering dome. She took him past the Fifty-Ninth Street entrance, past ranks of bicycles standing like steeds at a starting gate; she took him all the way around the grand edifice of the Women's Building, scrutinizing each door and window, and she was just pausing to negotiate the passage beneath the viaduct when Henry pulled her back.

"Eva," he said. "Stop."

"No," she said. "No, we have to—"

"Listen to me!"

Eva turned, and her eyes filled up with Henry.

"I trust you, Eva," he said. "I do. Just let me help. Just tell me what we're looking for."

Something flared in Eva's chest, bright and warm. It had never occurred to her that Henry would want to help—that he could be anything other than an audience to persuade. And so she told him what she could: that they were looking for an Impossible place; that it was warm, almost hot; and that if they looked for long enough, then surely they would find it.

Henry, eager and uncomprehending, nodded his head. And with that, they passed into the Midway Plaisance.

A water-powered monorail shooting passengers along at a hundred miles an hour; a huge tethered hot-air balloon floating above; a farm full of ostriches; the Zoopraxographical Hall. Here could be found whole streets and villages from distant places—Tunis, Ireland, Java. Everywhere the unctuous aromas of cooking food rose to the music of a dozen lands, and men and women in lederhosen, saris, dashikis, kimonos passed by on every side.

Other fairgoers browsed amongst the tinkling souvenirs at the Libbey Glass Company, but Eva could only smell the heat rising from the glassblowing furnace. Others stopped for a cooling dip in the great Natatorium, but Eva could only see the ripples—surely, surely there must be a way in through the water—and all the while, Henry was by her side.

When the turnstiles at the far end of the Midway came into view, Eva was surprised to find that it was not he but she herself who spoke.

"I give up," she said. "Maybe we need to come back tomorrow."

Eva fully expected Henry to agree—if it had not yet passed, four o'clock was quickly approaching—but Henry hadn't heard: he was several steps behind, stuck in his tracks. At first, Eva didn't understand what he was looking at, but she stepped back, and carefully tracing the aim of his gaze, she saw:

Set into the wall between the Hungarian Orpheum and the Dahomey Village was a simple door. It was entirely unremarkable but for the small copper lions—only the size of house cats—flanking the doorframe. One of them sat alert, the other lay sprawling.

Come.

"It moved its tail," said Henry, unblinking. "I could swear."

Eva crossed the dusty ground slowly. Her heart was pounding. "Henry," she said. "Henry, you found it!"

Beside her, he swallowed.

"Are you ready?" said Eva.

Henry's head shook softly. "No. But let's go anyway."

And this was the perfect answer.

Eva put her hand in Henry's and led him forward.

But the Pavilion was not at leisure.

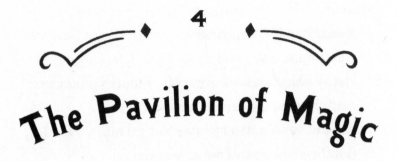

4
The Pavilion of Magic

Eva and Henry found themselves in a high, narrow entryway.

The air on this side of the door was different—denser, somehow more substantial. The sunlight fell in thick beams, and the hulking house seemed to pull them in, as if they were constantly walking gently downhill.

Even the silence here was heavy.

Eva turned back to ease the door shut, but it was no longer there; there was only a turnstile, spinning lazily in the breeze.

"Eva," said Henry, "what is this place?"

On their right, a low table held a spray of thin pink peach blossoms. Eva reached out and found them cold and hard—tinkling leaves of glass so thin and delicate that they bent beneath a single finger.

Eva smiled. "This," she said, "is the Pavilion of Magic."

The dam in her mind burst as they stepped over the threshold, and she spoke now with full fluency: how she'd stumbled onto this estate through the lions in Manufactures and Liberal Arts, how she'd met the man on the porch not an hour past.

"But have you ever been *here* before?" said Henry. "Inside?"

She couldn't keep a grin from creeping into her cheeks. "Come on," she said, and pulled him forward.

It wasn't that Eva had forgotten what Mr. Magister had said—that she was expected only tomorrow—but there was just so much excitement: Henry's astonishment, her curiosity. The scheduling seemed like such a little concern. What were a few hours between friends?

Beyond the entryway was a great front hall, all wooden beams and marble floors. Here the hefty silence almost echoed.

On the far side of the hall stood a broad staircase, its steps lined with thick red carpeting. Halfway up, where it split in two, there was a tall window of shining stained glass depicting Mr. Magister, gemlike in waistcoat and tails. The likeness, however, was unfinished, and a panel of plain glass, oddly clean and white, peered out like a blank skull where his face should have been.

"That's him," said Henry. "Isn't it? The man that I was drawing?"

Eva nodded. "Part of him, at least."

The light in the hall was very odd, and as Eva's eyes continued to rise, she soon saw why: the beams and pillars that formed the vaulted rib cage of the hall were real live oaks, Spanish moss hanging down like royal banners from their boughs. Eva was sure that she could see sunlight glimmering through the densely woven foliage.

Shards of sunlight above, stained glass ahead, but still, something nagged at Eva's eye: all of the illumination did not seem accounted for.

It was only when she looked down that she understood.

In the very center of the marble floor, beneath Eva's feet, an emblem had been worked in colored granite: a great flaming bonfire that itself, somehow, contributed to the brightness of the hall.

Each time she looked away, the arrangement of the flames seemed to shift.

Gingerly, she stepped back.

"Eva," said Henry, whispering to avoid disturbing the hush, "are you sure we're supposed to be here?"

"Of course," replied Eva, as if she were a good deal more confident than she really felt.

Beneath the overhanging mezzanine, two parallel archways led back into the house. The left, to which Henry was drawn, seemed to show a dim and flickering light, and the right, which called to Eva, looked misty and cool.

If they hadn't been there together, they would've taken different paths. But Henry had a way of seeing things clearly.

"Wait." His heels echoed against the marble floor like a battery of distant cannon fire. "We ought to stay together. It's all too easy to get lost."

Eva nodded.

Side by side, they passed through the right-hand arch, and on the far side, they found a sitting room, all cushy furniture and long creamy curtains. Henry seemed very taken with the view from the windows, but Eva's attention was soon pulled away.

Someone had just left the room—she was certain of it. She could smell linen, perfume—did she know that smell?—and there was a presence, surely, just out of sight through the next doorway.

Someone was there.

Eva wanted to see her.

"Hey," she called, so softly that only she and the house could possibly hear, "come back." And without a second thought she went through the door.

In the dining room, a heavy table seemed to have grown up out of the very floor, its gnarled-root toes twining into the grassy green carpet. On the surface of the table, a banquet had been laid: It was a summer's worth of peaches, pale pink and white, rich red and gold, some as big as melons, some as small as pastilles. There were carafes of effervescent peach wine and great seared peach steaks steaming from the grill; a tureen in the middle of the table held a fragrant peach consommé, and small silver bowls at each of the many places were heaped with scoops of peach-colored mousse. The aroma was so thick you could almost touch it, and Henry, following in from the sitting room, swallowed hungrily.

But Eva could scarcely pay attention.

Someone—she was sure—someone had just gone through.

Eva followed eagerly into the library.

This room was a dark glory, armored in walnut and swaddled in scarlet. The smell of ancient volumes hung thick in the air—leather, paper, a light peppering of dust—but nearly as strong in Eva's nose was the swirling scent of the man who seemed just to have left, as different from the smell in the sitting room as could be, and yet just as strangely, deeply familiar: soap and sweat, tobacco and spice.

Something stirred beneath the surface of her memory.

Across the room, Henry was speaking, reading out the titles of volumes on the shelf: "*The Magus, or Celestial Intelligencer . . . The Triangular Book of St. Germain.*" Fire flickered in the hearth, sending the shadows of armchairs and reading desks leaping up across the bookcases.

"*Secretum Secretorum . . . Lives of the Necromancers.*"

These were intriguing titles, and at any other time, Eva might've lingered to look, but there was someone just outside the library—someone she'd been waiting her whole life to meet.

She was moving rapidly toward the next door when she heard rustling overhead.

"Henry," she said, her voice taut and trembling. "Henry, stop."

His hand was half-extended, reaching for a thick book. There, on the dim upper ledge of the bookcase, its eyes fixed upon Henry like gleaming silver dollars, sat a great preening eagle.

It snapped its hooked beak.

Henry froze.

Long breathless moments passed before Eva noticed the firelight reflected in the eagle's varnished plumage. The bird, it seemed, had been carved from the same wood as the bookcases.

Henry backed away slowly, the eagle's sharp talons

following, clacking along the upper ledge of the bookcase until he and Eva made their way into the next room.

Now they found themselves in the game room, where billiard balls grew from small ivory trees. Cloud formations of fragrant cigar smoke drifted just below the ceiling, and Henry, enchanted as ever, couldn't resist stopping to marvel.

But Eva didn't linger. He was there, just ahead, once again, just through the door: not Mr. Magister, not Uncle Jefferson, but someone far better, far more important.

She had to catch him—she just had to.

"Come back," she murmured. "Come back."

Door after door, turn after turn, room after room after room after room: here a workshop scattered with heavy tools; there a music chamber full of strange instruments. There was a great loom that chittered and champed as if it were hungry to weave; there was a humid glass conservatory planted thick with green; and always just beyond, just out of sight, the feeling of someone—Someone Very Dear.

It was in the vaulted kitchen that she finally slowed her feet. She was sure she'd heard someone in here—the clang of a wooden spoon on the side of a copper pot— but, of course, she'd only just missed them. She always seemed to in this house.

There was something on the stove—a steaming concoction that gave off the aroma of parched earth after rain—and on the cutting board nearby, someone had cut neat, even slices from a large stone.

"Henry," she said. "Look." And only in that moment did she realize that she'd left him far behind.

Where was she?

The next room was the servants' hall, and there Eva paused before the bell board. Small silver bells wore labels to indicate where help was wanted: DINING ROOM, MORNING ROOM, MASTER BEDROOM. These were all sensible enough, but farther down, the names grew strange: INCENSE VAULT, ANTIQUE STABLE YARD, GREATER CRUCIBLE.

One bell, labeled ELSEWHERE, was twitching violently, somehow unable to ring.

If they had truly been here at all, the man and woman Eva followed seemed to have gone on from this room. Idly, Eva peered through the next doorway: parquet flooring giving way to reeds and cattails and a sprawling pond beneath the canopied ceiling.

Eva was terribly frustrated. No matter what she did, no matter how many rooms she traversed, they were never quite there. Or rather they *were*, but always just out of reach.

Well, she was done playing this game. She wouldn't go any farther.

In a huff, she sat down in a creaky wooden chair.

And it was only here that she began to understand.

Her mind wandered, running back through the rooms she'd traversed, and she tried to string them together in an orderly sequence. The longer she thought, though, the more they seemed to resist consolidation, as if each room in the Pavilion were a universe unto itself.

Gradually, the particular pleasant fog that surrounded the Pavilion settled about Eva's mind; the lap of the water and the croak of the frogs in the room next door echoed in her ear, and soon, tired and sore, she lifted her feet onto the table.

Time passed—who could say how much?—and Eva felt peckish. She was just about to call out and ask when dinner would be when out of the corner of her eye, Eva saw, passing by on the sunlit tiling, the single most extraordinary thing she'd ever seen in her life.

Her breath caught in her throat.

It was her mother. She'd never seen her before, of course, never known her, but now she knew her for certain, as unquestionably as she knew her own self: her mother, wiping her hands on her apron, bustling with the business of the day. Tears sprang immediately to

Eva's eyes, and it was a moment before she recognized, through the lap and croak in the pond room, the whirring of Father's fishing rod.

Mother on one side, Father on the other, and Eva safe and sound between.

What was it like to have a family? What was it like to be at home?

This. It was like this.

Perhaps the Pavilion had not brought her parents back to her, but it had given her the next best thing. This: this feeling in her heart.

Time passed—who could say how much?—and deep within the house, another sound rose to her attention.

Raised voices.

People were arguing.

Eva turned her head sharply, eager to hear more clearly, and without warning, Mother and Father were gone, just as they'd always been.

Where was Henry?

Eva leapt to her feet and darted out of the servants' hall, following the sound of the echoing argument through the empty kitchen as quickly as she possibly could.

Room after room, corridor after corridor, and eventually the formless voices began to resolve themselves into sharp, angry words.

"Because," she heard Mr. Magister say, "that is what is required of you. I owe you no explanation."

A boy's voice piped up in aggravated response. "But it makes no sense," he said. "Why on earth do you need more? What good could it possibly do?"

Eva charged down a long gallery, its walls lined with strange art that seemed somehow to breathe, and she was just about to call out when a handful of cold, strong fingers closed around her wrist.

Eva spun around. For a silent, dizzy moment, she thought she had been seized by the ibis-headed bronze idol now facing her, but then she understood—the hand that had taken hold of her was coming from right behind the statue:

Henry.

He put his finger to his lips and beckoned her into the statue's nook.

The voices were growing closer. Swiftly, Eva wedged herself in beside him.

But if Henry was here, then who was arguing with Mr. Magister?

The answer came barreling down the long gallery before she had a chance to catch her breath: the boy was slight, his pale cheeks glowed scarlet with anger, and his straw-colored hair shot out in many directions at once, almost willfully unruly.

"But you don't understand," he was saying. "It takes everything I've got inside of me." He seemed on the verge of tears.

"Of all people, Vaclav, you think *I* do not understand?" said Mr. Magister. "Do not confuse your own weakness for my ignorance."

Vaclav spun on his heel. "Don't you call me *weak*."

Eva's mouth hung open. She couldn't possibly imagine speaking to a man like Mr. Magister in such a manner.

"Denying your weakness—yes, Vaclav, your weakness—will not save you from it. You know the terms of our agreement. Either do what is required of you, or what you have taken from the Pavilion will be reclaimed."

Vaclav scoffed. "I don't know how you think you can—"

But Mr. Magister cut in. "I do."

There was a heavy pause. "I'm going home," said Vaclav, and turning away once more, he charged around the far corner of the long gallery.

"Go, then," said Mr. Magister. "I have never sought to stop you. But do not expect the doors of the Pavilion to open easily unless you return to pay what you owe."

Henry darted softly up and out, eager to hear what was said. Eva tried to grab hold of him, but he was out of reach before she began to move, and with a sigh, she followed him.

Vaclav and Mr. Magister were standing before a great door at the end of the adjoining hallway, its stone arch richly carved: gears and hammers, wreaths and rosettes of railroad track and telegraph wire. At the peak of the arch, a lion's head stared open-eyed, and the copper hinges that held the door in place were grasping gloves.

There was no doorknob.

"I want to go home," said Vaclav to the door.

The lion at the peak of the doorway blinked; behind Vaclav's back, Mr. Magister gave a gentle nod, and the gloves that Eva had taken for hinges flexed and grasped, pulling the door open. From her position, Eva couldn't see the place beyond the door, but there was a shift in the light and a crunching of footsteps, and an acrid stench began to pervade the hallway.

"Vaclav," said Mr. Magister. "I warn you: there is no hiding from Magic. Not even where you go now."

"Goodbye," said Vaclav, and he went through the door. Softly, it swung shut behind him.

Mr. Magister sighed and mopped his brow. His bow tie undid itself, and his deft gloved fingers unfastened his uppermost button. After a moment, he retrieved the golden pocket watch from his waistcoat, muttering to himself as he popped the case open. "Foolish boy," he said, and he was just about to turn when something on the watch face caught his eye. His eyebrows fell, and then, to Eva's horror, he peered down the hallway.

He peered toward them.

"Eva?" he said. Beside her, Henry's eyes widened.

Again, louder: "Eva? Is that you?"

Panic lit Henry's face. Eva took a deep breath and stepped out into the open. "Hello," she said.

"Why, Eva," said Mr. Magister. "I didn't expect you until tomorrow."

Eva nodded eagerly. "I know," she said. "I know. But I was just so excited."

Mr. Magister gave a wan grin. "I understand," he said. "But I'm afraid I am rather weary tonight. Did you . . . ?"

Again, his eyes fell to his watch, and something there caught his concern.

"Eva," he said. "Are you alone?"

Eva tried to draw a breath, but it stuck in her throat. Her cheeks began to burn, and before she managed to speak, Henry stepped out into the hallway behind her.

"Ah," said Mr. Magister. He was already in motion, his golden watch slotted into his waistcoat pocket, his nimble fingers fastening his collar. "What is your name, young man?" The bow tie retied itself with a sharp *snik*.

"P-P-Poole," said Henry. "Henry Poole."

Mr. Magister bowed gently. "What a delight," he said with a smile. "Welcome to my house, Mr. Poole. I do not believe you have visited us before?"

"No," said Henry. "I haven't."

Mr. Magister nodded. "Then Miss Root must've brought you inside."

"Yes," said Henry.

"Of course," said Mr. Magister. "I see. It may be, then, that this is our only opportunity for acquaintance, young Mr. Poole. I regret that my house is generally rather particular about whom it admits."

"I can't come back?" There was something just short of panic in Henry's voice.

"Why, Mr. Poole, nothing would please me more, but I am afraid my desire is not the only consideration in the matter. The house is accustomed to welcoming only those candidates with a demonstrated aptitude for the practice of our Impossible Art. But I shouldn't worry—it is altogether unlikely that the disappointment shall linger. In fact, I should be surprised indeed if you even remember this conversation."

"But, Mr. Magister," said Eva. "On the train, he showed me sketches—incredible sketches of the fairgrounds that—"

Mr. Magister smiled gently. "Very nice," he said. "But not every artist is a Magician, I am afraid."

"No," said Eva. "No, but he drew them before he'd ever seen the Fair."

This seemed to pique Mr. Magister's interest. "Before? Really?"

Eva nodded.

"And you'd seen no photographs? Nothing?"

"No, sir," said Henry.

Mr. Magister held out his hand, and Henry lifted his sketchbook. Mr. Magister paced idly as he leafed through it, nodding and frowning at the fairground sketches before him.

He didn't seem entirely convinced.

"Please," said Eva. "Please," she said again. "He has Magic—I'm sure of it. He even managed to draw you."

Oddly, this assertion seemed to comfort Mr. Magister. "Ah," he said, shutting the sketchbook. "You must be mistaken. I'm afraid that is simply not possible."

"But it looks just like you," said Eva.

"No," said Henry softly. "No, Eva, I don't think it was him."

Eva's eyes grew wide in disbelief. She knew what she had seen.

"Remember that fellow at the Michigan Building?" said Henry. "He said it was someone else."

"There," said Mr. Magister. "You see?" But Eva's mind had snagged on the man at the Michigan Building: Gabbermann.

What name had he given to the face in Henry's portrait?

Beside her, Henry's eyebrows dropped; Eva could see the same confusion massing in his mind.

What name had it been?

And then, like a sudden match in the darkness, it was there: "Coagulo!" she said. "Jack Coagulo."

Mr. Magister stopped. He stood staring for a long moment, and then abruptly he opened the notebook and flipped rapidly until he found the portrait in question.

"Ah, yes," he said. "There it is." Now he turned his eyes to the facing page. "And what is written here?"

Henry cleared his throat. "The name and lodgings of the fellow who—"

"Yes, yes, yes," said Mr. Magister, interrupting brightly. "I see. Why, how pleased I am to have been wrong! You are evidently a young man of great talent, Mr. Poole, and I shall be very glad of your further acquaintance."

A broad smile spread across Eva's cheeks. "So, he can come back?"

Mr. Magister nodded graciously. "I shall count on it. Henry—I hope you will allow me to keep this portrait as a memento of our meeting?"

And without waiting for an answer, Mr. Magister tore two pages carefully from the sketchbook, folded them away neatly, and returned the book to Henry's hand.

Henry blinked.

"Terribly kind of you," said Mr. Magister. "Now, where can I ask my doorway to deposit you? I should like our further acquaintance of all things, but as I say, I am fairly wrung out this evening, and I am afraid we shall have to wait."

"Overstreet House," said Eva. "Prairie Avenue."

Mr. Magister nodded and turned to the arched doorway. "Overstreet House," he said. The lion at the height of the arch gave a heavy blink.

"Please, sir," said Henry. "I am afraid we were meant to meet our driver at the Sixty-Fourth Street turnstiles, and if we arrive home without him . . ."

Mr. Magister nodded. "Yes, I see. What time was set for your meeting?"

"Four o'clock," said Henry.

Mr. Magister winced. "Goodness," he said. "But we shall see what we can do."

Fortunately, Willie was still at the turnstiles when they arrived, waiting testily behind a well-thumbed newspaper. They were over two hours late, and his face fell into an expression of concern and disapproval when he saw them approaching.

But Mr. Magister got to him first.

Eva didn't hear everything that was said, but she made out a bit—words like *waiting* and *distressed* and *explanation*—and as she watched, Willie's irritation melted into confounded apologetic concern.

"I don't know," she heard him say. "I must've—must've fallen asleep, or, or . . . Anyhow, thank you, thank you, sir, for looking after them."

It all made Eva feel a bit guilty.

"Eva!" Henry beckoned frantically from inside the coach. Willie was ready on the box. "Come on!"

She turned back to say goodbye, but Mr. Magister was already gone.

Eva climbed into the coach; Willie urged his horses on. The veil of darkness was beginning to fall.

She had so much to say to Henry, so many questions to ask—about the Pavilion, about the rooms he had seen, about the boy in the long gallery and Mr. Magister and everything—but it all disintegrated on its way to her tongue, and when she opened her mouth, nothing came out.

She stared at Henry; Henry stared back in identical confusion.

There was no telling what Magic lay beneath the Fair.

Before long, Eva and Henry turned from one another, unable to speak of what mattered, unwilling to speak of what didn't. Eva gazed out the window; Henry began to draw, his eraser as busy as his charcoal.

Outside, night descended on soot-stained Chicago.

The peculiar thing was that Eva's memories seemed somehow to *hide*: there had been a bird, a great bird of prey—an owl, perhaps, or an eagle—she could still see its cold eyes shining in her mind, but she didn't know in what circumstances she had encountered it. Where had it been? In the front hall trees?

But how could there have been *trees* in the front hall?

The farther they went from the fairgrounds, the more this fading advanced, until all Eva had left were sharp little promontory images jutting out through a fog of uncertainty: the eagle eyes; the sloshing pond. She was so distracted by her shrinking memory that she didn't notice the warmth of Henry's head on her shoulder until he began to snore, and she turned and saw what he'd been drawing.

It looked just like her fractured memory.

Henry woke, silent and blinking, when the carriage came to a stop at Overstreet House. Eva saw the very moment in which his foggy recollection descended— a kind of perturbed stillness. She wished she'd been able to

speak of it, but there was some small comfort, at least, in knowing that they were together there in the impenetrable fog.

Dinner was as bright and friendly an affair as ever, but neither Eva nor Henry had much to say. Mr. and Mrs. Overstreet seemed to take this for exhaustion, and she heard sharp words directed at Willie as she climbed the stairs toward her room. Willie was, of course, embarrassed and apologetic at having been so late to get them, and Eva felt a renewed pang of guilt as she readied herself for bed, though she couldn't quite say why.

Sleep came quickly.

There was a flash in the morning of unqualified pleasure—the sunshine, the soft pillows—but it didn't linger. Overstreet House had been so magnificent at first, so sweet and so warm, but Aunt Isabella was not her mother, Uncle Jefferson was not her father, and the invariable aftermath of Impossible warmth is a quiet, unshakable chill.

Eva rose, dressed, washed her face; it all seemed terribly insignificant. There was something bigger, deeper, realer waiting for her, if she could just manage to remember it.

She had to get back to the Fair.

Eva was about to open her bedroom door when

her eyes fell on the scrap of paper that had been pushed underneath. She knew, of course, the moment she saw it where it had come from: it was a page, twice-folded, torn out of Henry's notebook.

She could almost hear the peach blossoms tinkling.

Eva tucked the sketch away and went out into the hall. Henry's door, beyond the stairs, was still closed, but the sound of pleasant chat rose up from below like the aroma of morning coffee.

Eva went down. A gout of laughter came rolling out of the parlor, and Aunt Isabella turned to greet her as Eva came in.

"Why, Eva," she said. "Look! Your Dr. Fludd has come to call."

"Dr. Fludd?" Eva had never heard the name before.

"Hello, Eva," said a voice by the hearth.

Eva turned.

It was Mr. Magister.

"Dr. Fludd," it seemed, was the headmaster of Eva's school, which, conveniently, had its campus in Hyde

Park, not at all far from the fairgrounds. Paying close attention to the flow of conversation, Eva learned that she had spoken so highly of the Overstreets' generous hospitality that Dr. Fludd had been moved to come and thank them in person.

She smiled bashfully.

This, of course, all seemed highly implausible to Eva. Hadn't Aunt Isabella met her as she'd climbed off the train? Hadn't Henry invited her to stay precisely because she didn't have a home in Chicago? Hadn't he even told his aunt that Eva lived in Philadelphia? But as Mr. Magister crossed the room toward the broad bay window, a beguiling aroma swept by with him—fresh, line-dried linen; the char of the hearth; the sweetness of peaches—and Eva found, suddenly, that Dr. Fludd seemed charming, eminently reasonable: very agreeable indeed.

His Magic was strong.

Dr. Fludd could not linger, alas—there was no end to an educator's work—and soon he took his leave, asking Eva to see him out the door. She went with measured step, careful not to speak too soon, and when they reached the curb, Mr. Magister gave a gentle sigh. "Very well," he said.

"Are we going back? Can I come with you now?"

Mr. Magister gave a fond chuckle.

"It is my hope that you will come and visit me again tonight—tonight and no sooner."

"Tonight?" said Eva. She couldn't imagine how she could possibly wait.

Mr. Magister nodded. "I think you will find that dear Mr. and Mrs. Overstreet have a tendency to assume that you and Henry are safe under the care of Dr. Fludd when you are absent from their home."

"Of course," said Eva. "Thank you."

Mr. Magister settled his top hat on his head and raised his arm to an approaching hansom cab. "You are a very generous girl, Eva. To try and share something as rare and precious as is found in our Pavilion speaks very highly of you indeed. And I am hopeful that Henry may yet manage some real Magic. But make no mistake—he is not what you are. You are special."

"I am?" said Eva, failing not to blush.

Mr. Magister smiled. "Of course you are. But I must tell you—I value my privacy very dearly. And as much as it pains me to imagine it, I am afraid that if I am forced to contend with another uninvited guest—another Henry, Eva—then I must consider the possibility that the Pavilion was wrong to trust you."

Eva's stomach lurched.

"Do I make myself clear?"

Eva nodded assiduously. "Yes," she said. "Yes."

But something reverberated behind the fog in her memory—a wooden spoon on a copper pot; the cast and whir of a fishing reel—and she couldn't help letting out the question she held inside.

"Mr. Magister?" said Eva. "Has anyone ever used Magic to bring people back? From, from . . . ?"

She trailed off. There was only one place people disappeared to, in the end.

Mr. Magister did not immediately respond, and for a long moment, he eyed her from his full, remote height. "Ah," he said presently. "Is that what the Pavilion showed to you?"

It sounded like a question, but it wasn't one; all the same, Eva nodded gently.

"Well, I shall not deceive you, Eva: it has not yet been accomplished. But we are in the practice of enacting the Impossible in our Pavilion, and if there is one place on earth where you might do what you suggest, it is with us." With that, he popped open the door of his cab. "Until tonight, then, Eva."

Eva nodded. "Until tonight."

She'd turned back toward Overstreet House, but Mr. Magister spoke out once more from the open hansom window.

"Eva," he said.

"Yes?"

"Come alone."

This sent a cold uneasiness shooting through her—it was all too easy to get lost if they didn't stay together—but Eva knew that bringing Henry to the Pavilion uninvited had been a bad mistake, and she was eager to atone. "Of course," she said. "Of course."

Mr. Magister's cab rolled off down the avenue.

Henry didn't emerge from his room until well after noon, his hands smudged with charcoal, his shirt rumpled and untucked. Even then, he only came down to raid the pantry, and though he didn't object when Eva followed him back upstairs, he didn't pay her much attention, either.

"What are you working on?" she said.

"Hmm?" said Henry. "Just a drawing. I can't seem to get it right."

Eva went around behind his chair for a better look.

There it was—the Pavilion of Magic: fragmentary, hazy, unfinished and unfinishable.

"Thank you, by the way," said Eva. "For my peach blossom."

"What?" said Henry, eyes fixed on his work.

Eva took the sketch from her pocket, carefully smoothing its creases. "Oh," said Henry. "Oh, yes. I'd almost forgotten."

Eva left Henry to his work—sketching and erasing and shading and erasing and erasing and erasing and erasing. Uncle Jefferson had long since gone off to the office, and Aunt Isabella was out paying calls. The house was quiet and still, and the only sound Eva heard all afternoon was the faint clatter of kitchen dishes and the rub and scratch of Henry's charcoal.

In an attempt to keep from counting every single passing moment, Eva occupied herself with an old issue

of the *Daily Columbian,* the newspaper printed and distributed on the fairgrounds. It was incredible to her how something as gargantuan and miraculous as the Fair had so quickly come to seem mundane—an intervening obstacle, the inert husk of the True Magic.

If only evening would come.

It was nearly four o'clock when Eva decided she could no longer stay in the house. She was itching for some distraction, and she knocked gently on Henry's bedroom door to invite him out for a walk, but he'd fallen asleep in his chair, charcoal in hand. At first, Eva was disappointed—she even considered waking him—but after a moment's reflection, it became clear that this was her opportunity:

Now she could slip away; now she could go.

And so Eva made her way out of the house and down to the lakefront. Here she turned southward, and for nearly two hours, she walked, following the bend of the lake, gradually shortening the intervening space and time that lay between herself and the Pavilion of Magic.

Slowly, her shadow reached farther and farther out toward the water; slowly, the day sloughed off its light like a summer cicada shedding its skin.

The light was dim when she reached the Sixty-Fourth Street turnstiles; dusk had arrived alongside her.

Eva stepped forward. Everywhere, bodies moved in

and out through the champing turnstiles, in and out, like human breath, and suddenly, there he was, his gloved hands spread wide, a smile smoldering beneath his mustache.

"Hello, Eva," said Mr. Magister. "Welcome home."

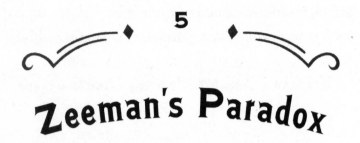

Zeeman's Paradox

Eva began to dig in her bag for her money, but Mr. Magister laid a hand on her shoulder.

"No, no," he said. "My friends do not pay here."

He strode forward; the turnstile spun. "Come," said Mr. Magister, and Eva followed, wincing instinctively as her thigh met the bar.

With a yielding click, however, she passed through.

"The Fair favors you," said Mr. Magister, and in a flash, he was moving, lighting out across the fairgrounds with bright intention. As he passed the open window of Hayward's Restaurant, he reached inside and took a fizzing glass of champagne from the hand of an oblivious gentleman. "Cheers," said Mr. Magister, and he drank deeply, emptying the glass in a single draft.

The gentleman inside the restaurant blinked, bewildered at his inexplicably empty hand.

"But come," said Mr. Magister. "What would you like? Lemonade? There has never been a summer day that could not be improved with lemonade."

Mr. Magister settled the champagne glass in Eva's hand, empty and light; in a sudden moment, it became heavy, filled to the sloshing brim.

"Cheers," said Mr. Magister with a sparkling grin, and once Eva began to drink, she found that she could not stop.

Sweet, tart, ice-cold lemonade slid easily down to fill her belly.

Everything whirled; everything swam. The glass was suddenly empty again.

"Excellent," said Mr. Magister. "Now come see the Fair as it ought to be seen."

And with that, he led her forward.

Magic kicked up in Mr. Magister's wake like dust swirling in a sunbeam: grand statues on their pediments bowed low as he and Eva passed; watercraft swam up seamlessly to catch them as they strode from the jetties. The blooms in the Wooded Island's great Rose Garden seemed to sing out their perfume in a composed harmony of fragrance, and in the Mines Building, Mr. Magister reached through the glass of a display case to make ice cream for Eva from a hefty lump of gold.

Everything sparkled; everything danced. Laughter began to bubble out of Eva, and soon it was impossible to see at all clearly through the shining haze of her joy.

On and on they went through the ecstatic evening, sailing from delight to delight: in the Stock Pavilion, the cattle capered and waltzed for their amusement, and on the Midway, Mr. Magister bid the huge scale model of St. Peter's Basilica in Rome to split open, revealing row upon row of tiny model choristers, bishops, cardinals—all celebrating a spectacular Mass in their croaking wooden voices.

On and on, faster and faster, more and more and more, until slowly, upon the observation deck high atop the Manufactures and Liberal Arts Building, Eva became aware of herself again. Above them, the blue velvet sheet of evening was beginning to darken at its edge. Mr. Magister was beside her there, reclining on one elbow, pulling apart a croissant from the French Bakery Exhibit into a long, unending ribbon of pastry. "Are you enjoying yourself?" he said.

Eva turned to him, dumbfounded. *Enjoying* seemed like such a meager word.

"Excellent," he said. "I am glad. Because all of this is meaningless without you here to share in it."

"Me?"

Mr. Magister nodded. "Magic must be experienced—witnessed—or else it is simply squandered potential, like electrical current run through an interrupted circuit. Without you, Eva, the Magic is incomplete; without you there is no Magic at all."

Could it truly be that there was something of her in all this Impossible beauty? Something essential?

"Tell me, Eva," said Mr. Magister. "How do you come to be here? What brought you to my house?"

Eva took a deep breath, meaning to say that she did not know, but instead she found herself speaking of Grandage's, her early aloneness, Mrs. Blodgett. Soon she began to pick up speed, telling of the séances that she had given, of the train and the Overstreets and everything that had been.

Eva looked up when she'd finished, as if waking from a dream. Mr. Magister was watching her intently, gloved fingers steepled beneath his mustache.

"Eva," he said. "I cannot say how happy I am that you have come. You must return as often as you can to my house. Come soak in the Pavilion as if it were a . . . a great vat of dye, and in time, you may find you have taken on a little Magic of your own."

Eva blinked softly. It was as if she had just been instructed to eat up all the chocolate in the world.

"Really? Me?"

Mr. Magister nodded. "You. And eventually, Eva, when your Magic is strong, you will find that the Pavilion calls upon you to add to it in some manner: to give back, in your way, some small measure of what you take. This you must do without reservation. It is the only price of your admission."

"Give back? How?"

Mr. Magister shrugged. "In whatever way seems best to you. Others have contributed gardening, machinery, renovation. It is not the particular gift that matters so much as the fullness of its giving. But I shouldn't worry just yet."

The sky above was growing dark; all around them, men and women crowded toward the edge of the observation deck, their conversation thick as blizzard snow.

"Look," said Mr. Magister. "There, below, is what we have been in your absence."

Eva turned her eyes down to the Court of Honor: monumental buildings filled with marvels barely visible in the thickening dim.

"Now look again," said Mr. Magister, "and see what we might be with your help."

And at just this moment, a rippling gasp ran through the crowd. Applause broke out.

The darkness had been banished.

Eva had seen electric lightbulbs once—three of them—as she disembarked, late and tired, on a train platform in Missouri. They'd seemed wonderful to her even then, like immortal fireflies trapped in their little glass domes. Now, before her waiting eyes, over one hundred thousand of them had come to life together, at the very same time. They were everywhere: mounted on pediments, nestled in corners. Massive searchlights dove high up into the sky, and all the Fair's fountains burbled with color.

It was like nothing she had ever seen before: a heaven's worth of light, twinkling and shining, giving shape and depth to all the wonders below.

"So," said Mr. Magister. "Will you join us?"

Eva nodded furiously, and the lights of the Fair turned the tears in her eyes into little glimmering starbursts.

Mr. Magister was positively giddy at her acceptance, and in his glee, he plucked the light from a nearby bulb—the light itself, somehow, through the unbroken glass—turning it, stretching it, rolling it between his fingers. Soon he leaned forward and tied it neatly around the first finger of Eva's left hand, like a ring, as a memento of the evening. The little bow glowed between them, and Eva's cheeks ached from smiling.

"Excellent," said Mr. Magister. "Now let us, for goodness' sake, get you home to rest."

They traveled down from the observation deck with a handful of other fairgoers, and though the two of them disembarked from the little elevator onto a floor that had not been there on the way up, no one seemed to take any notice. Eva knew precisely where they were, though—there was something in the smell of the place, some sweet, dusty electricity—and when the arched door beneath the lion's head came into view at the end of a corridor, she was ready to go home.

"Shall I expect you tomorrow, then?" asked Mr. Magister.

Eva nodded.

"And Henry—you will bring him with you?"

"I will."

Mr. Magister nodded. "I thank you for coming alone tonight. It is an admirable thing to trust in one's friends, of course, but like all virtues, it has its limits."

Eva nodded.

"Very well," said Mr. Magister, and to the lion above the door, he said, "Prairie Avenue."

The door swung open.

Slowly, Eva stepped forward. She was suddenly very weary indeed.

"Understand me, Eva," said Mr. Magister. "You have brought Henry to my halls, and now you must answer for him. He is your responsibility."

Eva nodded. "I understand."

"Very good," he said. "Until tomorrow."

But Eva hesitated. "Mr. Magister?"

"Yes?"

"There was something in the Pavilion: a kind of feeling . . . Different. Better."

It wasn't that she didn't want to mention her parents directly; it was just that she didn't see how she could quite explain what she meant to an adult, and every moment she spent stammering seemed like a diminishment of the good, clean warmth she'd felt.

"What I mean is," she said, "do you think that I might be able to carry it out with me someday? If my Magic is strong enough?"

Mr. Magister gave a dazzling smile. "Why," he said, "you must come and find out."

Eva's ring gave a buzzing throb as she passed over the lion's threshold, and when she looked up from her hand again, she found herself alone on the sidewalk in front of Overstreet House.

A shiver ran down her back in the sudden dim.

It was time for bed.

Eva was woken the following morning by a sharp rapping at her bedroom door. Before she could even answer, Henry had stepped inside.

"Eva," he said. "Eva, we have to go back."

Henry tossed his sketchbook onto the bedspread.

"I don't understand how it works," said Henry. "I have to get a second look."

Eva wanted to tell him what had happened the night before—to reassure him that Mr. Magister was expecting them—but she wasn't quite sure how she could explain. Earlier, on the way to the fairgrounds, Eva looked up to find him staring at the plain copper ring on her left forefinger. She thought he was going to ask where it had come from, but he turned his head to look out the window instead.

She'd always worn that ring, ever since she could remember—hadn't she?

Willie dropped them off at the gate. Eva watched Henry pay for his admission, only to feel the sudden jangle of his coins arriving in her pocket the moment he went through the turnstile.

She pushed in after him, not bothering to pay.

They began to search for a way into the Pavilion immediately, but it was only after long looking that Henry found it behind the reproduced Yucatán ruins at the southeastern extremity of the grounds.

"Eva," said Henry. "Eva!"

There, on the other side of a low stone archway, was not the vision of the rippling South Pond that they ought to have seen, but a high, narrow entryway paneled in dark wood.

"I knew it," Henry said.

Eva smiled and pushed him forward. On either side of the arch were two weathered geometrical lions carved into the stone.

As soon as they were inside, Henry began to sketch fluidly, mapping out the floor plan as best he could. Eva stepped into the front oak hall, eager to see through which door she might feel her parents again, and she stopped, listening, waiting, making herself as still and quiet as could be.

No—whatever whisper of warmth there had been on her earlier visit was hidden from her now. But all the same, the world smelled different here—toasted, tingly, electric—and she could feel, somehow, the whisper of multiplying possibilities on her skin.

Soon she felt herself drawn onward.

Eva found Mr. Magister in a scarlet study upstairs, bent low over a table strewn with schematics and diagrams.

"Ah," he said. "Hello, Eva."

He'd evidently been hard at work—his jacket was slung over a nearby chair, and beads of sweat dotted his ruddy brow.

"Hello," said Eva. "Are you feeling all right?" There was something ashen in his appearance that she couldn't quite ignore.

"Not to worry," said Mr. Magister, shrugging into his jacket. "Something is slightly out of balance in the Pavilion—that is all. I shall be fine. Is Henry with you?"

Eva nodded. "He's trying to draw a floor plan downstairs."

At this, Mr. Magister gave a chuckle of genuine amusement. "Bless him. I think he and I ought to have a little talk, don't you? Just so that he understands?"

Eva didn't quite know what this meant, but she nodded nonetheless.

"Good," said Mr. Magister. "I trust you and the Pavilion can fill a bit of time together until we return?"

Eva nodded. "Yes," she said. "Oh, yes." Already she found herself peering through each passing door, wondering who might be waiting on the far side of each labyrinthine corridor.

"Wonderful," said Mr. Magister with a grin, and as his footsteps faded away, Eva felt a tingling throb at the first knuckle of her left forefinger.

She had worn a ring there once—long, long ago. Hadn't she?

Eva thought she could tell when Henry and Mr. Magister left the Pavilion. There was no sound, of course, and she did not see them go, but something in the atmosphere, in the feel of the house, seemed to relax; it was like the lowering of the shoulders she'd always felt when Mrs. Blodgett left a room.

Oddly, the thought of Mrs. Blodgett made her laugh.

Slowly, Eva began to move from room to room, passage to passage, staircase to staircase. There was an undeniable warmth in the air, a kind of brightness, as if the house were preparing for a great holiday party, and she was slightly surprised each time she came into a new room and found it silent and still.

In a nursery on the second floor, she decided to try summoning the presence of her parents by coming to a stop the way she'd done in the servants' hall, but Magic rarely works the same way twice, and soon she grew bored of waiting.

There was an intricate music box in the shape of a carousel on a shelf, and when Eva opened it, she saw a stableful of tiny horses who ran a full race each time the lid was lifted. She held it in her lap for some time, opening and closing the lid, watching the tiny jockeys vie for victory with genuine excitement.

She thought she recognized the tune, but she couldn't quite say what it was.

When she looked up, she was surprised that from the nursery window she did not see the tangled grass beyond the front porch, but a stunning view of Lake Michigan. The day was clear out there, and the border between the sky and the water was as crisp as an autumn apple, but when she looked again only moments later, the water had an entirely different aspect: hazy, steely pale. There was a sail on the horizon, and high in the sky, a bar of light pink bespoke the shoreward sunset.

Sunset?

It was still morning, wasn't it?

Eva looked down at the music box and back up again.

Now the water beyond the window was dark, full of crinkling moonlit waves.

Eva shivered. Was this the imbalance in the Pavilion that Mr. Magister had spoken of? It almost seemed that the window was looking at her—somehow watching.

Eva pushed herself to her feet. She was getting hungry, anyhow, and she wanted to find a route back down to the dining room. If only she'd thought to ask Henry for her peach pit back, she might've had a snack for the long, uncertain way. . . .

She was nearly there, down in the great glass-walled conservatory, when she felt it a second time: the undeniable sense that she was being watched. At first, she thought that Henry and Mr. Magister had come home, but that didn't feel right. And it wasn't warm, like the shadowy presence of her parents had been, either.

What, then, was this feeling?

Something rustled deep in the leaves.

"Hey," said Eva softly. "Come back."

But there was no answer.

Eva was eating peach mousse from a small silver bowl when Henry and Mr. Magister returned, and she rushed out into the front hall to greet them. Mr. Magister was very pleased; Henry had a far-off look in his eye.

They were both exhausted.

"Good evening, Eva," said Mr. Magister.

Evening? It only felt like midmorning. But all the same, Eva smiled and said, "Good evening."

"I shall look forward to hearing how you fared today, but just now, I imagine that both Henry and I could use a bit of rest."

Henry nodded blearily.

"You may sleep in whatever room appeals to you," said Mr. Magister. "We don't stand on ceremony here." With a nod, Henry wobbled forward into the sitting room. Eva very much wanted to hear what had happened, but he was practically asleep on his feet.

Mr. Magister was already beginning to climb the stairs.

"But, Mr. Magister," she said, hot on his heels. "Won't Mr. and Mrs. Overstreet miss us?"

Mr. Magister frowned and shook his head. "Recall, old Dr. Fludd has cast a very convenient ambiguity for you two. I am quite certain your absence will go unnoticed."

Eva nodded.

"You are welcome, of course, to go back and sleep at Overstreet House whenever you choose, but I imagine you might begin to rather resent the commute. And now, Eva, I am quite exhausted. . . ."

Eva smiled. "I'm not." What weariness—and wariness—she'd felt seemed to have been eaten away with her peach mousse. "It barely feels like noon to me."

"Yes," said Mr. Magister. "Our Pavilion has only the most casual acquaintance with the flow of time. It is quite easy to lose track of it here."

"Is that why you're always looking at your watch?"

"My what?"

Eva gestured to the golden pocket watch in Mr. Magister's waistcoat.

"Ah," he said. "That is not a watch."

"What is it?" said Eva.

"A sort of pressure gauge, I suppose."

"A pressure gauge?"

Now Mr. Magister stopped. "I appreciate your enthusiasm, Eva—truly, I do. But I am afraid I am terribly tired now. I must rest."

Eva nodded. "Is it the imbalance?"

Mr. Magister blotted at his sweaty brow with a pocket handkerchief. "Possibly," he said. "I shall put it right just as soon as I am able. For now, Eva, a good night. You will find yourself ready enough to rest when you lie down, I think."

They had come to the end of the long gallery, and Mr. Magister turned up the adjoining corridor toward the lion-headed door. "Bed," Eva heard him say, and with a creak, the door swung open and shut.

All around her, the paintings in their frames seemed to let go a sigh.

Navigation in the Pavilion was not easy by any means—the seemingly infinite rooms had a way of jumping about, of changing places as if they themselves were apt to go wandering—and the challenge of finding her way back to the sitting room was daunting.

In the end, however, it was much simpler than she'd worried. Henry acted as a kind of anchor to her: all she had to do was think of him, and her feet turned in the right direction.

By the time she reached the sitting room, Henry was snoring in an armchair. She'd hoped she might be able to hear about his time with Mr. Magister before he dozed off, but all that would have to wait until morning.

It was odd, though: standing there beside him, watching his breath roll in and out like the waves on Lake Michigan, she felt something soft, familiar, warm—not precisely like the feeling she'd had in the servants' hall when she'd visited the Pavilion before, but not entirely different, either.

It was a comforting feeling; it was good, and with a stretch, Eva slipped her feet out of her shoes, curled up on a chaise, and closed her eyes.

When Eva woke, it was in the bright light of morning. Henry was already up, peering out the window on the far wall.

"Good morning," said Eva.

"Mmm," said Henry.

Eva stretched and slipped into her shoes. "So," she said. "How was it?"

A long moment passed before Henry responded. "How was what?"

"Your time with Mr. Magister?"

Again, a heavy pause, and then Henry said, "Come look at this."

Eva made her way to the window.

"The sun," said Henry. "It's over there, you see?" He pointed off diagonally through the windowpane in the direction from which the light was coming. "But in the dining room, it comes straight in."

"So?" said Eva.

"Well, the windows are on the same wall."

"Really?"

Henry nodded, then trotted to the dining room door. "Look."

He was right—the sun was coming in at different angles in the two adjacent rooms. "Well, it is the Pavilion of *Magic,* after all," said Eva.

"I know," Henry said. "But I think there's something wrong."

Eva frowned. "Mr. Magister did say there was a slight imbalance."

"Imbalance? Of what?"

She shrugged. "He said he'd fix it."

Henry squinted one eye and tilted his head.

"Are you hungry?" said Eva, eyeing the dining table.

"Yes," said Henry, taking Eva's peach pit from his pocket. He held it gingerly, almost reverentially, in his open palm. "Can you . . . ?"

"Of course," said Eva, and she closed his hand in both of hers.

Come back, she said in her heart. *Come back,* and no sooner had the peach returned to its pit than Eva and Henry sat down beneath the window to eat.

The sun warmed their backs. They didn't talk. Henry's shoulder leaned gently against Eva's, and they passed the peach back and forth, back and forth, trading bite for bite.

When the peach was finished, Henry led the way farther into the house, sketching in big broad strokes as he went. Eva tried a handful of times to ask what he and Mr. Magister had done the previous day, but Henry couldn't seem to concentrate on anything other than the Pavilion, and all of his answers sputtered out like a candle in the wind.

And there was something in his sketching, too, that had shifted. On the train, at Overstreet House, even at the Fair itself, Henry had seemed entranced whenever he set charcoal to paper: enchanted, enthusiastic. Now he moved his hands sharply across the page, as if he were angry—as if he were preparing an argument. Eva tried to shake him out of this dark mood, gleefully calling him over to see a chessboard in the library peopled with salesmen and senators rather than knights and bishops; she even suggested a game, but one of his pieces insisted it wouldn't work for a player who wasn't even old enough to vote for it, and by the time Eva looked up, Henry had already moved on, returning relentlessly to several well-thumbed pages in his notebook, sketching, erasing, redrafting maps and floor plans and exterior views of the Pavilion.

She tried not to let his indifference hurt her—after all, she knew the way the Pavilion could intoxicate, could draw a person forward. All the same, she felt a pang as he wandered off without her.

Did her friendship not mean as much to him as his did to her?

But just as soon as this question had arisen in her mind, the answer followed: Of course not. How could it? Henry had never been as alone as she'd been before they met.

He'd never even been as alone as she was now.

But then again—was she really alone? At every turn, the Pavilion seemed to be leaning in to suggest otherwise. Through the walls of the loom room, she heard someone playing slow, deliberate hymns on an ill-tuned piano, and later, passing through a long branching corridor, she thought she felt someone passing down an adjoining hallway. Thinking it was Henry, she went back for a closer look, but when she arrived, there was no one there.

It was in the machine shop, though, its workbenches strewn with tools and gears, that the sense arose most distinctly:

She was being watched.

There was someone present—surely—just there, over her left shoulder.

Cato.

Eva had no idea where this name had come from, but there it was, solid in her mind, like a hefty stone at the bottom of a water glass.

She moved gently, just as she might've around a skittish horse, only allowing herself to turn her head slowly, and gradually a distinct image began to resolve in the corner of her eye: a boy in a leather apron and round, shining spectacles.

He was staring straight at her.

Eva whipped around, terror in her heart.

But there was no one there. On the bench at which the boy had stood, a small dismembered cuckoo clock was laid out, its workings spread wide. Dust was thick upon the gears.

"Cato?" breathed Eva.

There was no answer.

Eva left the room as quickly as she could without running, and as she went, she felt a kind of tickling whisper at the base of her skull, just below the hairline: *Come back,* it seemed to say. *Come back.*

Now Eva reversed direction, picking her way toward the more familiar precincts of the Pavilion. Perhaps Henry was right—perhaps there was something more seriously wrong here, and if there was, then Mr. Magister should know about it immediately.

But before she managed to find him, Eva came upon another problem:

Henry.

He was in a little bedroom on an upper floor—

probably staff quarters, she thought—with a narrow bed, a low wooden table, and not much else.

She was surprised at how quickly he had deteriorated, wild-eyed and worried. Even his hair seemed to have grown shaggy, and something at the back of Eva's mind wondered how long they'd truly been apart.

"Henry?" she said, and he came straight across the room.

"I don't understand it," he said, as if they'd been in the midst of a conversation only a moment before. "I just don't understand."

"What?" said Eva, and in answer, Henry handed her his sketchbook.

"I can't see it," said Henry. "I can't see it. Or maybe I see too much?"

Eva looked down at the mad tangle of charcoal and then up at Henry's bewildered face.

"Eva—I don't know what to do." There were tears in his eyes.

Eva nodded. "Stay here," she said. "I'll get Mr. Magister."

But when she turned, he was already standing in the door, as if the mere mention of his name had brought him there. Eva had to stop herself from gasping at the sight of him, sweat-soaked and ruddy in an undershirt and trousers. Still, his spotless white gloves were on his hands, and in them he carried a pair of round spectacles.

"Henry," he said, and as he crossed the room, Eva thought she smelled something burning. "Here we are," he said, and bending low, he settled the spectacles gently on Henry's face, then smoothed down his unruly hair.

Henry blinked, squinted, turned his head to and fro. "Oh," he said. "Oh."

Mr. Magister rose. "Better?"

"Yes," said Henry. "Yes, I think so."

"What happened?" said Eva.

Mr. Magister sighed. "If the Pavilion is an image, Eva—which in a certain sense, it is—then the angle from which it is viewed is of paramount importance. A great amount of havoc can result if the perspective does not line up properly, and Henry's initial approach was, shall we say, unconventional."

Gingerly, Henry crossed the floor and laid his hand on the bedroom wall, as if to assure himself that it was solid.

"Now," said Mr. Magister. "If you'll excuse me . . ."

And, wincing, he strode from the room.

"Wait," said Eva. "Wait!" So much was unclear to her, so much uncertain. She clattered out into the hallway in pursuit of Mr. Magister, but he was already gone.

One thing—perhaps only one—was clear: she had seen the shining spectacles before.

They belonged to Cato.

Where There's Smoke

It was a long walk back, but Henry needed rest and quiet, and Eva knew where to find it: the parquet pond room. She slowed her step to let Henry take his time, and now and again, he stopped to wonder through his spectacles at an artifact anew—the bookcase eagle in the library, a sequence of tapestries depicting jousting knights in tailcoats. But even if they had clarified Henry's vision, these spectacles seemed to be causing new problems. He stopped often to rub at his temples, the charcoal on his fingers leaving dark smudges behind. Occasionally, he had to take them off altogether, then blinked blearily, as if he were surfacing from deep water in order to breathe.

When they finally reached the banks of the pond, he sat and took the spectacles off again. They were in a room with no windows, but even so, a gentle breeze ambled through the reeds.

"Eva," said Henry suddenly. "I don't think we should stay here anymore."

"What? Why not?"

Henry folded his glasses and rubbed at his eyes. "It's wrong. Something's wrong. And he knows it."

"Who? Mr.—?"

But Henry held up a hand. "Don't say his name."

Eva was bewildered. There was no question that Mr. Magister behaved in a peculiar manner sometimes. But the Pavilion, even Magic itself, was often peculiar, too.

"You don't trust him?"

Henry frowned. "I want to, very much. But I can't seem to make myself. I need to get away from him— without him knowing. Just for a little while. Just to see."

"But, Henry," she said. "He came to help you."

"Maybe," said Henry, considering the folded glasses in his hand. "But these make me see less, not more. And I don't think that's an accident."

Eva frowned. "Can I look?" she said, and Henry passed the spectacles to her.

Mrs. Blodgett had used a pair of reading glasses, and Eva remembered peering through them once—the way they'd rendered the world soft, fuzzy, big, like a smothering blanket. These glasses, however, did something very different indeed. The house itself seemed dimmed through their lenses—dulled, uninteresting. The walls and ceiling of the room were barely evident, but the lake, the cattails, and the reeds all glowed with a hidden, internal light. Of everything in her field of vision, Henry was shining brightest, radiating waves of flame, and it was beautiful to see. But there was a growing ache in her head, as if someone were slowly pushing an infinite icicle up into her brain, and she pulled the spectacles off with a wince.

Gently, Henry took them from her hand.

"Yes," she said. "I see."

Henry nodded.

"Where are you going to go?"

"I don't know," said Henry. "Not far. And it might not be for good. It's just that there comes a time in any drawing when you've been looking so hard for so long that you have to take a step back. It's the only way to see."

"Maybe Overstreet House?"

"No," said Henry. "It's too difficult to remember the Pavilion once you leave the fairgrounds. But we'll find somewhere."

Eva blinked. "We?"

Henry was surprised, even hurt, by this question. "You're coming with me, aren't you?"

Eva's head shook back and forth. She couldn't imagine leaving, particularly not sneaking away. What if Mr. Magister found out? What if he barred her from reentering? What if she never found her way back to the Pavilion, to Magic, to her parents?

"I—I don't think I can."

Henry's eyebrows dropped. "Why not?" he said. "He told you we were free to go and sleep at home, didn't he?"

This was true—he had. And yet now that the thought of really doing it came up, she wasn't at all sure that he meant it—or that she wanted to invite the consequences.

"Eva," said Henry. "You can't possibly be telling me that you trust him."

Eva swallowed. "Well, I trust the Magic," she said. And it was true.

But Henry knew the difference. "Eva . . ."

"I'm sorry," she said. "I just can't risk throwing it away on a suspicion."

Henry took a deep breath and slotted the spectacles back onto his face. "All right," he said. "Then I'll go and find proof. Can you cover for me while I'm gone?"

"I can try," said Eva.

Henry nodded. "I think I might have to use the lion's door to get out."

Eva grimaced. That lion had wide eyes. "Is there no other way?"

"Well," said Henry, "there's the front turnstile. But I haven't been able to get past the lions on the porch, and even if I did manage it, I'm not sure where I'd be. I haven't seen any other exterior doors. None of the windows on the ground level open, and the idea of trying to climb down from above frightens me—I have the feeling that you could start falling here and never, ever stop."

This possibility was both horrifying and all too plausible. Idly, Eva put her hand into her pocket; her fingers found the peach pit.

"Henry?" she said. "You're not going to leave me here, are you?"

For comfort, she closed her hand around the pit in her pocket, its keen edges pressing against her flesh.

"Of course not," said Henry. "I'll come back."

And at the sound of these words, the peach in Eva's pocket began to regrow.

Henry knew he would have to ask the lion above the doorway to let him out, but Eva thought they might be able to buy its discretion with a gift.

"Meet me in the long gallery," she said, and he was there when she arrived, sitting in a Dantesca chair, spectacles off, head in his hands.

"Did you get it?" he asked, and she nodded as she went by.

"Bring the chair."

The lion peered down at them as they approached. "A gift for you," said Eva, and it blinked and opened its mouth.

Eva climbed up on the chair and pressed the squirming little music box racehorse, saddle and all, into the lion's maw.

"It's not *alive*, is it?" said Henry.

"I don't think so," said Eva. "Not really." But the snap and crackle of tiny bones filled the hall as the carven lion chewed.

"Please," she said when it was done. "We'd like to see the fairgrounds."

The lion stared for some time, looking from Eva to Henry and back, but eventually it gave a demonstrative blink, and the door creaked open. Henry stepped forward and pushed with his fingertips, swinging the door wide, and the bright sunlight over Jackson Park came streaming in. Oblivious fairgoers passed to and fro before the archway, and after a moment, the elevated train came rumbling by high above.

Henry pulled the spectacles from his face, sighed, and walked through without another word. The door swung shut, wafting the aroma of the sunbaked path into the hall.

Eva had missed that smell.

Turning toward the stairs, she took the regrown peach from her pocket. It looked lovely, as ripe and colorful as ever, but when she bit into it, she found it mealy and dry. After the second bite, she chose to pull the remaining flesh from the pit with her fingers, discarding it into a wastebasket in a schoolroom full of vacant desks on the second floor.

In later days, she would wonder if this had been a mistake.

She passed by the open door of Cato's machine shop— even now, she could not get his name out of her head, like a catchy strain of melody—but she didn't go in.

Not far from the top of the stairs, she found a door sitting ajar upon which someone had chalked the date *October 8, 1871*. Inside, a space the size of a ballroom was overhung with gloom, and in the dim above, she could hear ticking. A great clockwork model of the night sky— stars, planets, galaxies—twinkled out, distant and near all at once.

Slowly, the arrangement of the stars inched forward, swirling, turning in imitation of the heavens above. As she stood watching, however, they caught, stopped, and, with a whir, reversed their motion.

Back and forth, back and forth, ran the great clockwork night.

It was very beautiful, but the ticking clockwork made her think of the dusty gears and pinions in Cato's workshop, and besides, she could see what seemed like the light of the blazing sun burning out bright from beneath the floorboards. It was too close in here, too stuffy. She needed air.

Maybe she should go and sit on the porch.

But Eva never reached the porch; Mr. Magister was in the library, and he called to her as she passed.

"Eva," he said. "How is Henry faring?"

The wooden eagle was perched on the back of a chair beside him, blinking intently.

"Oh," said Eva, "he's much better, thank you," and this, she supposed, was true.

"Good."

Mr. Magister was hard at work reorganizing his books, and though he was still not entirely well, he must have found an effective method of managing his pain: a large cut-glass pitcher sat on the table, its side beaded with condensation, and from time to time, he poured himself a glass and drained it away in one gulp. This seemed, at least, to minimize his discomfort.

"I apologize," he said, "for leaving you unattended so long. The Pavilion's imbalance has proved far more formidable than I first imagined, but I am hopeful that this may help to relieve some of the ill effects." Here he gestured to the pile of unshelved books on the table before him.

"The books are causing the problem?" said Eva.

"Causing it?" said Mr. Magister. "Why, no. But there is more than one way to address an imbalance, and in matters of Magic, the entire system must be taken into account—including the placement of every last book and paper." He frowned at the spine of the volume in his hand. "Thomas," he said to the eagle, "where is *The Grimoire of the Angel Raziel?*"

With a sound like the creaking of great oaks, the wooden eagle spread his wings and flew across the library to a shelf by the fire.

"Ah," said Mr. Magister, and after crossing the thick carpet, he placed the book in his hand first to the left of the grimoire, and then to the right. "But tell me, Eva," he said. "Have you not felt moved to try your hand at a bit of Magic?"

There was the peach, of course, but Mr. Magister had already seen her do that, and besides, its texture had been so disappointing last time. Eva felt her face redden. "Oh," she said. "I—I suppose I wouldn't know what to do."

"Have you not felt any invitation?" said Mr. Magister.

"Truly? Has there been no way in which the Pavilion has reached out for you?"

Eva frowned. "Who is Cato, Mr. Magister?"

At this, Mr. Magister flashed his gleaming white teeth; it might've been a smile if there had been any joy in it. "Ah," he said. "I shouldn't worry about him. A loose thread in the weave, nothing more. I imagine that all shall resolve once this imbalance has been corrected."

This didn't seem right to Eva. She couldn't say for sure who or what Cato had been, but he certainly hadn't seemed like a loose thread. "But, Mr. Magister—"

"I'm afraid I really must concentrate on this task," said Mr. Magister. "In the meantime, I advise you not to waste your time traveling down dead ends."

Eva intended to object once again, but a call rang out in the entryway.

"Eva!"

She knew that voice.

That voice belonged to Henry.

Eva was shocked.

Henry looked quite different, his clothes clean, the color high in his cheeks. He even seemed to have had a haircut.

"Eva," he said. "Thank goodness. I'm sorry I took so long."

But from the Pavilion perspective, he had left only that afternoon. "How long has—?"

"Never mind that," said Henry. "I just saw Vaclav— the boy from our first visit."

There was a pronounced rustling in the library, and Mr. Magister, shrugging into his jacket, strode into the hall. "Where?" he said. "Where did you see him?"

Henry had clearly not expected Mr. Magister to be there, let alone listening, and he blanched.

"Come, come," said Mr. Magister. "Time is of the essence. Where is Vaclav?"

"The Fifty-Seventh Street turnstiles," said Henry. "He wants to come in, but he can't figure out how."

"Good," said Mr. Magister. "Good. You've done us all a great service, Henry," and with that, he turned and raced up the stairs, taking them two at a time.

Eva was boiling over with curiosity, but Henry leapt off without another word, chasing after Mr. Magister as quickly as he could.

"Henry," she called. "Henry!"

She caught up with him where the long gallery met the lion's corridor, just in time to see the tails of Mr. Magister's jacket disappearing through the archway.

Henry didn't lose a moment; he turned, immediately

on the hunt, consulting several pages of his notebook, switching rapidly between spectacles and bare eyes as he surveyed the Pavilion around them.

"Henry," said Eva. "What's going on? What are you looking for?"

"How many fireplaces are there in this house?" said Henry.

Eva balked. They were innumerable. "There are fireplaces in almost all of the rooms, aren't there?"

Henry nodded. "Have you ever looked into one of them? I mean, really looked?"

"I suppose not."

"Here," said Henry, passing her his notebook. "No wood, no coal. The fire's coming up from below."

Up from below. Eva thought of the sun beneath the floorboards of the October 8 room.

"But think—if the fire's coming from below ground level, then it means there's got to be a basement or something down there. And if I can find the foundations, then I can tell what the true shape of the house is. I can figure out what's going on."

"So, what was all that about Vaclav? A distraction?"

"Oh, no," said Henry. "He's there: Vaclav Schovajsa. He doesn't remember, of course—not really—but you'd be surprised by what he *does* know."

Henry led Eva around a hallway corner. "Ah," he said. "Here we are."

The spot in which they found themselves must've been the single plainest in all the Pavilion: three bare walls without windows, doors, even decor—a stubby dead end of a featureless hallway.

"Where?" said Eva. "I don't see anything."

Henry was smiling. "Me neither. Yet." And taking off his spectacles, he paced toward the wall. "You see, the spectacles only show me *your* view—the view from the audience. And this Pavilion has a backstage, as well."

Now Henry reached out his hand and closed his fingers around a doorknob that wasn't there. The claw of his open fist turned, and as he pulled the unseen knob into the hall, the wall tore open in a perfect rectangle.

"Look," said Henry.

Behind the door was a set of simple stairs plunging down through numberless switchbacks. Far, far below, Eva saw a warm, flickering glow.

"Shall we?" said Henry.

Eva nodded; slowly, they began to descend.

At the very bottom of the stairs was an open doorway. Henry led Eva through.

Seven hearths surrounded the great brick chamber, a chamber so cavernous that though there was a fireplace on every side, darkness held the territory in between. In four of the seven hearths, blazing fires burned; two of the others were still under construction, and the final fireplace was ready, the fuel carefully arranged in its open mouth, just waiting to be lit.

At the very center of the room, a single bare lightbulb stood on a copper pole, flickering weakly.

The air felt loamy and moist.

It was not a comfortable place to be.

Henry walked in a wide circle around the edge of the room, surveying the fireplaces one by one, but Eva was more interested in the lightbulb. There was something strange about it; she couldn't quite tell what, but the socket into which it was plugged seemed to be figured in some way—sculpted. She wanted to see, but she was also hesitant to get too close, and she rocked from one foot to the other, trying to catch it in the hearth-light.

This was how she noticed the glint.

The mortar between the bricks of the floor shone

dully in the dim; when Eva bent low to examine it, she found that it was copper.

She reached out her left forefinger to touch it, and drew back with a shock. Her knucklebones buzzed madly at the contact.

"Eva." Henry had come to the completed, unlit hearth. "Look at this."

Eva made her way over. "What?"

"The wood."

And when Eva crouched down for a closer look, she saw that it was not wood at all, but a jumble of tools and construction materials—a hammer, a wrench, a hand-saw; nails, rivets, iron.

"That won't burn," said Eva. "Will it?"

Henry frowned. "Look at the others." Sure enough, none of the four fires in the foundation room were burning conventional fuel. One seemed to be fed with the keys and strings of a piano; another by a shining bolt of fabric that unwove into flaming swatches and threads as it traveled up the chimney. The third hearth contained a green shrub that appeared to be growing berries of flame, and the fourth and final burning fireplace held a tiny steel furnace fitted with an elaborate clockwork lock.

"Do they look the same in your spectacles?" said Eva. Henry checked. "Yes."

And it was then that the unlit fifth fireplace flared.

All the detritus of construction within it went up quickly in a blaze of bright heat. The copper mortar lines beneath their feet flickered in unison like a great strand of faulty filament, and Eva yelped, grabbing hold of Henry's arm. Her bones were buzzing, and for a moment—just a moment—she thought perhaps the veins in her wrist had flickered as well.

"Eva," said Henry. "Look."

The lightbulb at the center of the room was now burning bright and strong, and even at this distance, Eva could see the shape into which its socket had been sculpted, its coppery mane dripping down the sides of the pole like rivulets of water:

A lion's head, the bulb between its sharp teeth.

"Come on," said Eva, pulling Henry toward the staircase. "He'll be back before you know it."

She didn't want to speak of it, but she swore she'd seen the lion blink.

They had barely staggered back into the dead-ended hallway above when they heard whistling on the ground floor. It seemed so strange, so incongruous there in that house of still mystery, but Eva recognized the popular tune: *Ta-ra-ra boom-dee-ayy, ta-ra-ra boom-dee-ayyy . . .*

She looked at Henry, and with a swallowed sigh, he settled the spectacles before his eyes. "All right," he said. "Let's go and see him."

They found Mr. Magister back in the library, and he broke off his whistling as they approached. "Ah! Come in, my friends. Come in!"

He was marvelously improved, and all around him, the library seemed to reflect his mood, the books neatly shelved, the heavy scarlet drapes thrown wide to admit the thick, rich sunlight.

"Did you find Vaclav?" said Henry.

"Yes," said Mr. Magister. "I did. It was quite a pleasant conversation, truth be told. We cleared up our misunderstanding, and in the end, I think, we shall both be the better for it. For my part, I feel uncommonly well. We ought to celebrate, don't you think? Oh, surely, we ought to celebrate. Have we taken a meal together since you came?"

Eva shook her head.

"A grave oversight on my part—you shall have to forgive me. Very well, then: if you proceed up the stairs out in the hall, I believe you will find chambers in which to make ready—Henry's to the left, and Eva's to the right. Let me busy myself with a few preparations, and at the sound of the gong, we shall reconvene for dinner. How does that strike you?"

Mr. Magister was so jolly and invigorated—at any moment only a hairbreadth from a bright chuckle—that Eva found herself beaming as he began to compose the sunset, wiping away the bright day's sunshine from the windows to reveal the peachy dusk beneath. He whistled again as they climbed the stairs, and Eva hummed along: *Ta-ra-ra boom-dee-ayy, ta-ra-ra boom-dee-ayyy* . . .

The door of her dressing chamber was clear and conspicuous, and she waved brightly to Henry as she pushed inside. He, however, hesitated on the far side of the hall, glancing at the door with glasses and without.

There had been something, hadn't there? She could only half remember: a feeling of concern—close, loamy air. Things had seemed dire before Mr. Magister had returned, but his jollity and bravado were so contagious that she could scarcely recall ever feeling anything but gleeful anticipation. . . .

Beyond the door, Eva found an ivy-lined dressing room with a soft, heather-colored sofa and a broad mirrored vanity. Through a farther door, she discovered a tiled chamber with a great marble bathtub. She turned the spigots on, and there was a glorious fragrance in the steam, like lilac and peppermint.

Eva left her clothes slung across the sofa and slipped into the water. Immediately, she felt her muscles relax, her skin growing warm and pink. There was a pleasant buzzing sensation all across her body that she thought must soon subside, but it never quite did, and the water stayed at just the right temperature as long as she was in it.

It was only at the sound of the gong that she reluctantly rose.

The prospect of putting her unwashed clothes back on hardly appealed to her, but this didn't blunt the surprise of emerging into the dressing chamber to find that they were gone. All the same, she could hardly complain: in their place an impossibly fine white gown had been laid out. There didn't seem to be a single seam or closure in all its material. She wriggled into it, thinking that it must be droopy and huge, but its measurements were precisely suited to her—it fit her like a tightening embrace.

It was nothing like her old clothing in any way, except that she found with satisfaction that the peach pit she had left in the pocket of her last dress had been moved to the corresponding pocket in this one—a sort of gentle welcome home.

It had been long minutes since the gong had rung, but still, Eva took a moment to run the silver brush on the vanity through her hair. Only a handful of passes seemed to render her hair full, light, and buoyant, and when she stepped out of the dressing chamber, she felt like an entirely new person.

The Pavilion itself appeared to have dressed for dinner, the front oak hall crisscrossed with patches of colored sundown, and the white fabric of Eva's gown whispered as she descended the stairs.

Mr. Magister looked delighted when she arrived in the library.

"Why, Eva," he said. "You look lovely. Doesn't she look lovely, Henry?"

Henry, who seemed to have declined to bathe or change, blinked at her from behind his spectacles.

"Henry has just been advocating on your behalf," said Mr. Magister. "He thinks you deserve a day off—an opportunity to return to the fairgrounds now that you have a bit more Magic under your fingernails."

"I do," said Henry, as if his throat were very dry.

"What do you say, Eva? Could you use a day out?"

In truth, Eva felt a disinclination to lose track of the Pavilion, as if it might just disappear entirely if she so much as closed her eyes to sneeze, but Henry's gaze was fixed on her expectantly, and whatever else she might feel, no one but Henry had ever come back for her before.

"Yes," she said. "Yes, I think I'd like that."

She knew Henry must have a reason.

Mr. Magister gave a shrug, and he turned toward the windows. "Very well."

Eva shot a glance at Henry and accidentally caught him looking at her over his spectacles. He reddened.

"I've always said you were free to come and go as you please. But enough of all this. Let us go in to dinner!"

The preparations Mr. Magister had made seemed to consist primarily of relocating the lion's door into the dining room. Once they were seated, he spoke to it in an imperious tone, calling for course after course: There would be oysters first, and then a rich soup of mushrooms. Next there was salmon mousseline, followed by a roast with dauphinoise potatoes, all brought in by waiters in spotless livery who moved as if lost in a dream. After the roast came pheasants, and then a salad that Eva was far too full to eat but somehow could not decline. Mr. Magister's wineglass was never empty—sherry, then Chablis, claret, and Madeira—and he drank happily and deeply. Dessert was a new dish invented for the occasion by Monsieur Georges-Auguste Escoffier of the Savoy Hotel in London: peaches poached in sugar syrup with vanilla ice cream and a smooth raspberry sauce. As they scraped up the last spoonfuls from their dishes, Mr. Magister waxed poetic about the fruit of his youth: how he'd spent his early years in Georgia, where his parents had kept an orchard; how he had a distinct memory of sitting, hot and parched, beneath the trees, feasting upon the peaches. It had been his very first inkling of Magic.

Idly, Eva touched the pit in her pocket.

"In truth," he said, "I sometimes wonder if the peaches I ate all those years ago were not the result of the Magic we are undertaking now."

Henry didn't understand. "What do you mean?"

Mr. Magister shrugged. "I don't see why we ought to expect Magic to unfold like orderly mechanical processes: causes first, and then effects. The longer you practice the Impossible Art, Henry, the more you may suspect that our effects may well *precede* our causes, or, indeed, follow them long after they have passed out of memory."

Eva rattled her head gently at this notion.

"Or, to put it in slightly more apposite terms: the magical current that runs between our causes and our effects is as often alternating as it is direct." He gave a little chuckle. "Yet another reason to be deliberate."

Soon thereafter, the coffee cups having been cleared, Mr. Magister, plainly feeling his wine, rose and bid them goodnight, staggering through the lion's door with a half-belched request for bed. Eva was terribly tired herself, full to the brim with food finer than she had ever eaten.

It had all been delicious, of course, but she thought,

given the option, that she might prefer to resurrect her simple peace and share it with Henry again, sitting on the floor by the windows.

The moment she was in the sitting room, Eva kicked off her shoes and flopped down on the chaise. Henry followed, but rather than turn in to sleep, he sat himself cross-legged in an armchair by the fire and began to consult his sketchbook, leafing back slowly over the stained and well-worn pages.

If she hadn't been so pleasantly full, Eva might've asked him what he was thinking of.

Slowly, she drifted off to sleep.

"Eva. Eva!"

She blinked. "Time is it?" she heard herself ask. The fire by Henry's chair had retreated low in its hearth, as if slumbering itself.

"I don't know," said Henry. "I need your help."

"What is it?"

Henry held up his sketchbook. "Look," he said in a hoarse whisper, as if he were afraid he might be overheard.

Now he lifted the cover and, in the lurking firelight, flipped through the most recent pages.

Each of these held an attempted portrait of Mr. Magister. Some of them were quite detailed, and all of them were very carefully executed.

None of them, however, succeeded.

"I can't do it," said Henry.

"What?" said Eva. "Draw Mr.—"

Henry nodded. "That's right. He has some standing protection. I think that's why he was so impressed with the first one I drew—the one he took away. And that's where you come in."

Now Henry flipped back to where Mr. Magister had torn out his portrait; jagged flags of paper peeked out of the binding like sharp, thin teeth.

"Can you help me?" said Henry.

Eva swallowed. This didn't seem like something Mr. Magister would want her to do.

"Do you think he'd mind?" she said.

"Yes."

"Then should we?"

Henry took her hand in both of his. It was incredibly warm. "Eva," he said. "Please."

And so, with a deep breath, Eva laid her hands atop the sketchbook's binding and shut her eyes.

Come back, she heard her mind say, and her lips moved, whispering the phrase aloud: "Come back." Eva's will rose, and beneath her palms, she could feel paper moving. When the motion stilled, she lifted her hands, and Henry gave a triumphant laugh.

There, on the surface of the regrown paper, was Mr. Magister's face, just as he had drawn it.

"Perfect," said Henry, taking up his sketchbook as if it were the hand of a beloved convalescent. "Perfect."

Eva felt an electric thrill running through her bones, and she couldn't keep a grin from splitting her face. She flexed her fingers.

So it wasn't just the peach. What else might she bring back?

But there was something strange about the book in Henry's hands: something shining, new.

"What's that?" said Eva, pointing at the binding.

"What's what?"

Protruding from the binding was a long, stretched strand of light, draped between two pages like a bookmark of ribbon. It hadn't been there before.

"Oh," said Henry. "When Mr. Magister took me out to see the fairgrounds, he made that for me from the light of one of the electric bulbs—a little welcome gift, I suppose. It must've fallen off and grown back when you resurrected the portrait. To be honest, I'd forgotten about it until now."

This reminded Eva of something, but she couldn't quite say what.

The joints of her left hand began to ache.

When she woke again in the light of morning, Henry was gone.

Eva, however, knew just where to find him.

Mr. Magister's portrait was not the only page that had been torn out of the sketchbook, and it was therefore not the only one that had been called back. When Eva sat up and found the neatly folded page that Henry had left between her open fingers, she couldn't help but smile.

This time, he'd folded it with the peach blossom on the outside, and within, he had written two simple lines:

Top of the Cold Storage tower.
As soon as you can.

Eva laid the note on a low side table and stretched; when she rose to go to the lion's door in the dining room, the note remained there.

It wasn't that Eva intended to leave it, particularly, or even that she'd forgotten it—it simply didn't occur to her that leaving it behind might cause any problems.

But it did.

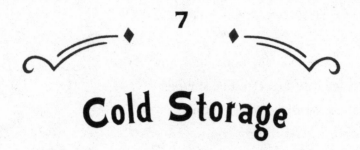

Cold Storage

The Cold Storage Building, a wide structure of five stories surmounted by a central tower of over two hundred feet, sat just inside the Sixty-Fourth Street turnstiles at the western extremity of the Fair. Much of its volume was taken up with the apparatus of ice manufacture—boilers, engines, condensers, filters—and with large cooling chambers for the refrigeration of the Fair's perishables. On the fifth floor of the building was an ice-skating rink—quite a novelty in the heat of the boiling Chicago summer—and there was a restaurant of some quality as well. But Eva passed by all of these things without interest.

Henry was at the top of the tower, where he seemed to have established a kind of studio in a disused room. Broad windows let in the daylight from all four sides, and when Eva arrived at the door after an interminable climbing of stairs, what little breath she had left was stolen away.

The walls of Henry's chamber were completely covered with sketches of the Pavilion of Magic, pinned-up scraps and broad slabs of board: oak-leaf shingles, scrollwork newel posts, elaborate window surrounds, the shifting patterns of the wallpaper.

And it was not difficult to see what Henry had been up to that morning. All around the room, set on window-sills, leaning against the walls, even flat on the floor, were sketches upon sketches of Mr. Magister: full-length, half-length, three-quarters. In a corner, one ashy portrait was giving off puffs of real cigar smoke.

"Good morning," she said, and with a start, Henry

looked up. The color in his cheeks rose like ripening fruit. She couldn't quite see it, but the sketch he was working on didn't seem to be of Mr. Magister or the Pavilion.

"Oh, hello," said Henry, shutting his sketchbook hurriedly. "I didn't hear you coming."

Eva turned her eyes to the drawings on the wall. "You've certainly been busy."

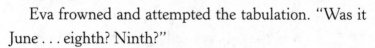

"Well," said Henry. "Yes. But it's also been much longer than you think. Do you recall when we first went into the Pavilion with Mr. Magister?"

Eva frowned and attempted the tabulation. "Was it June . . . eighth? Ninth?"

Henry nodded. "Today is July tenth."

Eva shook her head. "What?"

She knew that the Pavilion was detached from the regular flow of time, but she hadn't expected to lose an entire month without noticing.

Henry strode toward the door. "Come on," he said.

"Where are we going?"

But Henry didn't answer, and Eva had no choice but to clatter down the tower steps behind him. When they reached the ground, Henry pushed his way out through the turnstiles onto Stony Island Avenue, and it was only once they reached the line of hansom cabs waiting at the curb that she caught up with him.

"Henry! I thought we were spending the day at the Fair."

Henry called up to the driver of the first cab in line without breaking his stride, and he popped the door open and gestured Eva inside.

"Randolph and Fifth, please," he said.

The coachman squinted down at Henry skeptically. "You got money, kid?"

"Of course," said Henry, and he climbed in after Eva.

Randolph and Fifth. Where had Eva heard that before?

As soon as the cab was rolling, Henry took a blank rectangle of paper from between the pages of his sketchbook and began to fill it in carefully, front and back. His work took long, concentrated effort, and he was just finishing when they finally pulled up at their destination.

All the details were in place, from the portrait to the patterning, but it was dull gray, charcoal-colored, and the stock was wrong, too thick and heavy to be the real thing. When Henry handed it up to the coachman, how-

ever, and told him to keep the change, the fellow flashed a broad smile. "Hey, thanks!" he said.

Henry hopped down and made directly for the blocky building on the corner. Eva followed behind. Down the long street before them, clanking bottles rolled in broad lazy arcs, and the wind stirred up a distinct aroma of vomit.

"Henry," said Eva as they drew near the door. "What is this place?"

"Briggs House," said Henry, pulling back the door.

And all of a sudden, Eva remembered: the fellow at the Michigan Building—he had recognized Mr. Magister's portrait.

Randolph and Fifth.

"Hello," said Henry to the clerk behind the desk. "We're here to see William Gabbermann."

"Henry!" Eva was half a flight of stairs behind him, somehow yelling and whispering all at once. "Henry, stop!"

"I'm just going to talk to him," said Henry. "See what he knows."

"You're not going to do anything stupid?"

Henry flashed a sly grin. "You'll just have to come along and make sure."

Eva shot him the sharpest look she could muster.

"But you really should be here," said Henry. "It was you who brought the address back. As soon as I saw it resurrected in my sketchbook, I remembered the whole thing—Mr. Gabbermann, how he recognized the portrait, even the name he used for Mr. Magister: *Jack Coagulo*. Before that, it was like the memory had been ripped out of my mind, just like it had been torn from my sketchbook."

Henry led Eva out of the stairwell and down a long corridor of numbered doors. "Here we are," he said, and raising his fist, he gave a sturdy knock on Gabbermann's door.

There was no answer.

He knocked again.

No answer.

"Mr. Gabbermann?" called Henry. A door down the hall cracked open to make room for a peering eye.

"Henry," said Eva, "maybe we should come back later."

But Henry was determined. "Mr. Gabbermann!" he called again, so loud that Eva was sure the whole hotel would hear him.

Now there was noise from down the corridor, and Eva turned to see a big man in checkered pants stumbling out of the stairwell, his eyes puffy and red. Wherever he'd slept, it had clearly been in the same swampy clothes that he wore now.

"Mr. Gabbermann?" said Henry, and the man's face split into a grin.

"Why, I know you," he said. "Old Bill never forgets a face. Come on in, let's talk."

Gabbermann's room was not tidy.

"I hope you'll excuse the mess," he said. "I try to keep my private space private—plenty of folks on the make out here, you know, and you really can't be too careful."

He moved a pile of dirty clothes to the floor, and once Eva and Henry were seated, he settled his bottom onto the creaking bed and gave them a second look at his grin.

"Now, then," he said. "What were we talking about? You'll have to forgive me, it's been quite a trip, and there's always so much to keep track of. Was it the automated thresher? No, you're too young for that line. The popcorn confection? Because I have to tell you, I'm just overjoyed to see you again. I thought we had a real connection last time we spoke, young Mr. . . . ."

Gabbermann squinted at Henry, who kept his expression admirably level.

"Overstreet," said Henry. "I'm Hiram Overstreet. This is my sister."

A spasm of surprise shot through Eva, but she, too, kept her expression as even as she could. "Jenny," she said.

"Mr. Overstreet!" said Gabbermann with a guffaw. "Why, of course. I never forget a face. And which was it? The electrostatic mimeograph?"

"No, no," said Henry. "We've come about Jack Coagulo."

"Ah," said Gabbermann. His shoulders fell, the broad mask of good cheer slipping from his brow, and he sat in silent thought now for a long moment. "You know, in a funny way, Jack Coagulo's the reason I come back to Chicago. I had this dream—"

"Mr. Gabbermann—" said Henry, cutting in, but Eva's hand shot out to stop him; she'd had a dream of her own, long ago: great white buildings, towers, domes; an unending forest of columns and archways.

"What dream?" she asked.

Gabbermann looked up suddenly, as if he was surprised they were still there.

"Oh, it was nothing," he said with a chuckle. "I dreamt there was this steam engine pulling my house along the railroad tracks—my little place back in Kentucky, you know—pulling it up the tracks. And in the cabin, there was old Jack, shoveling coal into the furnace in his fine clothes and all, and the train whistle seemed to be calling out, *Come see the Fair! Come see the Fair!* Anyhow, it got me thinking about the old days up here by the lake, and, well, the next day I went out and bought a ticket up to the Exposition. Feels silly now, I suppose, but that's what happened."

"You seem to have known Jack pretty well," said Henry.

"None better, in our heyday," said Gabbermann. "I was his first investor. We was gonna make each other *millionaires.* And we might've done it, too, if it hadn't been for the fire."

"The fire?" said Eva.

Gabbermann gave a sigh. "I suppose you won't have been born yet—twenty-two years back. It was all the world could talk about when it happened: the Great Fire of Chicago. Whole damned—excuse me—the whole city, practically, burned to the ground. It felt like the wrath of God. Maybe it was, even."

Henry leaned forward. "Why did the fire stop you? What did you invest in?"

At this, Gabbermann seemed to come to himself, and he sat up straight.

"Begging your pardon," he said. "I don't know as I think Jack Coagulo is a person you go telling tales on. He's always liked his privacy pretty well, better than most, even, and as I recall, you still haven't told me how you're connected with him, Mr. Overstreet."

There was a sharp edge to this; Henry swallowed and didn't speak.

Eva turned to look at him. Long seconds were dragging by, and he had been quiet for far too many of them. Gabbermann's eyes had begun to narrow.

Henry needed help.

"I hope you'll excuse my brother," said Eva, improvising. "He's very upset. Our mother's ill, you see."

"Yes!" said Henry, cutting in. "Yes. And Mr. Coagulo's got the money for her treatment."

"Ha!" said Gabbermann. "Well, I'm afraid you'll have to get in line, there. Old Jack still owes me a tidy bundle, and I don't expect as I'll see it again in this lifetime."

Now Gabbermann rose from his creaking bed and went to the window.

Henry frowned. "If you can help us," he said, "perhaps we might recover what you're owed, too."

Gabbermann turned back slowly. "You know, that's an excellent point."

"Anything you can tell us would be—"

"Well, to begin with," said Gabbermann, a sudden fire in his eye, "he ain't really called Coagulo."

"Oh?" said Henry.

Gabbermann shook his head. "When I met him, he was traveling with a company of actors out of Georgia. I think Jack Coagulo was just a stage name. Got that sound to it—a little too grand, a little too self-important, just like old Jack hisself. He used to do tricks to amuse the crowd before the performance, but he was much too subtle to really get anyone going. Half the crowd was always talking during his act, and of those that watched, only a few ever really got what he was up to.

"Now don't get me wrong, his stuff was wonderful—really beautiful—but I thought he needed to go bigger, broader, if he ever wanted to make a stir. I told him so, too, but he said that wasn't his line. He wanted to make little miracles: things that people could hold in their hands, that they could pay a few dollars for and take home with them, bring a little enchantment into their dusty old lives. Well, I told him I'd be happy to partner up, but only if he was going to make miracles as people would at least *notice*. He said to me, 'Bill,' he said, 'I'll send one of them miracles home with you tonight, and if it ain't good enough for you, well, then, you win.'"

Gabbermann gave a wistful little giggle.

"You know what that old bastard—excuse me—that old fella, you know what he done? He turned my Sally's eyes from brown to violet. It was three days' time before I noticed it, lying right next to her there in bed. Just about took my breath away."

Eva couldn't help but chuckle. The coy quiet, the subtle beauty of the effect—that was Mr. Magister's Magic. "Sounds just like him."

Gabbermann nodded. "Well, I told old Jack, I said, 'You go right on ahead and make what you're thinking of making, and whatever it is, I'll try and sell it for you.' I brought him up to Chicago then, thinking we'd be shipping huge quantities within the year, rented a big old warehouse to hold all the stock, and even set him, Kate, and the baby up with a little place to call their own. Well, he got straight to work, and what he was making was as good as I could've expected. I remember a rocking chair that was a perfect fit for anyone who sat in it, and a map of the lake that showed the tides moving, right there in blue ink . . . but it all took so damn—excuse me—it took so very long that I couldn't imagine how we'd ever make any money. The chair alone took four months. One chair! I told Jack so, but that only made more trouble, see, because as soon as I complained about the rate of production, well, he started spending half his time working on plans for some great Machine that would grow his Magic—some kind of a magical bank. Don't ask me— I never saw hide nor hair of it, despite as I was paying his bills and all. Anyhow, I told him he had to be turning out more product or I couldn't continue to support him, and he took it to heart—started working day and night, like a madman. That was 1871. And then October rolled around."

"October of 1871," said Eva. She'd read that date somewhere. Where had it been? "The eighth?"

Henry stopped scribbling in his sketchbook and looked up.

Gabbermann nodded. "The fire," he said. "You think you can imagine. You think it's just like what you've got at the end of your little candlestick, but that's not it at all. It grows and it grows, and it takes everything in its path. I'll never forget that night. Don't think I ever could."

He gave a deep rattling sigh.

"The fire started down near our warehouse and spread north real quick. There'd been a drought, see, everything dry, and so much built of wood—even the streets, paved with wood blocks. I remember going to

Jack's place to decide what we ought to do, but Kate said he was already down at the warehouse. I told her I'd try to bring him back, but I didn't make it three blocks. I remember the lakeshore—so many people out there, keeping themselves by the water while the city burned, sitting on trunks and wagons, whatever they'd been able to haul out in time. It was incredible: terrifying and horrible and weird and beautiful, the smoke as dark as the fire was bright, everything glowing and orange. There's an odd thing as happens when the air gets real hot: narrow little cyclones kick up, and they draw the flame into the sky all thin, like a lightning storm in reverse. *Fire devils,* they call 'em. I remember, I was watching one rise with the water around my ankles when I saw him, sitting in the surf, covered in soot. He had bad burns all over his hands, and he was weeping, weeping."

Gabbermann took several quiet breaths.

"It was days before the wreckage was cool enough to even go back in, but right then and there, looking at him in the lake, I knew somehow—I knew that Jack's little family . . . well, they didn't make it."

There was a long silence now. Gabbermann blinked, and a tear rolled down his cheek.

"Jack and I split up after that. Nothing in the warehouse survived. I went back down to Kentucky. I don't know where he went. He tracked me down in Louisville a few years later with some harebrained scheme about buying up the fire—he said he'd found a way he could purchase a memory, make it real, like. He'd never been exactly what anyone would call conventional, but honestly, it seemed like he'd gone a little daffy to me. All the same, I'd recovered all right, so I gave him a hundred dollars just for old times' sake, and I ain't seen him since. I never expected any return on that particular investment, of course, but times have gotten a little tighter, and if it's out there, well, I wouldn't mind having it back. Where you might find him now, I don't know. Once in a while, I hear something through the grapevine—he's up in Newport working in service, he's out in Asheville recovering from the consumption. Never put much stock in the rumors, though. A man like that—well, stories crop up."

Henry underlined something three times in his sketchbook. "And do you have any idea what his real name might be?"

Gabbermann frowned. "I think—"

But they never found out what he thought.

There was a knock at the door.

"Just a moment," said Gabbermann, and he went to answer it.

"There," said Henry in a hoarse whisper. "Now, aren't you glad we came?"

Eva shook her head. "I don't think this is a good idea at all."

Henry rolled his eyes. "We have a right to know who he is," he whispered.

"Henry, just because this fellow—who doesn't seem to have any Magic of his own, by the way—just because he thinks that Mr. Magister was going crazy sometime before we were even born . . ."

"Eva . . ."

"As far as we know . . ."

"And just because you feel bad for Mr. Magister," whispered Henry, "it doesn't mean that we can trust him."

Eva tsked in exasperation. If Henry only knew how many sad stories about dead wives she'd heard in her séances . . .

But at just this moment, he took hold of her fingers and squeezed—hard.

Gabbermann was in the entryway, door closed behind him, watching them both with narrowed eyes.

In his hand, he held a gray bowler.

"Forgot my hat," he said.

Slowly, Gabbermann walked into the room. On the bureau by the window, there was a pitcher and a grubby, finger-smudged glass, and he laid the hat beside them, then poured himself two full glasses of water and drank them down without stopping.

He opened the top bureau drawer.

"I'll be honest with you," said Gabbermann. "I've been afraid of Jack Coagulo a long time. I told you I gave him money for old times' sake, but as much as anything, I was just dead scared of what he might do if I said no. And that's why I went out and bought me this."

Gabbermann reached into the bureau drawer and turned back to them; Henry stiffened.

In his hand, Gabbermann held a snub-nosed revolver.

"You said, little missy, that it was just like Jack to change the color of my wife's eyes. And I thought that was strange. How on earth would you know that? But the real thing of it is—you're *right*. It *was* just like Jack. And I thought, shucks, maybe I'm being paranoid—you're just two kids trying to help your sick mama. But when Hiram and Jenny start calling each other Henry and Eva, I gotta start wondering."

Gabbermann cocked his pistol.

"Just what in the hell is going on here?"

Eva swallowed hard; the barrel of Gabbermann's gun was quivering.

It all happened so fast.

Henry's closed eyes snapped open, his flat palms shoving out hard into the empty air. Gabbermann flew backward, flung across the room by an Impossibly strong force, and his pistol went off, spitting bright flame at the ceiling. Henry was pushing Eva, yelling, *"Go, go, go!"* There was plaster and dust in the air, Gabbermann halfway through the back wall, and Eva tore open the door of the room and ran, Henry behind and then beside her, doors opening in the corridor all around them, eyes and voices, and they were back in the stairwell, the lobby, the street, racing through traffic, pushing pedestrians, dodging and sprinting, turn after turn, deeper and deeper into the city.

Blocks away, they slid to a panting, heaving halt. All around them, the city rumbled and clattered. "Oh my goodness," said Eva. "Oh my goodness."

Henry's eyes were wide, his cheeks red; the corners of his lips had begun to curl into an unbelieving grin.

"Henry," said Eva. "Henry, what did you do?"

"I don't know!" said Henry. "I don't know. I just felt all this, this tingling power, and I thought, I just thought, *No*, and, and . . ."

Eva peered back in the direction from which they'd come. "Is anyone following us?"

Henry shook his head. "I don't think so."

"Oh my goodness."

Henry gave a little chuckle, and Eva slugged him in the arm. "I told you this was a bad idea."

"Sure," said Henry. "But it wasn't me who invented our sick mother."

Eva spluttered unsuccessfully for an excuse. Who was this brash boy in Henry's clothing? Not the quiet observer she had come to know, not her contemplative artist—a live wire.

She watched him run a hand through his rumpled hair.

"Well, whatever else is the case," said Henry, "it's clear to me now that Mr. Magister isn't what he seems. He's hiding something."

"Hiding what?"

Henry set his jaw. "I'm not sure yet. But if we don't find out in time—mark my words, we'll regret it."

He had just reached out to hail a cab when Henry realized with shock that he'd left his pencils in Gabbermann's hotel room; he couldn't draw up the fare to the grounds even if he'd had the energy, and he certainly didn't now—once the exhilaration of escape wore off, it became clear quickly that pushing Gabbermann like that had utterly depleted him.

This wasn't a complete disaster—he had more pencils in his Cold Storage chamber—but neither of them had any cash on hand, Eva having left her bag beside her chaise in the Pavilion.

This meant that they had to walk back down to the Fair—and it was very hot.

The way was long—eight miles, give or take—and Henry soon grew red and sweaty, his pace slackening with every passing step. Eva insisted that they ought to stop in at Overstreet House on their way down ("just for fifteen minutes—just to rest a bit"), but Henry flatly refused. There were too many questions: Why had Mr. Magister wanted to collect the fire? What was his true name? And what, in the end, was his Pavilion meant to accomplish? He had to get back to the Cold Storage tower, where he could sketch and think, and the longer he stayed away from the fairgrounds, the further his memory would fade.

By the time they reached Jackson Park, Eva had begun to worry in earnest—what had seemed at first like enthusiasm had begun to look disquietingly like delirium—but once they passed the turnstiles, Henry improved quickly: the favor of the Fair was strong.

It was past noon when they arrived, and they made

their way to the Midway directly. Henry had three servings at the French Cider Press in quick succession, his hands shaking as he raised his glass. Eva kept waiting for the girl at the counter to ask them to pay, but she never did—an extension, perhaps, of the favor of the Fair— and when they made a beeline for the Ostrich Farm to indulge in giant omelets, she ordered without worry. But despite the bolstering effects of the food and fairgrounds, Henry was consumed, his mind ablaze with thought. Eva could hardly keep his attention, and he drifted away over and over again into his own mind, his eyes darting back and forth foggily, as if examining a drawing on some unseen page. Cato's glasses still hung from the open neck of his shirt, and the sight of them there reminded Eva of an image, like a fragment of a dream: one of the round lenses splintered, cracked.

They seemed to shine, those spectacles, with some reflected light, and only now did Eva begin to wonder about its source. It was warm—saturated, like a bonfire or a thick sunset.

When they'd finished eating, Henry turned immediately toward Cold Storage. There was something off with him—something, perhaps, jarred loose in the confrontation with Gabbermann—and he said he wanted to sleep.

Eva considered going with him, but the prospect of sitting idle on the fairgrounds while Henry napped hardly appealed to her. There were several nearby sites she had neglected that called out to her now: the Japanese Hō-ō-den, or Phoenix Hall, on the Wooded Island; the Electricity Building at the bottom of the lagoon.

And so they split up, Eva taking the bridge to the Wooded Island while Henry wandered down past the Horticulture and Transportation Buildings toward Cold Storage.

It had become a bad habit with them, splitting up; it was all too easy to get lost, and the longer they were apart, the more Eva worried. She worried her way across the tatami mats in the Hō-ō-den; she worried her way along the island's placid walking paths; she worried her way amongst the bloody blossoms of the Rose Garden.

Something was wrong. And when she reached the end of the island's southern bridge, only three-quarters of an hour after parting company with him, Eva turned not leftward toward the Electricity Building as she'd planned, but rather rightward to make her way back to Henry.

But already it was too late.

Just beyond the Transportation Building, a thick black plume of smoke had begun to spread into the sky.

The Cold Storage Building was burning.

Eva had never moved so quickly in her life.

Tears crowded her eyes, streaming back across her cheeks, and she shoved, pushed, bashed her way through knots of people without regard, the squeezing fist of her chest ratcheting tighter and tighter with every passing moment. Everyone at the Fair—everyone—was staring at the blazing tower, gathered together in twos and threes, pointing their fingers over rooftops and trees, and as Eva came nearer, the gawkers grew thick, and she wormed her way between the people, tearing, clawing her way forward.

Henry was in there.

The Columbian Guards had established a cordon at some distance from the Cold Storage Building beyond which Eva was told she could not pass. A uniformed gentleman barred her way, and she found with some surprise that she was speaking, pleading through a clenched throat: she had, she had to get inside, he was inside, she had to get him out, and the man was shaking his head, and still she begged because the tower, she could see the tower blazing, flame above and flame below, licking up the walls, and there were firemen up there, tiny with the distance, caught between fire and fire, panicked, trapped, and a sound somewhere between a gasp and a yell tore through the tight-packed crowd because one of the firemen had jumped, leaping from the top of the tower rather than stay there to burn alive, and Eva's mind spun, spun, how could Henry get out, what could he do, he had been so tired, so exhausted, and even the firemen were trapped, what could he do alone, one boy, one frightened, exhausted, beautiful boy?

Something flared, bursting through the windows at the peak of the tower; a spray of glassy smithereens fell toward the ground, and at the very same moment, Eva felt something shatter inside of her.

Henry. Henry.

"Hush, now." Strong hands took hold of Eva's shoulders. "Hush."

Someone had been screaming, and closing her mouth, Eva realized it had been she.

"We must go," said Mr. Magister into her ear. "We're no longer safe here. Come."

The sudden weight of enchantment spread across Eva's chest, heavy and soothing. The quiver and shake of her sobbing slowed, and her feet began to move beneath her.

"I know," said Mr. Magister. "I know."

The crowd parted unwittingly as Mr. Magister steered Eva toward the nearby train tracks. They climbed a set of access stairs, and Mr. Magister led her toward the far end of the platform, where a lone Pullman car sat waiting, untethered to any engine.

The air smelled scorched.

Mr. Magister opened the door to reveal a set of steps leading up into the well-appointed car, and leaning down to bring his eyes level with hers, he spoke.

"Eva," he said. "I cannot say how sorry I am. I promise you, I shall get to the bottom of this terrible accident as soon as I am able."

Eva sniffed, blinked.

"My Pullman car will carry you to a safe place. I shall meet you there."

A new spasm of panic stole into Eva's heart. "You're not coming?"

Softly, Mr. Magister shook his head. "I am afraid there are things here that I must see to. Urgently."

Eva tossed her head as if Mr. Magister had spoken in an incomprehensible language. "You're not coming?" she said again.

Now Mr. Magister drew himself up to his full height. "Do not fear," he said. "You are under my protection."

With a gentle hand, he guided Eva up the steps that led into the opulent train car.

The door closed behind her.

Retreat

Time passes differently on trains.

The wheels thrummed beneath the Pullman car. Beyond the windows, the prairie spread out to the horizon and slowly began to crinkle, gathering into jagged hills.

Hours passed, and the sky grew dim, yet Eva seemed stuck in a single smoldering moment:

Henry was burning.

Henry was dead.

She'd sat herself down in the first available seat—an upholstered bench behind a polished wooden table. There was a geometric pattern inlaid in the wood and Eva traced at it idly with her finger, but her eyes barely saw.

All she could see was Henry: across the table from her only hours ago, the massive ostrich omelet cooling to rubber on his plate; sketching in the tower, collar loose, sleeves rolled to the elbows, his hand, swift and sure, skating lightly across the page.

The Cold Storage tower in flames; the force of the explosion; the heat on her face.

Henry.

Something had been wrong. She should've known. And his words echoed in her mind: *You can't possibly be telling me that you trust him.*

She swallowed hard.

I trust Magic, she thought. *I trust Magic.*

Hours barreled by like a train passing on a neighboring track. Outside, the sky lit up—lavender and coral and mulberry and mauve, all the colors of a fading bruise. The sun was setting, but on which horizon Eva didn't know. If only she could remember where the light had been coming from, she might've been able to say.

Henry, of course, would have known.

This thought ought to have made her cry—she felt the surging ache in her head, the tightness and grip in her throat—but whatever heavy dam Mr. Magister had laid about her held firm, and she could not.

But, oh, how she wanted to.

Eva sat quiet and still.

Slowly, as if descending from the very midst of the sky, darkness fell like a grand curtain.

There had been no sign of civilization since Eva had rolled out of Chicago—no city, no settlement, no station—but now, ahead, she saw, tiny in the distance, a little pool of light cast down by a lone streetlamp in the gloom.

The brakes began to fire, grinding and squealing beneath her. The car slowed and, as the streetlamp drew up beside her, stopped.

The door popped open.

A man stepped into the light.

"Good evening," said Mr. Magister.

Quietly, Eva began to weep.

"Oh," said Mr. Magister. "Oh dear."

Mr. Magister led Eva across the platform of unhewn rock and down a short dirt path.

"Come," he said. "We shall be there shortly."

At the end of the path was a dense thicket set beneath an impenetrable canopy. Not even the moon's light could reach through the trees, and the roots and brambles below seemed to drag at Eva's ankles.

For a moment, she thought she might never reach the other side.

And then, suddenly, they were out.

The lawn beneath her feet was patchy, balding of its tawny summer grass. There was a small stand of trees ahead, and in their midst stood an L-shaped farmhouse, tall and narrow. The hearth fire flickered through the window of the parlor, and what should have been a welcome warmth in the midst of the darkness was instead a reminder:

The heat on her face; the force of the blast.

Where was she? What was this place? And as if in answer, Mr. Magister laid his hand on her shoulder. "We shall be safe here, for a time," he said. "Welcome home."

Not long ago, the word *home* would've filled Eva with passionate longing. Now it only wearied her.

She followed Mr. Magister forward.

The house was clad in clapboard, the same weathered gray as the barn behind. It did not seem to have been tended or inhabited in quite some time, and all about the perimeter, bushes and brambles had grown up in an unchecked tangle. A vine snagged at Eva's toe as she stepped up onto the low platform of the porch, and at the front door, Mr. Magister turned to survey the sky. Eva took a look for herself and found it unexpectedly beautiful: the starry spray of still light; the vast spill of the Milky Way—comforting, familiar.

Mr. Magister had made his best effort at preparing the house for her, but still, the heavy scent of dust lingered, tickling sharply at the back of Eva's throat. He led her through the house's rooms: the parlor, the dining room, the ancient kitchen—tarred and feathered in dust and grease. There was a small pantry behind a rickety door, and up the moaning stairs were three bedrooms. Mr. Magister had laid his hat and coat on the bed in the first; in the second, he had deposited Eva's bag, rescued from the Pavilion. But this left one bedroom unoccupied, and Mr. Magister saw the expression on Eva's face:

There would be no argument. That could only be Henry's room.

Gently, Mr. Magister eased its door shut.

Without a word, Eva went into her own room, curled up on the bed, and began to sob.

It was only once Mr. Magister's footsteps had moaned back down the stairs that Eva rose, silent and light, and went to open Henry's door.

Eva slept and woke, slept and woke. Sometimes she could hear Mr. Magister moving about in the parlor, sometimes not. Crickets keened outside her window by night, and when the morning came, the birds twittered meaninglessly.

She had never felt a pain like this before. It was like she was rotting from the gut out.

Once, Mr. Magister came up and stood in her doorway. Eva had her back to him, curled up still on the covers. She didn't turn.

By and by, he left again.

It was dim outside when the smell of bacon rose up to Eva's bedroom, and she felt a stabbing pang in her stomach; she had almost forgotten about food.

Mr. Magister was sitting by the parlor fire reading an old book when Eva came down the stairs. He raised his eyebrows. "Hungry?"

Eva nodded, and tucking his book under his arm, Mr. Magister went to the kitchen to fetch her a chipped bowl of steaming beans and a slab of buttered toast.

Eva sat quietly, chewing without pleasure. Presently, Mr. Magister spoke:

"Tell me, Eva, have you ever heard of a man called Gabbermann?"

Eva swallowed.

Mr. Magister knew that she and Henry had met him on the fairgrounds—they had spoken of it. So why was he asking?

But then she recalled what Henry had said at Briggs House: *It was like the memory had been ripped out of my mind.*

She wasn't supposed to remember.

"Gabbermann?" she said, and with a sigh, Mr. Magister sat forward and laid his book aside.

"William Gabbermann is a very, very dangerous man, Eva—a dark Magician of great power."

Eva kept her expression studiously level.

"Long ago, I labored under his influence, and at great personal cost, I managed to escape from him. It is his most fervent wish now to steal back all the power that belongs to me. I fear it may've been he who got to Henry."

"Henry?" said Eva. "What would he want with Henry?"

"No one comes to sojourn in the Pavilion of Magic, Eva, who is not possessed of magical talent. You, for example, have quite a knack for bringing back what is gone. And though I did not, to my detriment, give it the attention it deserved while I had the chance, Henry's talent—the transcription of those things that cannot be clearly seen—was also quite considerable. But it was not only Henry's own power that he carried to his death, Eva—it was mine as well."

"Yours?"

Mr. Magister nodded. "Just as the shining sun ripens the fruit on the tree, my Pavilion of Magic grows the power of those young Magicians who walk in its halls."

Eva thought of her peach, of the sketchbook—of the boy Cato. It was true: perhaps she'd brought her talent with her, but the Pavilion had fostered it, without question.

"So, Henry had your power?"

Mr. Magister nodded. "Some of it—in a manner of speaking."

Eva frowned. "But what good would it do for Gabbermann to burn him?"

Mr. Magister scoffed. "What good is a lump of coal left unburned?"

This was crass, and Mr. Magister saw it in Eva's face.

"Forgive me," he said. "I do apologize."

Eva looked down and stirred her beans, her mind circling around to what he'd said:

She had a knack for bringing back what was gone.

"Mr. Magister?"

"Yes?"

"I asked you once if it was possible to bring back—to bring back people."

Mr. Magister neither moved nor spoke.

"Can you tell me—?"

But he broke in before she finished. "I told you, Eva, that it has never been accomplished. Even amongst

Magicians, death is an impenetrable barrier—a puzzle we are simply incapable of thinking our way around. The best have tried, but I am afraid it is simply not possible."

Eva swallowed. "Yes. But isn't that what we do? The Impossible?"

"There are," said Mr. Magister, "limitations. Human beings have a way of thinking themselves into corners, you see—even Magicians—and death is rather a hard cage to climb out of. You ought to know that as well as anyone. How long were you engaged in your swindle with Mrs.—What was her name? Mudgett?"

"Blodgett," said Eva. She set down her beans in sudden disgust.

"I am sorry, Eva," said Mr. Magister. "Truly I am. And I promise you: if Bill Gabbermann is to blame for Henry's death, then I shall see to it that he pays. Trust me."

And Eva found that she did—in this matter, at least.

"Before I search him out, however, you must answer a question for me, a very important question indeed."

Eva took a deep breath.

"Did you go and see him?"

Eva blinked at the empty space between her bowl of beans and Mr. Magister's book.

She didn't answer.

Mr. Magister shifted in his chair. "I understand, Eva, that moving in and out of the Pavilion can trouble the memory—you must take your time and think carefully. But whatever transpired, I shall discover the truth in the end." Now Mr. Magister rose, reclaiming his book gently from the table. "Do not forget who your friends are," he said.

And with that, he made his way up the stairs.

But Eva had only one friend. And tonight, he slept in ashes.

She could never forget.

Mr. Magister was reading when Eva came trudging up the stairs, the door of his room hanging open, but she passed by without a word.

She couldn't stop thinking about it. If she could bring Cato back without meaning to—even for just a moment—and if she could bring her parents back by just sitting idle, what might she accomplish if she really tried?

She had to at least try.

And so Eva lay down on her bed to wait. Mr. Magister's door squealed shut; she waited. His bedroom floor stopped its squeaking, and still she waited.

Finally, when the farmhouse had held its silence deep into the dark of night, she rose.

It was there in her bag, just where she'd left it: the candle that had begun it all, tall and smooth, its wick curled into a tiny singed question mark. In order to begin her private séance, she would need to blow this candle out, and in order to blow it out, it would first have to be lit.

Perhaps there were matches in the kitchen.

Eva took a deep breath and turned toward the moaning stairs. Down she went, creeping slowly, laying her feet on the edges of the steps to keep her passage quiet, and she was just about to go into the kitchen when, out of the corner of her eye, she saw the roaring parlor fire.

Turning aside, she bent toward the hearth.

It was odd—she had never seen such a healthy blaze fed by so little fuel, only a few glowing coals left in the grate despite the leaping flames.

This reminded Eva of something, but she couldn't say quite what.

She lowered her candle gingerly toward the coals; its wick sputtered like a clearing throat and then, suddenly, caught.

Carefully, quietly, Eva carried the flaming candle back up the stairs. She paused on the upper landing, waiting to hear if she had inadvertently woken Mr. Magister, but nothing moved; all was silent.

The candle's flame wobbled, sending the inky shadows on the corridor walls dancing out from their places.

Eva crept forward, past Mr. Magister's bedroom, then hers. She hadn't been able to keep from thinking that Henry belonged in the third, vacant as it was, and if she was going to bring him back, it would be there.

Henry's room.

Inside, there was a bed and a window. A small standing mirror sat on the table by the foot of the bed, its glass slumbering beneath a thin layer of dust. Eva turned it away before she sat herself down.

It felt like forever since she had done this—forever and no time at all.

She evened her breathing and stilled her mind. She shut her eyes softly, and when she opened them again, she was ready.

The candle flame filled her vision, bright and steady.

Was this truly the stuff that had taken Henry? It seemed so little here, so insubstantial at the end of her candle: a raindrop to the sea. How could *this* have destroyed something so beautiful, so singular, so good as Henry?

And suddenly, the words were there, chasing one another about her mind:

Come back.

Eva pursed her lips and blew; the candle flame guttered and died.

"Come back, Henry," said Eva into the darkness. She

was surprised by the size of her own voice, and softly, quietly, after long moments of still silence, she said, "Please come back."

But Henry—if there was such a thing anymore—did not appear.

After what seemed like an interminable wait, Eva pushed out of her chair.

What was she doing?

What on earth was she doing?

Slowly, she trudged back to bed, not even bothering to quiet her footsteps.

The candle she left smoking on the table.

When Eva's eyes opened in the morning, she didn't bother to move. She couldn't see the point.

Thin, gray light filtered in through the cataracted window. Downstairs, Mr. Magister was whistling— *Ta-ra-ra boom-dee-ayy, ta-ra-ra boom-dee-ayyy.* Eggs were frying in the kitchen, and Eva found the aroma somehow revolting. She let out a strangled sigh, rolled over, and pulled the covers up to her chin.

She wanted less light, less noise—less Everything.

She wanted as little Everything as possible.

But Eva had rolled over on top of something—

something small and hard, pressing stubbornly into her hip—and she brought it up from her pocket:

The peach pit.

It seemed like a mistake, its presence here.

Its tip was perfectly pointed, needle sharp, and she pushed it into the pad of her thumb over and over again, savoring the little starburst of pain.

Would the fruit come back if she called it now? After her failure last night, she was hardly sure. And besides— it seemed like such a useless thing to do. She had no appetite, and no one to share with.

Why would she even want to bring it back?

She had just put the peach pit down on her bedside table when Eva felt a shock rocket through her body.

Someone had walked past her bedroom door— someone strange.

Quickly, she leapt up, eager to look out into the empty hallway.

A girl had gone by. Eva had seen her clearly: red hair, freckles, straw-colored dress, dirty white apron.

But no one was there now.

Eva opened her mouth. She wanted to call out, but she couldn't let Mr. Magister hear her downstairs.

"Meg?" she whispered.

Meg? Who was Meg? She'd meant to say *hello.*

Everything was still. Upstairs, there was no movement

of any kind—all Eva could hear was the pacing of Mr. Magister's feet below.

She must've imagined it.

Could she have imagined it? In such detail?

And then, behind her, in her very own room, something shifted.

Eva whirled about, backing into the hallway so quickly that her back jammed into the rickety banister.

There was a plant in the corner with broad, flat leaves and its terra-cotta pot had suddenly cracked, sending a narrow spray of soil across the rough floorboards.

Eva advanced slowly. How had that happened? Pots didn't just crack out of nowhere.

Besides—wasn't it strange that a potted plant would be green and alive in a house so long neglected?

And as she drew closer, things grew only stranger. The plant's broad green leaves had begun to spill out of the side of its pot, pulling the entire arrangement off balance.

And yet, somehow, it hadn't toppled.

Because the roots had grown down—right out of the bottom of the pot—and into the floor.

Eva tugged lightly at a root. Yes, it had wormed its way between the floorboards. It barely budged, so she yanked harder, once, twice, three times, beginning to grow concerned that she might break it off, but in fact, the opposite occurred: with a splinter and a crack, the floorboard popped up before her.

Eva gasped.

The floor was filled with thick black earth.

Using her fingers, Eva dug quickly through the soil, and what she discovered there was very strange indeed: it seemed that the pot had served as a sort of conduit connecting the plant to the house, its massive root system spreading out far and wide. She dug on, clawing back more and more earth, until finally she encountered a horrible snarl of interwoven roots tangled all around a long, straight plumbing pipe.

It took her a moment, but then Eva saw:

Something was gleaming.

Here, deep in the second-story earth of this house, the plant's branching roots had become a lustrous red.

Copper.

Eva reached out her finger to touch them and felt a buzzing in her knuckles, strange and violent. She pulled back sharply.

"Eva?"

Mr. Magister was calling from downstairs.

Hurriedly, she pushed the soil back into the floor and replaced the floorboard atop it. She worried about dirt stains on her fine white dress, but miraculously, there seemed to be none, and with no other option, she wiped her hands thoroughly on the foot end of the bedspread.

Only the dirt beneath her fingernails could tell on her now.

Mr. Magister was seated in the dining room reading a book, the remnants of his breakfast before him.

"Ah," he said. "Good morning, Eva. I thought I heard you rustling about up there. Are you hungry?"

Eva shook her head.

Mr. Magister gave a curt nod. "I am afraid I have some business in town today that I cannot avoid."

Eva blinked. "Town?" she said. There had been no sign of settlement outside the train windows as she came. This place might've been almost anywhere: Pennsylvania, Arkansas—even Ontario. "What town?"

"Oh, I wouldn't worry about that," said Mr. Magister. "The point is that I shall be gone, and that I shall return."

"All right."

Mr. Magister rose, slotting his arms into his jacket. Eva turned toward the stairs.

"Eva," said Mr. Magister. "Remember what I told you: there is no use in traveling down dead ends."

Eva stiffened, but said nothing.

"Have you had a chance yet to think about Bill Gabbermann?"

Eva shook her head. "No."

Mr. Magister sighed. "Suit yourself. There is bread and cheese in the kitchen, if you want it."

And without looking back, he strode through the house, out the door, and off across the front lawn. Eva watched him go, and when he pushed his way into the thicket at the end of the property, she followed out onto the low porch.

Everyone else had abandoned her, one by one: her parents, long before she could even remember; Mrs. Blodgett would've, given half a chance. And now Henry had gone on where she couldn't.

Mr. Magister had said he would return. But they always said that.

Why on earth should she expect him to come back?

Why on earth should she trust him?

With a sigh, she turned back toward the house.

She wanted to be in bed.

The screen door snapped shut behind her with a sound like a lion tamer's whip, and slowly, Eva made her way across the hall to trudge up the steps. When she reached the landing above, however, she found herself not turning for bed but standing face to face with the closed door of Mr. Magister's room.

Something had hardened in her—something sad and angry. Henry had wanted to see; Henry had wanted to know.

And she wanted Henry.

Eva reached out, turned the knob, and pushed the door open.

A rumpled nightshirt on the bedpost; half a cigar in a saucer; a water glass on the windowsill. A small foldout secretary desk stood against the wall, and Eva could see the corner of a piece of paper protruding from its closure.

There was little indication here that Mr. Magister did not mean to return. She could not, it seemed, even rely upon the deadening comfort of abandonment.

She almost felt disappointed.

What was in that desk? What was that paper?

Eva strided into the room, crossed the floor, and pulled down the lower jaw of the desk.

Nothing. It was entirely bare. Nothing at all was inside.

But how was that possible? Eva shut the desk once more. The paper that had peeked out only a moment ago was absent now, and almost without thinking—almost—Eva spoke.

"Come back," she commanded, her voice bracingly

loud in the silence of the farmhouse, and instantly, the desk flopped open once again.

Mr. Magister's book fell to the floor, carrying a ream's worth of papers with it.

The book was familiar enough: thick, heavy, bound in red cloth. Mr. Magister had scarcely put it down since they'd arrived, but the title—*A Tabulation of Crop Yields in Farms of the American Prairie with a Technical Explication of the Pertinent Factors Contributing to Their Surplus or Dearth*—was itself so long and boring that Eva could barely bring herself to flip through it.

She was not wrong: inside, Eva found long columns of figures, solid blocks of prose, scarcely an illustration anywhere.

With a sigh, she put it back into the desk and bent to retrieve Mr. Magister's papers: lending prospectuses, bills for food or lodging, legal documents, the occasional business card. There were several letters, addressed variously to a *Doctor* or a *Mister* or even *Jack Coagulo, Esq.* at the Hotel Florence in Pullman, Illinois. One of these bore a return address in West Orange, New Jersey, for Mr. Thomas A. Edison, the famous inventor, and Eva was about to open the flap and read it when her eye fell on an envelope that was quite different from the rest.

She thought she knew the handwriting, but the address was an almost illegible scrawl:

old Devil Jack
wherever the hell yer hidin out
Chicago, Ill.

Somehow, this letter had made it through the mail;
the commemorative World's Fair stamp on the envelope
had been canceled.

Eva's fingers began to tremble as she took the letter from its envelope. The page had been crumpled; she
could almost smell the smoky anger on it.

well you ol rat bastard you done found
me again, didn't you. I said I wasn't
never gonna tell nobody what you did,
and I meant it, Im a man of my word,
you know thats true, but you just
couldn't stop yourself could you. I aint
givin you no more nothin. You already
owe me plenty. I gave you more than
you deserve, and not because nothin was
my fault, I told you, I warned you
you had to slow down but you wouldn't
listen to me, never would. It wasn't me
as told poor ol Katie to stay put until
you come back. thats on you.

Now listen here. I aint afraid of you and I aint afraid of your little kiddies neither. I told you to stay away from me and I meant it. It didnt have to be like this, but I aint havin it no more. Im goin to the cops. Im gonna tell them everything I know, and by the time you read this theyll be searching every little hidey hole in Illinoy so you better head for the hills.

Hope to God that this is the last you ever hear from me, Elijah, because if I ever see your smug little face again, Ill bust it up so bad they wont know where to put that stupid mustache.

Go to hell,
Bill Gabbermann

P.S. Yes I said Elijah.

Mr. Magister knew.

He knew that Eva and Henry had been to see Gabbermann. Which, horribly, terribly, meant that he had been testing her.

What would he do if she failed?

What if she already had?

Eva swallowed and packed the rest of Mr. Magister's papers hurriedly away.

She needed help. She couldn't do this alone.

She needed Henry.

Henry's room was just as she'd left it last night, the door ajar, her candle lying on the table.

Eva stepped inside and cleared her throat.

Outside the weepy rippled window, the wind rushed by as if late for an appointment.

"Henry," she said softly.

She was just going to talk—to tell him about how she was frightened, about how she was alone. She was going to say that she didn't know whom she could trust, that her faith in everything—in Mr. Magister, in Magic, in life itself—had been shaken.

She was going to tell him that she thought she was in trouble.

But she didn't get the chance to say anything other than *Henry*.

Suddenly, her candle rolled off the table, clattering to the floor with a loud clunk. Almost by instinct, Eva lunged forward, bending low to retrieve it.

But she stopped cold, halfway under the table, her arm stretched out long.

There, on the floor, lying in the accumulated dust, was a pair of round, shining spectacles.

One of the lenses was scorched and cracked.

Henry's.

Eva scuttled away, pressing her back hard up against the cold brass bedstead. She rubbed the heels of her hands into her tear-stung eyes.

They weren't there. It was a mistake. She would open her eyes again and they would be gone, or they would be something else.

But Eva blinked her eyes open and there the spectacles were, solid and weighty and undeniable. They were upside down, askew, as if lying just where they'd fallen. Their arms were open.

Eva's chest shook with sudden swallowed sobs. She was torn in half: she wanted nothing more than to press herself into those spectacles, to feel on her face the weight and warmth of what had so lately held on to Henry.

But she wasn't sure she could withstand the pain.

Slowly, Eva crawled forward.

The spectacles were warm, almost hot, between her fingers, and she shut her eyes as she put them on her face. She blinked her eyes open; a red-hot spike of pain pushed into her brain.

It was the left lens that had cracked, and through the half nearest her nose, the farmhouse looked entirely ordinary, just as it had a moment ago.

But the outer half of the left lens—and the entirety of the right—showed something quite different.

In this second view, Eva could clearly see a dull glowing light seeping forth from between the floorboards, a throbbing warmth that almost seemed to buzz.

But there was something else shining out in that house—something far brighter—and like a flitting, bespectacled moth, she found herself drawn irresistibly toward it.

In the hallway, she saw that the light was coming from behind Mr. Magister's bedroom door; in Mr. Magister's bedroom, she saw that it was coming from inside his desk.

And inside, she saw the origin of the light at last.

In between the pages of Mr. Magister's book, draped like a bookmark, was a ribbon, a filament of Impossible brightness.

It was not Mr. Magister's book at all.

It was Henry's sketchbook in disguise.

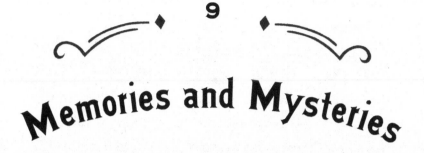

9

Memories and Mysteries

Eva lifted the sketchbook from the open maw of Mr. Magister's desk.

Her urge was to tear it open, to let herself drown in the drawings inside, but she found that she was hugging it to her chest, and she wasn't ready to stop.

How, how, how was it here? How had it survived the fire?

But the answer became quickly apparent:

It hadn't.

The volume that Henry had carried had been worn, the corners of its covers rubbed raw. This volume, on the other hand, was tight, new, and all the pages sat crisp and creaseless within their covers.

All the pages but one.

The volume fell open easily to this exceptional page,

and immediately Eva felt she could smell him there beside her: warm sand, wind-dried linen.

Henry.

A knot tightened in her throat.

The paper of the singular page was worn several shades darker than the rest, and somehow, there in the binding, it had been folded. On one side of the page was a neat drawing of a peach blossom. On the other, in Henry's hand:

> Top of the Cold Storage tower.
> As soon as you can.

The knot in Eva's throat gave a sudden snap, and grief oozed deep into her gut.

She was the one who had left Henry's note in the Pavilion; Mr. Magister must've used it to resurrect the rest of the sketchbook, just as she'd resurrected the peach from its pit.

What had he learned from its pages?

What did he know?

The first pages of the sketchbook were full of unfamiliar studies—still lifes, self-portraits—which must've been drawn in Philadelphia, before Eva and Henry ever met. Soon, however, Eva came to the spread depicting the mammoth Manufactures and Liberal Arts Building, all arches and banners on the waterfront, and she went quickly through the collection of pages that Henry had filled with the Fair: buildings, exhibits, people. When Henry had made these drawings, he'd never even seen their subjects, but from Eva's perspective, it was all very familiar: the Merchant Tailors' Building on the lagoon; the Japanese Phoenix Hall at the top of the Wooded Island. Here was the high tower of oranges in the Agriculture Building; here was Herr Krupp's great 122-ton cannon.

And suddenly, there was she—Eva herself, dozing on her arms.

Henry, oh, Henry.

There were others, too, a fact that Eva had missed the first time around: someone who looked like the boy Cato, round spectacles gleaming over his cheeks; freckle-flecked Meg; even Vaclav, his feathery hair rising up willfully at improbable angles.

Vaclav.

It had been some time since Eva had thought of Vaclav, and somehow his memory seemed to resist her even now, as if she were trying to haul up a heavy anchor bodily from the murky deep.

Eva turned the page and felt a sudden stabbing anxiety. There he was: Mr. Magister, staring out at her. On the opposite page, in Gabbermann's own loopy scrawl, was written Bill Gabbermann, Briggs House, Randolph and Fifth.

She should never, ever have brought these pages back.

Now the sketchbook began to fill with Pavilion: the sprawling front elevation, erased and redrawn and erased and redrawn and erased; crown moldings and window surrounds and detail after detail after detail; the floor-plan delirium; the fireplace sketch.

But here were other things, too. Henry had drawn Eva many, many times, often quickly, appended at the edge of some more developed work: her hands holding a peach or tucking back a lock of hair; her contrapposto twist to see through a window.

There were some sketches that made her blush.

On one page, amongst a thicket of ornate table legs, Henry had written and circled the following note:

Vaclav Schovajsa
Back of the Yards, here in Chicago

Once more, Vaclav stirred in the murky deep of her mind, and she ran her eyes back over the circled words:

Vaclav Schovajsa
Back of the Yards

Soon Eva came to the flurry of failed Mr. Magisters. They looked particularly sinister to her now, their floating eyes and ears seeming to take sharp notice as they went past.

When she arrived finally at the sheet of notes Henry had taken during their interview with Gabbermann, she knew she was coming to the end. It was terribly unfair. There were so many blank pages left in the book.

The interview notes were completely different from anything else Eva had seen in the sketchbook, straight and square from top to bottom. At the head of the page, Henry had written Bill Gabbermann, July 10, 1893, and below, in a column of orderly bullet points, he had recorded the following:

- "Investor"
- M.M. has debts
- Coagulo is M.M.'s stage name
- True name?
- ~~Kate and the baby??~~ The Fire
- "Great Machine," "Grow his Magic," "Magical bank"
- October 1871—the Fire
- The Fire, the Fire, the Fire

And this, it seemed, must be all. Henry had left his pencils in Gabbermann's hotel room and had burned to death that very afternoon—the tenth of July. It seemed impossible that he would've had the time to write or draw anything else.

But Mr. Magister's bright bookmark lay between the next two pages, shining through the paper, and just in case, Eva flipped the interview notes over.

There, on the next page, was writing.

Almost without thinking, Eva went to flick the bookmark aside, but an angry buzzing ran through the joints of her hand when she drew near to it. She pulled back instinctively, stopping to shake out the sensation.

The handwriting on the final, terrible page was undoubtedly Henry's, but it was rushed and sloppy, a scrawl. It was not, of course, in Henry's usual charcoal pencil; the words had not been marked atop the paper at all, but had, instead, been scorched in with something sharp, hot, and metallic—perhaps a stray nail.

This was what Henry had written:

The Machine—we are the Machine.
Gabbermann knows more than he's saying.
What happened to Vaclav?
The Fire, the Fire, the Fire.

And at the very bottom of his final entry, in letters larger than any others in the sketchbook, letters that had burned straight through the page:

EVA: FIND PROOF.

There is no saying how long Eva sat there, the book propped up on her knees. Those three words, tiny and gargantuan, stared her in the face, challenging, commanding, pleading: Henry's last—and for her, by name.

All of a sudden, Eva looked up in shock.

The sound of the screen door shutting below like the crack of a lion tamer's whip; feet pressing into the moaning stairs.

Mr. Magister had come back.

Eva leapt to her feet. With every passing moment, Mr. Magister was climbing closer; there was no way now that she could get out of the room without being seen, and though it felt like a betrayal to part with the sketchbook, she could see no other way.

Gritting her teeth, she laid it back in its place and shut the desk up behind it.

Mr. Magister was close; he had reached the top of the stairs.

With a shock, Eva realized that Henry's spectacles were still upon her face, and she snatched them off and shoved them deep into her pocket. She darted down behind the bed, and the glasses crunched and crackled beneath her.

Eva winced.

Mr. Magister had reached the bedroom door now, and he swung it inward. Slowly, he made his way into the room, and turning his back to the bed, he pressed the door shut again.

Eva's heart clattered in her chest. No escape.

What was she to do?

Mr. Magister paced wearily past the foot of the bed and his little desk until he arrived at the washbasin by the window.

Somehow, somehow, he had not yet seen Eva.

He rolled his shoulders, rubbed at his neck. Gingerly, he pulled off first one of his spotless white gloves, and then the other.

Eva was horrified by what she saw beneath.

Mr. Magister's hands were burned to a crisp, scorched and bubbled; as he stretched and massaged them now, she thought she could hear the crackling of toasted skin.

She gave an involuntary gasp. Mr. Magister stiffened.

Without looking back, he fluidly replaced his gloves, and slowly, he turned in her direction.

"Eva," he said. "Whatever are you doing here?" He did not seem remotely pleased.

"I—I . . . ," Eva stammered. "I'm sorry, I—"

Mr. Magister raised an eyebrow.

Eva felt panic overtaking her. What could she say? What could possibly excuse this invasion of privacy? There was something cold and hard in Mr. Magister's expression, and for the first time, Eva worried about what he was capable of doing to those who angered him.

Tears welled up in her eyes, and in a sudden moment of inspiration, she seized upon them to her advantage.

"I was so afraid," she sobbed. "You left—you left so quickly, and I thought what if Gabbermann comes to get me like he got Henry, and I wanted to be near you, I just wanted to be safe, and—and—"

Fortunately, Eva did not have to go any further.

"There, there," said Mr. Magister, opening his arms and beckoning her in.

With quiet terror, Eva stepped forward. Mr. Magister wrapped her in a close embrace. She was overcome by his heavy aroma: woodsmoke and whiskey and linen and sweat. His hot hands fell on her back, and Eva tried desperately not to recoil.

"Don't worry," he whispered. "I won't let Gabbermann get you."

Eva sniffled demonstratively and said something cloying like *Really? You promise?* but she had little attention to pay to his assurances.

Her bones were buzzing. She was growing sweaty and hot.

It wasn't Gabbermann who worried her at all.

Mr. Magister had come home quite tired, and having comforted Eva at length, he begged her pardon and lay down for a nap.

Eva herself was restless, however, and she went downstairs, her mind spinning like a dynamo.

Proof.

She needed proof.

But where could she find it?

Mr. Magister's desk: there were certainly secrets there, but she could hardly hope to gain access to it now. Perhaps he could forgive the intrusion once, but if he caught her there again, who knew what Mr. Magister would do?

And this turned her attention to the biggest question in her mind:

Proof of *what*?

The air was close and warm inside the farmhouse, and with every pace, the antique floorboards squawked beneath her feet.

Eva needed air, she needed room to think, she needed a place where every move she made wasn't audible and obvious—and in a sudden burst of energy, she made her way through the kitchen and out the back door.

The weather-beaten edifice of the barn stood stark against the afternoon sky.

There—perhaps she could find room to think there.

Eva's lips twitched softly as she strode across the crispy brown lawn, running through the final notes that Henry had written for her over and over:

The Machine—we are the Machine.

Gabbermann knows more than he's saying.

What happened to Vaclav?

The Fire, the Fire, the Fire.

The Machine—we are the Machine.

Gabbermann knows more than he's saying.

What happened to Vaclav?

The Fire, the Fire, the Fire.

The Machine—we are the Machine . . .

The glaring sun had raised the sweat to Eva's skin by the time she reached the shadow of the barn. It took the whole effort of her body to get the great door sliding, and her fingers strained at the smooth wood of the handle.

What she saw within stopped her in her tracks.

If she only looked upward, the barn seemed entirely normal. There was a broad hayloft to be reached by a sturdy ladder, and the dusty sun shone through the gaps between the timbers.

The floor, however, could scarcely have been stranger.

Where there ought to have been dirt and hay, stalls and troughs, a wide pond stood instead, bordered by reeds and cattails. Eva could hear the croaking of frogs and, somewhere deep inside, the call of a waterbird. A gentle breeze bent the green grass; outside, where Eva stood, the brown lawn sat still in the hot, unmoving air.

It was strange—very strange—but it was also just the kind of place that Eva needed to think.

She heaved the great door shut behind her, and stepping gingerly to avoid the softening of the moist ground, walked toward the hayloft. The grass was thick, tall, and tangled, and it took some effort for Eva to fight her way through to the ladder. Perhaps she would ask if Meg could rein it in a bit—it might benefit the overall impression.

But what a peculiar notion—how could she ask *Meg* for anything?

Eva shook her head. She couldn't allow herself to be distracted.

Proof.

She needed proof.

But where could she find it?

It was obvious, of course, when she really considered it: Gabbermann was at Briggs House, Vaclav in a place called the Back of the Yards, and both of these lay in the city that had been ravaged twenty-two years before by the Great Fire:

Chicago.

If she was to find the proof that Henry had desired, it would be in Chicago.

But even if this answer was obvious, it was far from simple. She couldn't just take a little jaunt into town like Mr. Magister. Chicago was far off, a journey of hours and hours by rail, and she didn't even know where she was starting from.

What was more, if Eva left without telling Mr. Magister, it would be an indelible act—an abandonment, a practical declaration of war. And she could hardly tell him why she wanted to go.

To this problem, there seemed to be no easy solution.

Slowly, she began to reel in her answer from the deep.

She would have to choose the moment carefully.

Mr. Magister was in the kitchen when Eva came back in, cooking in a boiling pot set over a high, hot fire.

"Eva," he said. "Where have you been?"

"Oh," said Eva. "I went to explore the barn."

"I see," said Mr. Magister with a nod, wiping his gloved hands on a kitchen towel. Improbably, they came away spotless. "And what did you think of it?"

Eva blinked. Was he testing her again? Was anything he did ever *not* some kind of test?

"Is it common in these parts," she said, "to build barns around water?"

Mr. Magister chuckled. "Not common, no. I believe the intention was to provide the livestock with ready access, but it causes all sorts of problems. The insects are unbelievable."

Eva hadn't noticed any insects at all in the time she'd spent by the pond, but then little about what Mr. Magister said accorded with her impression of the barn. It had not been built around a preexisting body of water—clearly, it was a work of Magic.

Mr. Magister, however, seemed intent upon convincing her that it was not.

Why?

"Very good," said Mr. Magister to his bubbling pot. "Nearly done. There are plates in the cupboard and silverware in the drawer, and if you will lay the table, Eva, I think we shall be ready to eat shortly."

It was early for supper and Eva still had not recovered her appetite, but she didn't protest.

All she had to do now was keep Mr. Magister happy until she could slip away.

Eva set the table. Mr. Magister brought out a steaming platter of boiled beef and potatoes, and Eva cut them up and pushed them around her plate.

She wanted to make small talk, to reassure Mr. Magister of her friendliness and goodwill, but nothing she could think of saying felt like safe territory.

What did you get up to in town? Nosy.

How long do you expect we'll stay here? Suspicious.

Which way to Chicago? Idiotic.

Mr. Magister cleared his throat.

"Did you sleep well?" said Eva.

"Hmm?" said Mr. Magister. "Oh. Oh, yes. Thank you."

But this was as far as the conversation went. A long period of quiet passed; the only sounds to be heard were the clinking of cutlery and the assiduous chewing of Mr. Magister's jaws, and in order not to do nothing, Eva put a bite of steaming potato into her mouth. It was incredibly hot, and she scalded herself, swallowing as quickly as she could.

Mr. Magister was filling his plate for the third time when he spoke. "Eva," he said. "I think it is time you told me what you discussed in your meeting with Bill Gabbermann."

Eva's stomach plummeted. She put a forkful of boiled meat into her mouth to buy a moment's time, and swallowing, she nodded.

"Yes," she said. "Yes, I think you're right."

There was no point in denying it; Mr. Magister had the sketchbook, and if he hadn't read Henry's notes on the conversation already, he could at any point.

"I am glad," said Mr. Magister, "that you seem to have come to your senses."

"It took me a while to remember," said Eva. "I didn't want to say the wrong thing."

"You?" said Mr. Magister with a smile. "Never." Eva couldn't quite tell if this was supposed to be friendly.

"But come," said Mr. Magister. "What did you and Mr. Gabbermann speak of? It has been some time since I saw him."

Eva took a deep breath. "The truth is," she said, "that I didn't talk with him at all, personally. It was Henry's idea to go and see him, and I stayed outside in the cab while they talked."

Mr. Magister raised his eyebrows. "Henry's idea?"

Eva nodded.

"Goodness," said Mr. Magister. "This is very peculiar."

"Peculiar?" said Eva. "Why's that?"

"Well," said Mr. Magister, pushing his plate away, "Henry said it was *your* idea."

Eva stiffened. How could that be? "I'm not sure I understand."

Mr. Magister popped a potato into his mouth with two gloved fingers. "Mmm," he said, mouth full. "I had the opportunity, you see, to speak with him in his Cold Storage studio the afternoon he died. He left a note in the sitting room indicating that I ought to come and meet him there, and so I went and I waited, and when he returned, he told me that you had provided him with Gabbermann's address, and that he had escorted you out to see him. So I'm afraid I am rather confused. Which of the two of you has lied to me?"

Eva's heart pounded at her rib cage as if it were trying to escape.

"The visit certainly wasn't my idea. I didn't even know where we were going until we arrived at Briggs House," said Eva.

Mr. Magister raised his eyebrows. "Truly?"

"Truly," said Eva. "And when I realized where we were, I argued all the way up to the door of Gabbermann's room."

Mr. Magister frowned. "I thought you said that Henry and Gabbermann talked while you waited in the cab."

Eva stammered, trying to find some explanation for this discrepancy. "Oh," she said. "Oh, I—I—I did, but—"

"Furthermore," said Mr. Magister, "you say that you waited in the cab, but when Henry arrived at his Cold Storage studio that afternoon, he complained bitterly of your long walk back from the Loop."

A sudden blush spread across Eva's cheeks. She was incredibly hot—Impossibly hot.

Mr. Magister stared directly at her; she thought she saw fire flicker in his pupils.

"I—I . . . ," she said. "I—"

She smelled burning hair, and for a tiny moment, Eva felt as if she might lose herself entirely.

But something cold and hard reared up in her mind:

Not yet, not yet, I need to find proof.

"I'm so sorry," said Eva. "It's all so confusing, and my memory is in terrible shape. You must be right—I must've left the cab: I remember the walk back now, so terribly hot, and that must mean that I *did* go in with Henry, but if I was present for the conversation, then I simply don't remember."

Mr. Magister did not move. His eyes were perfectly still, focused in on Eva like an eagle's.

By and by, he spoke.

"I am very weary, Eva. I have had quite a long and

challenging day. I mean to go to bed now. Perhaps in the morning your topsy-turvy memory will have righted itself."

He rose, tossed his napkin on the table, and began to make his way toward the stairs.

Eva let go the deepest breath it seemed she had ever held.

Without looking back, Mr. Magister said, "See to the dirty dishes. There is quite an accumulation."

Slowly, deliberately, Eva washed every last dish in the kitchen, and when she had finished, she washed them all again. She did it to fill the time—until the sound of Mr. Magister's tossing and turning broke off above, until the sunlight outside the windows dimmed and died—but just as much, she scrubbed and scoured to use up the angry energy trembling in her arms.

There had been a moment under the interrogation of Mr. Magister in which she had felt the distinct temptation to fly away, to let go and yield to the burning blush that had seemed to spread all throughout her body.

Everything felt unstable. She just wanted firm ground beneath her feet: true, real, mundane things that did not shift Impossibly with every passing breath.

She thought perhaps she was beginning to under-stand.

But she needed proof.

Her hands were trembling; they trembled through the double washing of each dish, through their final drying, through their return to appointed shelves, cupboards, and drawers, but only when the task was finally finished and her hands came to rest did they shake in earnest.

The floor above her was silent and still; the night outside was dark.

It was time.

At first, it hadn't seemed worth it to go and retrieve her bag from her room upstairs—every part of the house creaked and moaned at the slightest movement, and waking Mr. Magister might lead to disaster—but the large wad of cash she had taken from Mrs. Blodgett was still in that bag, and if she had any hope of reaching Chicago, she would need it.

Up the stairs, then, gingerly and slow, careful not to make too much noise. She found the bag just where she'd left it, slung over the back of a chair, and breathlessly she took it and went back toward the stairs.

She was two steps down when she realized that her sé-ance candle was still in Henry's room. She regretted the loss, but it was too late now.

She would have to leave it.

Carefully, Eva dismounted at the foot of the stairs; carefully, she crossed the front hall. The door itself squealed excruciatingly, but she managed to ease the screen open and shut without making a sound.

The air outside was warm and breezy, the night thick and clean. High above, the stars hung immobile, as if stopped there midbreath. Eva shot her gaze to the left and the right, almost incapable of believing that she'd made it outside.

Slowly, she edged toward the end of the low porch. She was just about to step down when she stopped:

What was that sound?

There was a rumbling in the bushes on either side like the idling of an ancient engine, and Eva peered into the branches to see where it might be coming from.

Eyes.

There were glowing eyes in the bushes.

Eva stumbled back in surprise, and she tripped on the low ledge of the porch, falling hard into the dust.

She fought to catch her breath.

From the bushes on either side of the porch, copper lions emerged, sparks flying from their coats as they came: the tangled bushes were not, as she'd thought, bare woody branches, but twisted capillaries of copper.

The lions circled and turned, blocking Eva's way out

across the lawn, and she scrabbled through the dust until the small of her back was pressed up against the porch.

With a rumbling growl, the lion on her left showed its teeth, sharp and white in the vast bulk of copper green. It crouched low, as if stalking, preparing to strike, and slowly crept toward her.

Eva hadn't counted on this; this was all wrong.

But she felt her will rising.

"No," she said. "No, I have to go back," and fighting to her feet, she raised her left hand against the approach of the lion.

It slowed; a familiar buzz began to shake the bones of Eva's fingers, and soon the lion stopped, inches from her trembling hand. The buzzing was growing, spreading through all the joints of her hand and wrist, and it was terribly uncomfortable, but she was the one advancing now, the lion backing down, and she went on, step by step, the buzzing in her elbow, in her shoulder, so violent that she thought her arm might simply fly apart.

The lion backed off and backed off until it came parallel with its partner; Eva continued to advance, and they split, opening a narrow path between them.

Eva dropped her hand.

A snarl flickered at the corner of the rightward lion's maw, but she said, "I'm going now. Goodbye," and at this, the lions circled wide about her and returned to the house, wading into the tangled wiring of the bushes until they were no longer visible at all.

Eva's heart was pounding, her arm numb, but she smiled as she turned her back on the door guardians.

She was on her way.

The thicket that bounded the wide lawn loomed up ahead, and Eva's approach slowed; blue moonlight drenched the grass at her feet, and yet almost no light at all penetrated the thick grove.

This was the only way forward; this was the only way back.

Eva drew a deep breath and plunged into the trees.

It was cool there—nearly cold. Little by little, she managed to wriggle her way forward, but the sharp twig ends reached out, tugging at her hair, scratching at her skin.

The air smelled metallic—like blood.

A crackling spark leapt out in the dim, and Eva felt the bite of static shock on her neck.

It was an age before she saw the gray light between the trees.

Fog, thick fog—and then rough stone beneath her feet. There was a narrow outlying tree beside her, so thin and straight that it seemed Impossible that it had grown from the ground, and this was because it hadn't: it was the lamppost beneath which Mr. Magister had greeted her upon her arrival.

Eva strode to the edge of the rocky platform. Mr. Magister's Pullman car appeared in the mist.

It was terribly changed.

When she had boarded at the Fair, the car had been a splendid, luxurious thing, crammed with amenities, polished to a high sheen. Now there was a thick layer of moss growing on the embarkment steps. Several of the windows had been shattered, the paint was peeling and worn, and vines and creepers twined amongst the wheels.

How, in just a matter of days?

Slowly, Eva climbed into the Pullman car.

Inside, everything was much as she expected: ragged, worn, the lightbulbs broken, the upholstery torn. But Eva had no time to make an accounting of the damage.

Her eye was drawn onward.

At the rear of the car, the door leading out onto the small balconied observation deck was ajar. Outside all of the car's windows, the foggy gray moonlight was visible, but on the observation deck, the light was different— thick and warm.

Eva strode across the car, pulled the door back, and stepped outside.

Immediately, she was overwhelmed with nausea. Everything seemed to be spinning, spinning, spinning, and Eva had to lean hard on the railing to steady her stomach.

She was indoors. How was she indoors?

"Hey!" called a man in a brusque baritone. "Come down from there!"

Eva looked up, and what she saw chilled her to the bone:

An officer in the unmistakable uniform of the Columbian Guards.

And in a flash, the illusion was broken: the long train ride to nowhere; the Impossible farmhouse.

The Columbian Guards only patrolled the grounds of the World's Columbian Exposition.

The fairgrounds.

Mr. Magister had been keeping her at the fairgrounds the whole time.

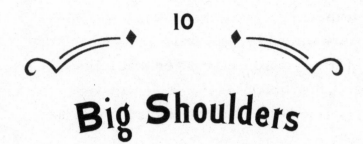

10

Big Shoulders

Eva's heart was pounding, her stomach tumbling over and over. She was dizzy, so dizzy, and her bones were buzzing in her body. She couldn't stop the world from spinning, and she stumbled out of the Transportation Building, staggering forward to the cold iron railing, and she heaved, vomiting into the thorny bushes on the banks of the lagoon.

The air was cool, the sky gray. Tiny flecks of rain swarmed about her like gnats.

A passing gentleman paused to ask if she was *okay, miss?* and she nodded, wiping at her mouth with the back of her hand, eager to be rid of him. She needed to think, needed to understand, but the world was turning so quickly, and everything she thought she knew was wrong.

Eva: find proof.

She lifted her eyes, and the grand sweep of the fair-grounds filled them up—the graceful bridges from the Wooded Island; the stately Mines and Electricity Buildings, varied and complementary, side by side—the world's most expensive prison, the world's most beautiful cage.

Her mind was as cloudy as the sky; her stomach lurched and moaned.

She had to get out.

Eva came crashing out of the grounds at the Sixty-Second Street turnstiles. Buffalo Bill's Wild West show was encamped just a block down, and she could hear the gunfire and the whooping of the crowd as she made her way to the line of waiting hansom cabs by the curb. Slowly, slowly, her stomach was settling, the buzzing in her bones resolving into a dull headache. She needed privacy, needed to think, and she climbed into the first cab without a word to the driver. Moments later, his ruddy face appeared at the window.

"You have to pay for this ride, girlie."

"I have money," said Eva.

"Oh?" said the cabdriver.

With a sigh, Eva flashed the fat wad of cash in her bag. The driver's eyes widened. "Where to, miss?"

But Eva hadn't thought this far ahead—she hadn't

had the time. Gradually, her mind began to grind into gear, reaching back through the mist for the words she'd read in Henry's notebook:

The Machine—we are the Machine.

Gabbermann knows more than he's saying.

Gabbermann.

Eva nodded.

"Randolph and Fifth," she said. "Briggs House."

Outside the cab window, the rain was growing strong.

Eva couldn't imagine that Bill Gabbermann would be very happy to see her; when they'd last parted company, he'd held a gun on her and, as far as he knew, she'd thrown him through the wall.

But this was the best way forward. She needed proof, and Gabbermann was as likely to have it as anyone.

What had he called Mr. Magister in his letter? *Enoch? Elias?* The farther she went from the fairgrounds, the thicker the fog between her and the farmhouse seemed to grow, and as the hansom rolled on, she ran over Henry's notes in her mind again and again, trying to pin them down:

The Machine—we are the Machine.

Gabbermann knows more than he's saying.

What happened to Vaclav?

The Fire, the Fire, the Fire.

There was something in Eva's pocket, and she had settled on it awkwardly. She reached in to feel what it might be, and the shattered glass of Henry's spectacles caught the pad of her finger. With a wince, she withdrew her hand in just enough time to see a drop of glossy red blood well up and drip onto her spotless white dress. She put her finger into her mouth and looked back down in annoyance, but she couldn't find the bloodstain.

Somehow, her dress was spotless.

By the time they reached the corner of Randolph and Fifth, the rain had thickened, drumming on the roof of the cab like a thousand tiny fists. Outside, an oily rainbow scum sluiced down the gutter.

The cabbie called from behind the carriage as she climbed out. "You going on or staying?"

Eva wasn't sure. She hoped to talk with Gabbermann, but in the event that he was unhappy to see her, it might be prudent to make a hurried getaway.

"Because I can wait, if you like. For a modest fee."

He was, Eva supposed, better outfitted for the weather than she—heavy coat, wide-brimmed cap. She overpaid him for the ride from the Fair, and he agreed to wait ten minutes or so before moving on.

Eva was very wet—just short of sodden—when she

stepped into the warm lobby of Briggs House, and she felt suddenly self-conscious. What if they recognized her and called the police? What if they threw her out as a vagrant before she'd had a chance to find her way to Gabbermann?

The clerk was busy filing mail into the numbered pigeonholes behind his desk, but his canny eye flitted over Eva, dripping by the door.

Loitering wouldn't help.

Summoning all her courage, Eva strode across the lobby.

But when she arrived before the clerk, she was derailed: on the desk was a short stack of newspapers, and there, beneath the words CHICAGO DAILY TRIBUNE, the date had been printed:

TUESDAY, SEPTEMBER 19, 1893

"Is that today's edition?"

The clerk didn't turn around. "Yes," he said. "Two cents."

Eva took the top copy in her hands.

September 19? How could that possibly be? The day before yesterday—the day of her last visit to this hotel, of the Cold Storage fire, of their flight from the Fair—it had been *July.*

September 19?

But of course—time moved languidly in the Pavilion

of Magic. And what else could the farmhouse have possibly been?

The clerk turned back over his shoulder. "Two cents," he repeated.

Eva tucked the newspaper under her arm and fumbled hurriedly in her bag, bringing up a dollar bill to lay on the desk.

The clerk raised his eyebrows, put his mail aside, and turned to make change.

"Please," said Eva. "I'm not sure if he's still here, but I'm looking for a friend of mine."

"What's the name?" The clerk didn't look up from his cash drawer.

"Bill Gabbermann."

The clink of coins broke off, and the clerk lifted his eyes. "Gabbermann?"

Eva nodded. "Is he still here?"

The cash drawer jangled shut, and the clerk began to flip through the thick ledger of his register. "Do you remember what room he was in?"

"I don't know the number. I think it was on the third floor near the back."

"Ah, yes," said the clerk. "Bill Gabbermann. I'm afraid he's out just now. Can you come back in, say, two hours?"

This seemed like an incredibly long time—who knew

what Mr. Magister might accomplish in two hours—but what choice did she have? "Yes."

"Very good," said the clerk, and he began to jot furiously on a notepad. "And what is your name?"

"My name?" she said. "Eva . . . ," and then thinking better of it, "Poole. Eva Poole."

The clerk nodded. "Eva Poole. Very good."

"Thank you," said Eva, and she turned to go.

"Miss Poole?"

Eva froze.

"Your change?"

"Oh," she said, giggling nervously. "Oh, yes, of course. Thank you."

The clerk counted ninety-eight slow cents into her sweaty palm. Eva's cheeks were burning.

"Two hours?" she said.

"Two hours."

The cab was still precisely where she'd left it, the horse steaming and stamping at the curb.

"Where to next?" called the cabbie from the cold.

Eva stood for a long moment, her hand on the carriage door.

Gabbermann knows more than he's saying.

What happened to Vaclav?

"Miss?"

Henry had circled it in his notebook, there amongst the table legs:

Vaclav Schovajsa

Back of the Yards, here in Chicago

"Do you know how to get to the Back of the Yards?"

The cabbie recoiled as if the words themselves had a pungent odor.

"The Back of the Yards? You sure?"

"Yes," said Eva. "Can you take me there?"

The cabbie sighed. "Get in."

The ride down to the Back of the Yards was long, and Eva soon found herself nodding. The rumble of the wheels, the sway of the carriage, and the drumming of rain on the roof all conspired to lull her into an uneasy slumber, and when she woke, it was because the cab had come to a stop.

Somewhere nearby, a train was rattling away, rough and bellicose.

"Are we there?" Eva called.

Outside the window, she could see that the sky had darkened, though whether it was the influence of evening, clouds, or smoke, she couldn't tell.

"This is as far as I go," called the cabbie. "Get out."

Eva climbed into the rain. "Is this it?" she said. "The Back of the Yards?"

"In there," said the cabbie, gesturing to a long, muddy alley. "Follow the smell. You can't miss it."

Even here, Eva couldn't ignore the stench: thick, rotten, acidic—almost juicy.

"Will you wait?" she said.

The cabbie shook his head.

"What do I owe you?" said Eva, taking the cash from her bag.

"All of it," said the cabbie.

Eva had quite a lot of money in her hands—more than enough for a hundred cab rides. "What?"

But it didn't take long for her to figure out what was happening. A metallic click echoed out above her, bright and high over the thrum of the nearby trains.

The cabbie was holding a pistol.

"You can try screaming," he said, "but I doubt it'll do you much good."

Somewhere in the distance, as if in mockery, the squawk of a steam whistle split the air.

"Just hand it over nice and slow now, and you won't get hurt."

Eva's eyes stung with sudden tears.

Slowly, she handed the wad of cash—all she had ever earned—up to the cabdriver.

"Thank you," he said; it was as if they'd just completed a totally ordinary transaction. "Good luck in the Back. I hope you make it out again."

And with a crack of his whip, he drove on.

One by one, Eva crossed over innumerable branching train tracks. Steam engines barreled in without warning, shaking the rickety wooden cottages on either side, their cars crammed with walking cargo.

When the wind was just right, Eva could hear what was being done down there at the stockyards—the rumble of the machines; the wail and scream of dying pigs. With every passing step, the odor grew stronger: animal waste, rotting viscera, the iron tang of blood.

She put her head down and pushed farther in, unsure of what she was looking for.

The rain began to pelt down harder; Eva held her newspaper over her head.

There was almost no one out on the tight and winding streets that night, but there were lights in the steamy little windows, and every so often she saw a pair of eyes gawking out. Here and there were open doors—mostly taverns—and into the already pungent atmosphere, they belched forth a bitter aroma of sour beer and man sweat.

Eva couldn't give them a wide enough berth.

On and on she stumbled, trying desperately to keep the hem of her dress out of the muck underfoot. Quickly, she lost her way, wandering on narrow, anonymous paths. The wood of the cottages had all been worn down to the same dull gray by the corrosive effluvia of the meatpacking plants, and the only inkling of direction she could glean came from the particular stench on the wind: from the east, the yards—blood and dung and animal fear; from the west, a massive rotting garbage dump, the biggest in the city.

Eva was exhausted.

Back and forth she went, the sky growing darker, the wind blowing colder. She began to wonder if she might not simply keel over there and let her corpse sink into the fetid mud.

And then, a sudden miracle: warm light from an open doorway and a woman calling out.

"Who you looking for?"

Eva was unprepared. She gaped and mumbled.

The woman chuckled. "Not from around here, are you?"

"No."

"Ain't many dresses stay that white in the Back of the Yards. Now, I seen you go up and down past my door five times in the last half hour—you looking for someone or what?"

Eva nodded hungrily. "Yes," she said. "Yes, please. Vaclav Schovajsa—do you know him?"

The woman gave a puckered frown. "Sko-vie-suh? Sko-vie-suh." She turned over her shoulder and called into her little cottage. "Jim!" she said. "You know a man Sko-vie-suh?"

"Ain't that old Iggy?" said Jim. "Angry Iggy?"

The woman's eyes widened. "Why, so it is, isn't it? Ignác. Big man, don't say much?"

Eva took a step forward. "Please," she said. "I'm looking for a boy—Vaclav."

"Oh, that'll be the son," said the woman. "Just a moment. Jim! Know where old Iggy drinks?"

The woman, who gave her name as Mrs. Malloy, dutifully led Eva to Whiskey Row, a broad avenue of taverns and saloons on the busy doorstep of the stockyards. Here the men of the plants and factories came to drink with ritual regularity—before work to grease their cleaver arms, after work to wash away the blood.

The kerosene lamps burned bright, but the gloom was almost impenetrable.

Mrs. Malloy stopped at the door of the first tavern along the row, a place called Kowalski's, and turned to Eva.

"You just keep your eyes front and follow me," she said. "They won't bother you much."

Inside, Mrs. Malloy caught the eye of the barman and asked if he knew Ignác Sko-vie-suh—old Angry Iggy. The fellow frowned and shook his head, so Mrs. Malloy thanked him and led Eva into the bar next door. It was in the fifth such establishment—a smoke-filled, half-empty room called Rapson's—that someone finally gave them an answer.

At Mrs. Malloy's question, the barkeep opened his mouth to answer, but he was preempted by a voice out of the smoke.

"He hated that. *Angry Iggy.* You'd've been angry, too."

Mrs. Malloy turned to the man, a short, squat, red-faced fellow drinking alone at a nearby table.

"You know him?" she said.

"Sure."

Mrs. Malloy crossed the sawdust-covered floor. "This girl's looking for his son."

"Vaclav," said Eva, tripping forward.

"Yes," said the man. "Good boy. Smart."

"Do you know where I might find him?" Eva said. "I need to talk to him. It's very important. Please."

Now the drunken man laughed—long and low and

lazy. By and by, he said, "Sure. Sure, I know where you can find him. Buy me a drink, I'll even take you there."

Eva swung her bag off her shoulder, but by the time she had it open, she'd remembered: she would find no money inside.

Her cheeks burned. She was so close—so close.

"No money?" muttered Mrs. Malloy.

Eva shook her head, and with a little nod, Mrs. Malloy rustled at the change in her threadbare pocket.

"John!" called the red-faced fellow. "Whiskey!" and then, his eyes glinting, "Make it a double."

Mrs. Malloy sighed and reached back into her pocket.

His sloshing glass in hand, the portly little man from Rapson's led them north and east. Eva found herself renewed now, her mind boiling with all the questions she would ask Vaclav: What had he suspected? Why had Mr. Magister sent him away? What had he said? What did he remember?

Before long, they arrived at the banks of Bubbly Creek, the stubby little arm of the Chicago River that marked the northern end of the stockyards. Even when the rain was not falling, the name was apt: the creek was choked with waste and sewage, blood and bile and chemical runoff, and the gases that rose up from the rot below the surface stirred and roiled the water in a constant motion. There the air was sharp and stinging, and it burned the hairs in Eva's nose, scratching at her throat like some swallowed rodent desperate to escape.

Eva coughed; Mrs. Malloy drew her lapel over her face.

Down a short alley crowded with ramshackle huts, the man from Rapson's stopped and swigged his drink.

"There we are," he said. "Schovajsa Manor."

"What?" said Eva.

The tiny lot seemed to be vacant—a perfect cube of rainy, empty air set between near-leaning neighbors.

"Have a closer look," said the man, and when Eva drew near, she saw, to her horror, what had happened.

There had been a house there once—a shack, probably no more than a single room. But it was gone. All that was left now was its footprint, the very bottoms of the gray wooden walls peeking out of the mud to show their scorched upper edges.

It had burned.

Vaclav's house had burned.

Something began to rise up inside of Eva.

"When?" she said.

"Oh, two, three months," said the man. "And in all that time, you're the first person I've known what's cared enough to ask."

"How did the fire start?" she said. Eva kept her voice soft and steady beneath the patter of the rain.

The man chuckled without mirth. "You know how many houses burn down in our part of town, missy? No one cares. An unattended hearth, a forgotten pipe. Take your pick."

But Eva already knew the true answer anyway: the Schovajsa house had stood only inches away from its neighbors, and yet not a single scorch mark, not a lick of flame, had marred their nearby walls of wood.

This fire had been focused; it had been sent with a job to do.

Eva heard a sniff, and with surprise she saw that Mrs. Malloy was crying.

"Why?" Mrs. Malloy said. "Why did you bring her here?"

The red-faced man spit on the ground. "Because," he said, "as far as *they're* concerned, there's no difference between the pens in the Yards and the houses in Back. Just as long as they all get fed."

"But she's only a girl," said Mrs. Malloy.

"So were you, once," said the man. With a swallow, he finished his whiskey, dropped the glass in the mud, and wandered away.

There they stood for quite some time. Rain collected in Eva's hair; Mrs. Malloy sobbed softly beside her.

It had been Mr. Magister, of course—just as it had been with Henry. Just as it would be, if she let it, with her. And how many more would he toss onto the fire before he was done?

As she stood before the ruins of Vaclav's little hovel, she felt something potent rise up in her: something that did not wish to wane.

"I'm sorry," said Mrs. Malloy, wiping at her eyes. "I'm sorry. I just . . . He's not nice, that fellow, but he's not wrong, either. My Jim, my little Alfie—it could've been them. It still could. Just burned up—like . . . like forgotten bacon. And no one seems to care."

Eva took a deep breath. "Mrs. Malloy?"

"Yes?"

"Can I tell you something in confidence?"

Mrs. Malloy nodded. "Of course, dear."

"Have you ever heard of a spirit medium?"

Mrs. Malloy's eyes widened. "Like someone as can speak to the dead?"

"Yes," said Eva. "I am a spirit medium, Mrs. Malloy. I bring back what is gone. *I* care. And I want you to know: I feel something now that comes back from Vaclav Schovajsa—something that I promise I will not let go of until it is satisfied."

Mrs. Malloy frowned. Her chin gave a little quiver. "What is it?"

Eva turned her eyes back to the patch of ground where Vaclav had lived and died, and as if taking a vow on the muddy ash of his grave, she answered the question:

"His anger."

Without money, Eva had no choice but to walk back to Briggs House, and she leaned forward into the stinging rain.

Every wet welt felt like a penance.

It had taken her so long to see what was right in front of her eyes—what Henry had seen and had tried to show her. And she could no longer deceive herself: it had been a choice. She had chosen to see the delight and not the danger, the Magician and not the murderer.

That was a mistake she would never make again.

After crossing over Bubbly Creek, Eva began to wend her way north and east. She didn't know quite where to look for Briggs House except that it was far away within the bend of the river, a block or two before it turned toward the lake. She would be late—very late—but with any luck, Gabbermann would still be there.

Gabbermann knows more than he's saying.

It was nearly an hour into her squelching trudge that Eva stumbled onto Prairie Avenue. Immediately, she felt a tightening in her chest.

The rain, of course, fell more lightly here—a genteel sprinkling in preference to the coarse, fat drops of the stockyards. These were the addresses of all the greatest names in Chicago: Sears, Field, Armour, Kellogg, Glessner—and Overstreet.

She could see Aunt Isabella through the front window, sitting in the brightly lit parlor. She was reading a magazine, an idle smile on her face, and Eva wanted to run to her, to bang on the door until they let her in, to cling to Aunt Isabella's skirts and tell her everything that had happened.

But Mr. Magister had been in that place—once, at least—to unseat Eva and Henry. Who knew what other malignant Magic he had left behind? And if Eva went there now, then surely he would follow.

A vision appeared before her eyes: the bright parlor in flames. How many kind people might she cause to burn?

The wind stirred across Eva's sodden skin; she gave a shiver.

Overstreet House had never really been her place, anyhow. Not really.

She turned and began walking again; the rain thickened once more. Soon the skyscrapers of the Loop began to crowd in around her, the jumping glow of kerosene lamps sending long phantoms flashing along the slick wooden sidewalk. Traffic rumbled by, and rattling trolley cars; Eva was no longer the only poor drenched soul struggling up the avenues.

By the time she reached Randolph Street, Eva was shivering wildly, her teeth chattering in her jaws. She was still several blocks from Briggs House, but Eva could see it in the distance, and despite her exhaustion, she sprang forward. Nearly twice two hours had elapsed since she'd last come out of that door, but now she was only a block away, and she was violently eager to arrive—so eager, in fact, that she nearly bowled over the gentleman who stepped in her way.

"Pardon me, miss," he said, but Eva shoved him aside. "Miss!" She could hear him approaching fast, following, catching up. "Miss!"

"I'm sorry," said Eva over her shoulder. "I can't stop now."

They were before Briggs House; the gentleman stood between Eva and the door.

"Excuse me," she said. "There's an important appointment that I'm very late for."

The man nodded. He was tall and broad, in a well-cut suit, a bowler hat, and a blocky, sensible mustache. Above his head, he held a wide umbrella that he extended forward, allowing the rain to soak the back of his calves so that Eva could be sheltered. "Your appointment was with me."

Eva shook her head. "No, sir," she said, squeezing past him. "I don't know you. My appointment was with—"

"William Gabbermann is dead."

The door handle was in her hand, the metal cold and slick. She had almost made it.

With a sigh, Eva let Briggs House go and turned back to the man with the umbrella.

"How?"

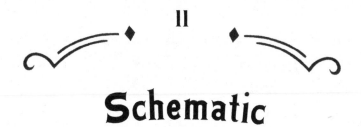

Schematic

The gentleman's office was only a block away: small, almost cozy, with a desk, two chairs, a little window, and far more paperwork than Eva had ever seen before. It smelled like tobacco and shoe leather, and the radiator in the corner ticked softly, quickly warming her rain-chilled skin.

"Now, then, Miss Poole," said the gentleman, gesturing to the chair opposite his desk. "I am Detective Webster. Harry at Briggs House told me you might have some information about William Gabbermann."

Eva blinked. "How did you know me? Out there on the street—how did you recognize me?"

Detective Webster's eyes had been scrolling across a sheet of notes, but he raised them now. "Harry gave a good description. And that dress is unmistakable."

The dress. Even now, despite her wading through all the filth of the Back of the Yards, it was spotlessly clean, and it was beginning to feel tight. Eva tugged at its collar.

"What did you mean to discuss with Mr. Gabbermann this evening?"

Eva shivered. "You never answered my question," she said. "How did he die?"

Detective Webster sat back in his chair and began to chew on the stem of an unlit pipe. "Were you well acquainted?"

"With Gabbermann?" Eva shook her head. "No."

"And what was the nature of your acquaintance?"

"We met once," she said. "He was a friend of a friend."

Detective Webster nodded and made a note. "Who was the friend that you had in common?"

"Why won't you tell me how he died?" Eva asked.

Detective Webster gave a tight sigh. "In truth, Miss Poole, because I'm not quite sure myself. What I do know is that he died in his own room, that he was holding his pistol when he died, and that the bullet that killed him seems to have come from the gun he had in his hand. In most cases, this would suggest a simple suicide. But this does not seem to be most cases."

The rain drummed like idle fingers on the window.

"Beside Mr. Gabbermann we found a rather large amount of money: exactly one hundred crisp dollar bills, neatly stacked."

One hundred dollars. Wasn't that how much Gabbermann had invested in Mr. Magister's fire scheme?

"What does that suggest to you, Miss Poole?"

"Well," she said, "it suggests suicide, doesn't it? If Gabbermann was murdered, wouldn't you think the killer would take the money?"

Detective Webster frowned and nodded. "My colleagues agree with you. But it happens that I spoke with Mr. Gabbermann the day before his death."

Detective Webster paused, surveying Eva's face carefully.

"It was, to say the least, an unusual conversation. He was clearly very afraid, but to tell you the truth, I didn't much worry—I assumed that poor Mr. Gabbermann wasn't entirely in his right mind. We see a fair number of people like that in this line of work."

"I'm sure you do."

"But Gabbermann said that the man he was afraid of wanted to buy out his stake in a joint enterprise of theirs—that he wanted to own it outright. And so this pile of money beside his body: To me, it doesn't say suicide. It says something much stranger."

Eva sat quietly in her chair, careful to keep her expression level.

Detective Webster watched her for a long time.

The radiator in the corner ticked along sleepily.

"Gabbermann also said that this man had sent two children to shake him down that day: a boy and a girl." Detective Webster pointed at Eva with the stem of his pipe. "You don't happen to know who that girl was, do you?"

Eva said nothing.

Rifling through the papers on the desk, Detective Webster soon came up with a folder.

"Gabbermann attempted several times to describe the man he was afraid of, but something seemed to stop him. Instead, he gave portraiture a try."

One by one, Detective Webster laid out three sheets of notepaper on the desk before Eva. The drawings were crude and unsuccessful—just as she'd known they must be—and yet here and there, in the curve of a shoulder, the length of a finger, the cut of a jaw, she could see him lurking, undeniably, in Gabbermann's memory.

"What name do you know him by?" said Detective Webster. "Gabbermann gave me several."

Eva sat back in her chair.

"Mortimer King? Vergil Silver? Haywood Grimm?"

And before she could stop herself, Eva shook her head.

"Or was it Jack Coagulo?"

She nodded. "That one I've heard."

"But it's not what you call him?"

"No," said Eva. "No, we called him Mr. Magister."

Detective Webster copied this out carefully into his notes. "Can you tell me anything else about him, Miss Poole?"

Eva gave a dry chuckle. "What do you know?" she said. "What on earth do you think you know?"

It came out slowly over more than an hour's negotiated conversation. Gradually, Detective Webster began to believe that Eva could be trusted; gradually, he revealed more and more of what Gabbermann had told him.

The story was strange: irreconcilable with what she and Henry had heard, and likely just as unreliable. But all the same, it had a savor of truth to it—of hidden facts scattered in amongst the fibs.

According to Bill Gabbermann, Mr. Magister's true name was Elijah Solway. They'd known each other casually growing up in the little town of Atash, Georgia, but they hadn't become friendly until after the war. Both of their fathers had died—Gabbermann's at Antietam, Solway's when Sherman's boys had burned the family orchard on their march to the sea. When they'd met back up, both Gabbermann and Solway had needed money, and they'd started out simply: a little shoplifting, some petty robbery. Gabbermann hadn't liked this, though—it felt coarse to him, dangerous and brutish—and soon enough they were grifting instead, running low-stakes scams and confidence games from Alabama up to the Dakota Territory and back again.

This scheme suited Gabbermann quite well; he had a way of holding people's attention, of drawing them in. But Solway was clumsy, nervous, and shy, and he gave up the trick as often as not.

It was at about this time that Solway discovered a volume called *The Impossible Art* in a secondhand bookshop. He had, it turned out, some talent, and he quickly became obsessed, spending days, even weeks, at a time in the silent study of Magic.

Now, Detective Webster was unclear on this point: he assumed that the art in question was simple legerdemain—illusion—but Gabbermann had spoken of Solway's Magic as if it were real.

He left room for Eva to comment upon this confusion, but she let it pass in silence.

There had been an agreement of some sort, a bargain. Gabbermann had raised—or more likely, stolen—a substantial amount of money to sponsor Solway's studies, and in exchange, he seemed to think that he was somehow entitled to a certain portion of the Magic that Solway learned.

It was at this point in his story that Gabbermann had begun to refer to Solway exclusively, almost compulsively, as *Jack Coagulo.*

Detective Webster regretted that he had not paid closer attention to Gabbermann's account, but the man had been prattling with full faith about Magic, and he didn't seem to have any crime to report—at least not anything actionable. Webster's ears had perked up, however, when Gabbermann mentioned a move to Chicago, and he'd offered his condolences when Gabbermann spoke of his losses in the Great Fire.

But nothing really made him sit up and pay attention until Gabbermann started talking about the girl from Quebec.

Alarming words had been used: *resurrection, burnt offering, human sacrifice.* Gabbermann alleged that in a mad attempt to bring his wife and daughter back from the fire, Jack Coagulo had gone across the border to Canada and fraudulently acquired an apprentice for the explicit purpose of bringing her to Chicago and burning her alive.

This word—*apprentice*—sent a shiver down Eva's spine. That, she supposed, was what she had been.

By now, Detective Webster had strongly suspected that Gabbermann was a crank, but still, he'd given some very specific information: the girl had come from Saint-Laurent in Quebec; her name had been Iphigénie Gagnon; she had been a tailor's daughter. It did no harm to check, and so he'd written to the gendarmerie in Saint-Laurent, and it was only after Gabbermann's death that he received the reply: Mademoiselle Gagnon had, indeed, gone off with a man who called himself Coagulo; her parents had not heard from her in nearly ten years.

This looked bad. And worse, Detective Webster had found a house fire out in Pullman that fit Gabbermann's timeline perfectly: only the brick basement had survived.

When he'd given Eva all the information that he was willing to share, Detective Webster laid out a level plea for her help. It was clear that she knew Solway. Did she have any knowledge of his whereabouts, any little scrap of information that might help bring him to justice? She had to understand, Solway was a very dangerous man, capable of kidnapping a young girl and burning her alive for his own dubious purposes.

At the mention of *a young girl* in the singular, Eva found herself laughing.

"What?" said Detective Webster.

Eva shook her head. "He's not *very dangerous*," she said. "He's the devil. Including your Canadian girl, I count at least three children he's burned."

"Three?" Webster's eyes were wide.

In truth, she thought the number was probably five— she couldn't help but think of the boy Cato and of freckled Meg, but of their lives and deaths, she had only suspicions.

"Who were the others?"

"A boy named Vaclav Schovajsa," she said. "His father, also—Ignác. And Henry Poole."

"Poole?" Detective Webster looked up from his notepad. "Any relation?"

The molten grief in Eva's gut gave a sudden lurch. "It's complicated," she said, because it was.

"Listen, Eva," said Detective Webster, "if you tell me where to find him, I can bring your Mr. Magister in. I can make sure he's brought to justice for all the things that he's done."

A sudden image of the detective stumbling haplessly through the wiry trees at the edge of Mr. Magister's farmhouse tore into her head; she imagined he'd be electrocuted before he even reached the lions, and if the trees didn't get him, then surely something else would.

"You don't understand," she said. "You don't understand his power."

Detective Webster gave a rough chuckle. "Is it that

magic business again? Because no number of card tricks has ever kept a man out of prison."

"No," said Eva. "No, Detective. You have to believe me—you have to understand—or I can't help you."

Believing her, however, seemed to be beyond Detective Webster's reach. He shrugged, grimaced, and opened his mouth to say so, but just then there was a tapping at the office door.

"One moment," said Detective Webster, and he rose.

In the hall stood an agitated fellow who introduced himself as Mr. H. H. Gross. "I'm terribly sorry," he said. "But I've been waiting to see someone all day. I didn't sleep a wink last night, and my building is still sitting unlocked. Can I tell you what's happened?"

Detective Webster flashed Eva a wide-eyed gaze as if to say, *The things we have to deal with . . .* , and he drew out his pad and pen.

Mr. Gross claimed he had been the victim of a robbery, and when Detective Webster asked him what had been taken, he began what seemed like a very long story: he owned and operated a very profitable cyclorama not far away, at 130 Michigan Avenue, and . . .

They were impressive things, cycloramas—massive paintings on rollers that surrounded the viewer on all sides as they scrolled seamlessly through their scenes. There had been a cyclorama on the Midway Plaisance depicting the eruption of the Kilauea volcano in Hawaii, and Eva had hoped to see it.

But she was not terribly interested in this fellow or his complaint. Mr. Magister was hot on her mind, and she had just begun to wonder if anything but Magic might ever stop him when Mr. Gross began to recite the impressive dimensions of his particular cyclorama— 47 feet high, 378 feet from end to end. The canvas itself had weighed eight tons, even before the application of paint.

"But how on earth could someone steal a thing so large?" said Detective Webster.

"No," said Mr. Gross. "No, no, no, they haven't stolen the *cyclorama*—they've just taken the *flames*."

At this, Eva sat forward. "Flames?" she said. "What flames?"

Mr. Gross shook his head in consternation. "Didn't you hear me? It's a panorama of the Great Fire."

The squat round polygon of the cyclorama building seemed to crouch amongst the high-rises, its windows cold and dark. Letters painted thirty-five feet high on its shoulders screamed CHICAGO FIRE, CHICAGO FIRE, CHICAGO FIRE.

The rain battered down on them as if it were trying to wash away an unseen stain.

The Fire, the Fire, the Fire.

"Come in," said Mr. Gross, pulling back the door.

There was an ongoing struggle with the lights—Mr. Gross seemed to have neglected certain repairs—and for a short time, Eva and Webster were left in the blue-dim lobby as he dashed away to a supply closet.

"You're sure this is connected to Solway?" said Detective Webster in a hoarse whisper.

Eva nodded.

"How can you be so certain?"

She took a deep breath. "I told you, Detective—if you want my help, you're going to have to trust me."

Soon enough, Mr. Gross returned behind the bobbing light of a lantern.

"Here," he said. "Follow me."

The exhibition room was huge—high and wide and echoing. The painted panorama that lined the walls seemed massive, filling Eva's eyes, drawing her into the scene, and the inconstant flicker of the lantern redoubled the effect.

The burning of Chicago stretched out and up into the murky distance, farther than the eye could see.

It was impossible not to notice what had happened— what Mr. Gross had described as "grand larceny." The pictures were still there: the ruined buildings, the flee-ing people, the choking black smoke that rose into the cloudy canvas sky. Eva could even see remnants of the fire's reflection, an orange glow cast upon painted walls and windows.

But the flame itself—every last tongue of it—was gone. In its place, the plain canvas, oddly clean and white, peered out like a skull where a face should have been.

Eva felt sick to her stomach.

Detective Webster approached the pictured wall, tak-ing the lantern from Mr. Gross's hand as he passed.

"It's incredibly precise," he murmured.

"Yes," said Mr. Gross. "Just the flame—nothing else. It's as if those portions of the canvas had never even been painted."

Detective Webster's eyes found Eva's, and he raised his eyebrows as if to say, *Care to explain?*

Eva kept her silence.

"Is it just this section?" asked Detective Webster.

"Oh my, no," said Mr. Gross. "Look." And stepping around the panorama, he threw a heavy switch. Deep in the basement, machinery grumbled and whirred, and the rollers that held the huge bolts of canvas began to turn.

Before their eyes, Chicago scrolled by, stripped of its Great Fire.

Presently, Mr. Gross stepped forward. "Excuse me," he said. "I'm going to go see about the lights."

Detective Webster offered the lantern, but Mr. Gross raised his palm. "I know my way in the dark."

Slowly, Mr. Gross's footsteps receded into the gloom.

The machinery ground away beneath their feet; the rain beat against the roof above. Detective Webster backed into the center of the room and laid the lantern on the ground.

The light flickered and leapt.

"Solway?"

Eva nodded.

"But why?" he said. "What good could paint do him?"

Eva sighed and stepped forward, the lantern sending her giant shadow jumping up the wall.

Of course, the paint didn't mean anything in and of itself. It was the gathering, the *taking* of the fire.

But how could she hope to explain this to the detective—to someone who refused to even consider the possibility of Magic?

All the same, it was a good question: Why *did* it serve Mr. Magister to have more of the Great Fire? Perhaps he'd had to use what he'd previously bought up in order to burn Henry and Vaclav? Perhaps he'd used more than he meant to?

Or perhaps it had to do with Gabbermann's repayment. Did Mr. Magister need to acquire the fire again in order to own it outright?

Eva had no idea.

Behind her, Detective Webster began to pace.

She was in over her head—out of her magical depth—and she felt suddenly hot, sweat beading on her brow.

She needed help.

Raising a trembling hand, Eva brushed her finger against the bare weave of the canvas. "Come back," she murmured, though whether she spoke to the paint, or to Henry, or even to the girl that she had been before all of this began, she didn't know.

What she did know was that she hadn't meant to call *him*.

First, the smell: crisp linen, whiskey, woodsmoke wafting in on the fresh air. He seemed to cast his own weird glow, lighting his passage into the hall. Detective Webster's eyes widened; Eva inched away until she could feel the painted panorama against her back.

But Mr. Magister didn't seem to see them.

No—no, of course he didn't. Whatever this was, it was canvas thin—not quite present, not quite full. Eva stumbled a few cautious steps closer, and from this new vantage point, she could see the brushstrokes at his jawline, the stippling in his mustache:

He was the painted memory of the cyclorama.

Mr. Magister strode into the center of the huge round room and stopped. He shrugged out of his jacket and doffed his top hat, and when his sleeves had been rolled up his forearms, he began gingerly to remove the spotless white gloves from his burnt hands.

He was preparing to work.

The painted Mr. Magister took a deep breath, shut his eyes, and lifted his hands from his sides. Slowly, the panorama rollers all around him picked up speed, whirring quicker and quicker.

Eva's eyes darted to Detective Webster, rapt on the other side of the room.

Now painted flames seemed to leap from the canvas, orange and yellow and red, flying through the air, collecting around Mr. Magister's hands. He winced, breathing in sharply through his teeth; his hands were burning all over again.

On and on the rollers ran, Mr. Magister collecting flame like iron filings to a magnet. Eva jumped back as the blaze around him grew, flickering, flaring, higher and higher; she could feel the heat of the growing firestorm on her cheeks.

With a slamming clack, the rollers reached the end of the panorama.

Mr. Magister's eyes shot open; Eva saw agony in

them. In either hand, he now held one half of the Great Fire of Chicago, the flames of paint burning high, nearly reaching the ceiling.

Mr. Magister cupped his palms and gazed into the inferno, its light blowing back the shadow from his face. Eva could see him searching, searching within it for something—for someone.

But what he sought, he did not find.

With a sigh, Mr. Magister shut his eyes and raised his cupped palms. In one deep draft, he drank the Great Fire of Chicago down.

Eva shuddered, shivered, and nearly exploded in agony.

She could feel it racing through every artery, every vein and capillary of her body: the fire, burning, burning, scorching her from the inside out. It was almost easier, better to burn, to let go and be consumed; she could not resist him, could never hope to overcome this man, this master Magician who imbibed fire and tragedy— never, not ever, not ever ever ever.

The painted fire was gone. Mr. Magister's hands were empty—dim and scorched.

His eyes flashed open. Where the darkness of his pupils should've been, there was only flame.

Eva squeezed her own eyes shut and screamed, and all the electric lights in the building surged on.

When she opened her eyes again, Mr. Magister was gone.

Mr. Gross came back to the exhibition hall. After several minutes of conversation, Detective Webster thanked him and tucked his notepad away.

Mr. Gross saw them out; Eva remained silent.

The front door of the building clicked softly behind them; the rain ran down in rivulets from the roof of the porch above.

Now, out of long silence, Detective Webster spoke. "What was that?" he said. "In there?"

But this was not a question that needed an answer. He knew.

"If I help you," Eva said, "if I agree to help—will you listen to everything that I say? Even if you don't understand?"

Detective Webster nodded. "I will."

She took a deep breath. "He gets his mail at the Hotel Florence in Pullman. I don't know if he keeps a room, but all his mail has that address."

Detective Webster took the small pad of paper from his jacket pocket. "The Hotel Florence?" he repeated.

Eva nodded. "Don't write it down."

The detective put his pad away.

"He'll be difficult to stop," she said.

"I'll take help."

"Take a lot. And move quickly."

"I'll go now," said Detective Webster, and after a long moment's pause: "If I stay in the rain, can his fire still reach me?"

Eva shook her head. "I don't know. Assume it can. Be careful."

"I will."

"And if he tries to lead you onto the fairgrounds of the Columbian Exposition, just let him go. Don't follow him into the Fair."

Detective Webster raised his eyebrows.

"You promised," said Eva.

"Very well."

Eva turned her eyes toward the inky-black lake. "I won't be able to sleep until I know you have him."

Detective Webster took a deep breath. "I'll let you know. Where can I find you?"

But Eva had no answer for this.

"Eva?" said Detective Webster. "Do you have any-where to go tonight?"

Her cheeks bunched up tight; her eyes stung.

She shook her head.

Detective Webster lived in a small house with bright windows and two young trees in the yard. His wife, Alice, and his basset hound, Toby, met them at the door, and it was hard to say which of them was more pleased.

He made it clear that this could only be for the night; in the morning, once he had Solway in custody, Detective Webster would call upon some friends at City Hall and see about getting Eva a more permanent situation.

She understood all of this, but she did her best not to think about it. It was such a cheerful little house—there was soup on the stove and bread in the oven, and it all smelled delicious.

Over his wife's objections, Detective Webster was continuing on to Pullman directly, without his supper. She didn't let him go, though, without first hiding a number of dinner rolls in the pockets of his coat, and as they watched him push out through the front gate, Mrs. Webster said that she regretted not putting in some loose soup as well.

She gave a braying laugh and turned back to the house.

Mrs. Webster insisted that soup was the only food for rainy days, and that anyone who thought otherwise should be subject to prosecution. Eva had a hard time disagreeing, and as they ate in the bright warmth of the kitchen, Mrs. Webster told her about her program of giving Detective Webster increasingly ridiculous hats as gifts—all ribbons and pom-poms and bright-colored bows. "He has to wear them, you see, because he's just too kind not to."

The soup was delicious, and it was rendered all the more enjoyable when Toby came to rest his fuzzy chin on top of Eva's feet. When they'd finished, Mrs. Webster showed her to the guest room and offered to draw a bath, and though this sounded lovely, to her embarrassment Eva didn't quite know how to get out of her dress. She politely declined.

Smiling, Mrs. Webster said she was going to go down and clean up. She turned in as early as she could on these nights when Detective Webster was out in the field—it was the only way to calm her anxious mind.

She was such a kind woman, so jolly and caring; Eva didn't know how to tell her that she ought to be much more anxious than she was.

Eva smiled, thanked her, and eased the door shut. But her smile faded away just as quickly as Mrs. Webster's footsteps. This was it. She'd made her choice now, declared her allegiance. She was against Mr. Magister—or Jack Coagulo, Elijah Solway, whoever he might be—and it felt like absolutely everything hung in the balance.

She wished she'd never met him. She wished she'd never come to Chicago, never even seen the Fair. Perhaps if Eva had simply stayed with Mrs. Blodgett, ignored the call of the candle, performed properly at the séance in Nadab—perhaps none of this would've happened, and Henry would still be alive, smiling and sketching blithely away in the parlor at Overstreet House.

Or perhaps the only difference would be that she never would've gotten the chance to meet him, to see his sketches, to watch him look.

And if that was it—if it was a choice between Henry and no Henry—well, then, even after all the pain and terror, she couldn't possibly wish him out of her life.

Eva sat down on the bed.

Had there ever been a moment as sweet as the one she'd shared with Henry in the dining room of the Pavilion? Just sitting there on the floor, passing a peach back and forth in the sunshine?

His shoulder had pressed against hers; she almost thought she could feel it now.

It had been too long since she'd attempted a peach.

But when she put her hand into her pocket, all Eva found was a pair of battered spectacles, a droplet of blood congealed on the shattered glass of the left lens.

A solid stone of dread dropped into Eva's gut.

Where was the peach pit? What had she done with it?

In a panic, Eva began to tear through her bag, but before she reached the bottom, she remembered:

The farmhouse—she had taken it out in the farmhouse and left it on her bedside table. She must've walked directly past it on her way out.

How, how, how on earth could she have been so stupid, so careless? There was nothing in the world that she wouldn't trade for that peach pit, even if it were inert, mundane, entirely without Magic, just to hold it. It was like the last living piece of Henry; more than that, it was a part of Henry and herself combined.

She had to go back and get it.

But this was foolish—foolish and impossible. She couldn't go back now. It was too late.

Wasn't it?

But the more she thought about it, the more it seemed that this was her final chance to recover the pit. Assuming that Mr. Magister had discovered her absence, he might be out in Chicago searching for her already.

And what if Detective Webster managed to apprehend Mr. Magister in Pullman? What would happen to the Pavilion then? Would she ever be able to get back in? Would the peach pit even continue to be?

And before she knew what she was doing, Eva's bag was on her shoulder.

She turned to face the door.

She had to get it back.

The streets were still.

The rain had stopped, leaving a gleaming blanket of moisture draped over everything. It was so late now that even the wind seemed to be sleeping.

Eva's heart began to pound as the fairgrounds came into view. Part of her wanted to return to the Sixty-Fourth Street turnstiles, her habitual angle of approach, but the Cold Storage Building—or what remained of it—lay just inside that entrance, and she couldn't afford a moment's distraction tonight.

Instead, she chose the Sixty-Second Street gate. She pushed hesitantly against the turnstile, but it whirred and turned smoothly, just as it always had, without the tribute of admission.

Whatever Mr. Magister's opinion, apparently the Fair still favored her.

Now all she had to do was find her way into the Pavilion.

Eva tried the Transportation Building first, wandering past Alaskan war canoes, antique laundry wagons, the gilded sleigh of King Ludwig of Bavaria. The total stillness of the grounds was even starker in here, and yet, somehow, she had trouble convincing herself that she was alone; the swish of her skirt, the clack of her heels seemed to multiply in the vastness of the space.

By the time she arrived in the section reserved for the Pullman Palace Car Company, all her muscles were stretched taut in anxiety.

Eva quickly found the car she'd returned through, but she could see before she was inside that it wouldn't take her back. It felt lifeless, mundane—just metal and wood and polish.

She left the Transportation Building via the gilded eastern door and made her way down the broad avenue before her. The Mines Building passed by on one side, the great lagoon and its Wooded Island on the other.

And the moment she realized which building came next, she knew exactly where she had to go:

The Electricity Building.

At its hub was an eighty-two-foot tower of colored glass that flashed and glowed with electrical light, and Eva was drawn toward it like a moth to a flame. She was terribly nervous, but at least the echoing of her feet was not as strongly pronounced here: the air was filled with fuzzy electric noise—the buzzing of copper wires.

Eva stopped short.

Copper.

All the wiring was copper.

Nearby, a display case had been erected under a large sign that read EXPLICATION OF THE ELECTRICAL CIRCUIT.

What Eva saw there seemed horribly familiar:

A circuit, the placard explained, was a simple electrical network consisting of a loop of conductive wiring, usually copper, that connected the various electrical components of that system. In Mr. Thomas Edison's direct-current scheme, the power flowed consistently in one direction, while in Mr. George Westinghouse's alternating-current scheme—used to electrify the fairgrounds—the flow periodically changed direction.

Eva couldn't catch her breath. With the horror of recognition, she thought of the roots in the walls, the snaking veins and arteries between the foundation bricks, the bushes that hid the sentinel lions at the farmhouse. *The Machine,* Henry had written, *we are the Machine.*

Eva's blood felt suddenly cold in her veins—almost metallic. She shook her head and stepped toward the center of the building, the confidence of understanding filling her to the brim.

On the side of the flashing tower was a thin metal

panel the size of a small cellar door. The bones in Eva's hand seemed to buzz as she took hold of it, but she didn't draw back, and when it was open, she saw very clearly:

Before her eyes was a mass of buzzing copper wire, twisted and tangled, like the nest of some electric eagle. At the end of each wire was a copper lion's head, and between their pairs of opposing jaws, the lions fought over many miniature things: a piano, a dress, a pair of spectacles, a tree, a hammer, a sketchbook. Just below the center of the massing, two lions had latched onto a single skeletal hand—left—its index finger bent as if to beckon. From the tip of the beckoning finger, one final wire led up to a massive, great-handled switch.

Without hesitation, Eva reached out, grabbed the switch, and pulled.

It wouldn't budge.

Eva tugged, yanked, pulling with all the fury and strength in her—so much, indeed, that for long moments, she didn't notice the sizzle and crack of her scorching skin, and even after she did, still she pulled, pulled and tugged as hard as she could until she could bear the pain no longer.

Eva stumbled back.

The palm of her hand was bubbling, weeping—burned.

The open door swung shut.

"Please," Eva murmured. "Please, I have to go back."

Now the electrical panel floated open once again.

What was inside, however, was entirely different: a darkened room, lit by a single, lonely candle.

Come, the silence seemed to say. *Come back.*

Eva took a deep breath and climbed through.

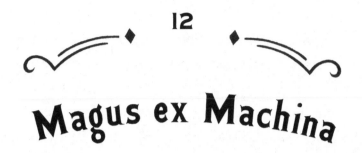

12

Magus ex Machina

The floorboards squeaked and moaned softly beneath Eva's feet. She was upstairs in the third farmhouse bedroom—the one she had thought of as Henry's.

Her left hand was in screaming pain, her palm scarred and burned.

But she didn't have time to worry about the wound.

Eva moved into the hallway as quietly as she could, and in moments she'd arrived at her own bedroom door. It was standing open, the bed still messy and unmade, and there, upon the nightstand, was the peach pit.

Their peach pit.

Eva lunged across the bedroom. The floor gave a loud squawk, but she hardly even noticed: she had it now, resting in her burnt left palm, and a shiver of warmth ran through her body like morning sunshine, like soothing bathwater.

Tears budded in her eyes. Perhaps everything could be all right. She just had to get away—she just had to get back.

Out into the hallway she went, and down past Mr. Magister's room. This was the moment Eva dreaded most—passing only feet away from his bed—but his door, too, was open, and the room was vacant and dim. He must've discovered her absence by now, must've gone after her into Chicago. There was a chance, she supposed, that he was downstairs waiting for her, but she hadn't heard any sounds other than her own since she'd arrived, and she saw no illumination below; the only light burning in the house was from the candle— her candle—there in Henry's room.

For a moment, the foolishness of this leapt into her heart—how reckless it was to leave a candle unattended in an old wooden farmhouse—but she found she didn't care: let the Pavilion burn behind her; she had what she'd come for.

Eva's descent of the staircase was the longest and most excruciating she'd ever made, her heart pounding harder and faster with each progressive step.

On the ground floor, all was still. Only the screen door lay between her and the outside.

Eva crossed the front hall quickly, eager to get back to safety as soon as she could, but something snagged her attention.

There, upon the dining room table, was a familiar book, thick and heavy, bound in red cloth.

That was the book that Mr. Magister had been reading.

That was Henry's sketchbook.

She knew she shouldn't have stopped; she knew she should've continued on out the door and across the lawn. But the thought of intentionally leaving the sketchbook behind felt like a betrayal—like an abandonment—and she turned into the dining room.

But something was off—something was different. This was neither Henry's sketchbook nor the dry agricultural treatise Mr. Magister had disguised it as.

This was a different book entirely.

The volume was laid open on the table, and Eva lifted it, slotting her finger between the pages as a makeshift bookmark in order to examine the words on its spine:

The Impossible Art.

Eva opened the book into her hand once more. It was the beginning of the seventh chapter—"The Alchemical Insight"—and facing the first page of text was an illustration: a snake in a loop, biting its own tail.

Eva read:

Alchemy, one of the most ancient and venerable tributaries to flow into the great river of the Impossible Art, has been attested distinctly in Europe, China, India, and Arabia. Vulgarly assumed to be devoted to the transmutation of base metals into gold, alchemy is, in truth, the occult science dealing with the perfection of the Self.

Though a fuller description of the alchemical process can—and perhaps should—take up entire libraries, it is possible to point to one discrete principle that unifies much of its theory: the doctrine of dissolution and resolution. This idea (that disintegration and reintegration, destruction and creation, death and life are fundamentally unified) is sometimes represented visually by the symbol of the ouroboros, or the serpent that devours its own tail, and it is most commonly known in the literature in its Latin form: *SOLVE ET COAGVLA*.

NB: In the articulation of all magical formulae, care should be taken to reproduce the pronunciation of the original speakers as nearly as possible. In this instance, therefore, the *V* ought to be pronounced softly, in the Roman style—as a *U* or *W*.

The letters squirmed and swam before Eva's eyes, as if resisting their reading, but Eva didn't stop.

"Solway," she read aloud, *"et Coagula."*

Outside, the breeze stirred as if waking, and a distinctive aroma rose to her attention: woodsmoke and linen and whiskey and sweat.

The screen door screamed and slammed shut again.

"Ah," said Mr. Magister, his smile smoldering. "There you are."

Eva dropped the book on the table and stumbled backward.

In his gloved hands, Mr. Magister held a wad of mail, and he sorted through it now, flipping envelope over envelope, scarcely even bothering to look at her.

"My word, Eva," he said, "but you have been a very naughty girl."

It was the first time Eva had seen his face since she'd left the Pavilion, and she searched it now for any hint of what she'd learned: the deception, the manipulation, the murder and lies.

But there was nothing. It was a perfect mask, each spotless tooth evenly placed beneath the trim hedge of his mustache.

"Elijah?" she murmured.

And at this, his face fell.

"Well, shit," said Solway.

Eva swallowed. Mr. Magister seemed to have changed before her very eyes, dissolved, revealing Elijah Solway like a snake sloughing off its old skin. Even his accent was different.

"You been talking to Bill Gabbermann?"

"Yes," she said. "And he told me everything."

Solway shook his head. "Old fool. It's *Eli*. No one ever called me Elijah but my mama."

"You killed him," said Eva.

"No," said Solway. "Bill killed himself. I offered him a way out, even gave him his money back, but still he wouldn't see reason."

"They're coming for you," Eva said. "They're going to arrest you."

"Who?" said Solway. "Them cops you sent up to Pullman? *Please.* I walked right by 'em, right past their blind little eyes. What do you take me for?"

A sharp lance of anger shot into Eva. "A murderer!"

"Now, that ain't fair," said Solway.

"They know," said Eva. "They know about Gabbermann and Iphigénie. . . ."

Solway gave a gentle sigh. "She was talented, that Iphigénie. A seamstress, I guess, or a weaver—don't seem quite right to call her a seamstress when her clothes have no seams. You see?"

Now Solway held up his gloved hands; there wasn't a stitch or seam on either of them.

"They're a set," said Solway. "These gloves and that dress you're wearing. They don't neither of them take scorch marks, which, let me tell you, has come in real handy."

With horror, Eva looked down at her body; the white dress she had put on seemed to stiffen.

"You burned her," Eva said.

Solway bobbed his head from side to side as if deciding whether or not to argue the point. "She burned, yes."

"And Vaclav? And Henry?"

Solway chuckled. "You don't have much time left, Eva. You really gonna spend it asking questions you already know the answers to?"

"But *why*?"

"I put a lot of Magic into them kids," said Solway. It was almost as if this question offended him. "Nobody faults a banker when he pulls the cash out of his accounts."

Tears stung Eva's eyes. "You're a murderer!"

"Now, I told you," said Solway. "I don't care for that kind of talk. I'm in business, is all, like any other man— only I'm building my capital with Magic instead of corn or coal or steel."

Eva was humming, vibrating with grief and indignation. "Don't you care at all?" she said.

Solway sighed as if this were the stupidest question in the world. "And here I thought you was clever. Of *course* I care. Every one of you that goes to the fire repeats the sacrifice—my wife, my daughter, my daddy, and now my students. I grieve for every one of you. That's why it works."

Eva felt a dark thrill, and she took a defiant step forward. "Not anymore."

"Oh, what?" said Solway. "You gonna stop me?" Eva could see the burning laughter in his eyes, and he raised both of his hands like a conductor before an orchestra.

Suddenly, Eva was searing hot—hotter than she'd ever been. She wanted to turn, to flee, to let everything out of her—the fear and the grief and the fury.

She gasped. "What are you doing?"

Elijah Solway laughed, a creaking, crackling sound like the weakening of great timbers, and in a blaze of light, his hands in their gloves burst into flame. "All right," he said. "It's time."

Drops of liquid fire dripped from his wrists onto the ancient farmhouse floor.

Eva turned and ran.

On and on, faster and faster, up the stairs, leaping, jumping, taking them two and three at a time, the thick red runner cushioning her footfalls, the moaning of the stairs following just behind. Eva looked back at blazing Mr. Magister, and her vision swam.

The narrow rustic hall; the broad marble entryway; the screen door; the turnstile.

The farmhouse and the Pavilion were bleeding into each other, both and neither at once.

Eva retched, her stomach heaving, and behind her, she heard Mr. Magister laugh. Up above, set into the shabby farmhouse wall, was a shining stained-glass window depicting a faceless Magician, and even there his hands were on fire, gemlike flames leaping from his gloves. Eva raced up in the direction of the window; the glass was beginning to melt, and at the top of the stairs, she spun around the banister, then pelted as hard as she could down the hall. She turned into Henry's room, but there was Mr. Magister waiting, the flame of the candle co-opted, the finger of his fire, and he reached out, and Eva spun again and fled, heat on her neck, vaulting over the banister, rolling, falling, tumbling back down the stairs onto the marble floor, and there was a seal of granite in the figure of a bonfire, and now its cold stone flames began to lift and leap from the ground, suddenly spitting, searing hot, and Eva slipped and slid away, into the library, and the scream of a bird pierced her ears like a needle, and there he was, the eagle, diving, striking, barreling into her like a cannonball, knocking her off her feet, beak and talons tearing into her, and she screamed, wrestling and ripping the bird of prey from her body, hurling it with all her strength across the room, where it crashed into the hearth with a cry of pain and came out flaming, its varnished feathers carrying the blaze, flapping out, spreading to the heavy curtains, and Eva turned and ran, out into the farmhouse dining room, out, out, and the library was burning, and she slammed into the great heavy table, spilling it, upsetting it, falling atop it, and it all came tumbling down into the cramped little hall, the banquet of peaches, the feast that had been laid atop the other table, and every dish and fruit and everything scattered on the floor, no flesh, no food, but a flood of wrinkled peach pits, thousands of them, thousands, and Eva slipped and fell, and her fingers opened.

Her pit, too, was lost amongst the flood upon the floor.

She could not see which one it was.

Eva screamed and she cried, and Mr. Magister came in from the hall, his hands so hot, and she had to go, had to leave it, run, and she dashed, bashed through door after door and room after room, Meg's glassy green conservatory, Cato's dusty machine shop, Iphigénie's chittering loom room, on and on, away, until she managed to circle back again to the hall, the front hall, the oak trees creaking and moaning, and she ran, slipping, sliding, headlong out through the snapping jaw of the screen door, out onto the broad porch, and the lions, the lions, one of them seemed dead, lolling empty-eyed and still upon the stairs, and the other triumphant, rattling green jaws tearing at the corpse of the first, and it raised its head and roared, roared like the rusty revving of every engine in the world, and she turned and fled inside, back inside through the smooth spinning turnstile, and there he was, in the granite bonfire, laughing and laughing, and she ran, deep into the walls themselves, deeper and deeper into a dark oak forest that shouldn't have been there.

A great gust of breath-hot wind tore through the scorched branches above.

Where was she?

Now a fiery light flared behind her, and more laughter, loud and strong and angry, and Eva kept running, but the hot wind stirred the dead leaves, and the forest began to spin, spin, spinning around and around.

The world swirled and she tripped and fell.

Everything spun.

Eva's stomach churned and rebelled. She retched again, and looking up, she saw where she was:

Inside the monumental Manufactures and Liberal Arts Building.

Everything was suddenly still and silent.

But the Fair seemed to have closed—all the wondrous displays and exhibits had been shut up and disassembled; crates and carts were everywhere, poised for the return of the morning workmen.

There could scarcely have been a better place to hide.

Eva plunged in, dodging deeper and deeper into the detritus. She had just climbed into a display case in the New South Wales section when the weighty silence was pierced.

Someone was whistling:

Ta-ra-ra boom-dee-ayy, ta-ra-ra boom-dee-ayyy . . .

And with a great rush, as if every throat in Chicago had gasped at once, the upper walkway that spanned the enormous building sprouted flames all along its edges. Fright burgeoned in Eva's chest, her hands beginning to quiver and twitch, but she kept as quiet as she could.

"Eva . . . ," sang Mr. Magister. "Eva . . ." She could hear his hard-soled shoes clacking upon the catwalk high above. "You've had a fine time of it, but your debt has come due. It's time to pay up. Be a good girl, now. Come on out."

Flames began to arc down onto the exhibit floor, and almost immediately, they caught—packing material, loose paper, crates and carts and shelving. Eva craned her neck to look, and with horror, she saw that the burning catwalk had ignited the roof of the building. Clods of molten metal had begun to fall, and new pockets of fire broke out wherever they landed.

Mr. Magister's voice seemed to echo from everywhere at once.

"Come, come, Eva," he said. "Do something useful for once. Show yourself."

She sat back as far as she could into the dark corner of her display case.

"Do you really think I won't find you? We're wired together, Eva—all of us."

Eva's heart sank.

The ring—a ring of copper and light.

We are the Machine.

Aspects of a system, organs of a body, components of a circuit.

"What is it they say? You can run but you can't hide?"

The fire was approaching fast—Eva had to move, but as soon as she stepped out into the aisle, there he was, emerging from flames not fifty feet distant, a chuckle in his cheek.

"Oops," he said with a toothy grin. "Found you."

She turned, running, running, dodging for cover in the Ceylonese and East Indian sections, but now the fire was everywhere and spreading fast, and wherever it was, there, too, was Mr. Magister, stepping out, spitting flame, mocking and taunting on every side, and she spun and tripped and scrambled at random, on and on and on amongst the burning parasols and toys, the molten silverware, the flaming silks and yarns, on, on, anywhere but into his hot hands, through raging showcases of glowing iron, past pillars and gates and arches and minarets that creaked and moaned with the pain of dissolution, until finally, somewhere deep in the American section, she saw a large strongbox standing open and she dove inside and swung the heavy door inward.

It was almost pitch-dark in the safe—only a wedge of jumping light stole in through the cracked door. Eva panted here in the close, hot air, panted and keened, and tried not to lose control.

Mr. Magister was near, but he seemed not to have seen where she'd landed; his footsteps circled around and around, and he called out again.

"Eva . . . ," he sang. "Eva . . ."

Her left palm was throbbing with pain. She was afraid that it must've been burned further in the mad dash through the growing inferno, and so Eva raised it up to examine it in the paltry light.

But she found that none was needed—the burn itself was glowing.

Eva lifted her hand nearer to her face, and sure

enough, wrapped around the exposed white knuckle of her first finger was a glowing wire filament—the ring that Mr. Magister had given her. It seemed to have spread, grown inside of her, twining like ivy around the neighboring bones of her hand.

How far had it gotten? How deep inside?

Eva shivered in the sweltering darkness. She wished she could grab it, pull it out, out, all the way, but even brushing against the burn left her in screaming pain.

Suddenly, she froze: crunching footsteps just beside the safe.

"Come, come, Eva," called Mr. Magister. "You've had your fun. Let me have what's mine, and your suffering will be over."

The will flared up in Eva's chest.

She did not want to be over.

"Eva . . ."

Now she saw his scrupulously pressed pant leg passing just before the cracked door of the safe, bare inches away, and she stoppered up her breath.

This was her chance.

With a heave, Eva shoved her full weight against the door of the safe, knocking Mr. Magister to the ground, and she jumped out, leaping toward the door at the end of the aisle, there, yes, she could make it, but now Mr. Magister was climbing to his feet, bellowing fire and fury at her, and she might just have made it if it hadn't been for the dress.

Far behind, the fingers of Mr. Magister's gloves closed tight.

All of a sudden, the spotless white dress was as immobile as cold marble—a prison, a cell.

Eva stumbled and fell flat, captured midstride, and she landed full force upon her left hand and cried out.

Mr. Magister chuckled.

"I had hoped," he said, "that you would cooperate. But I see now that you never deserved the honor of sacrifice."

Eva was Impossibly hot.

"If I had to choose again," he said, "I would find someone better to burn. I would leave you alone— without friends, without a home, without my Magic. I would've let you die in the gutter."

Mr. Magister flipped Eva onto her back with the toe of his shoe. The glowing wire wrapped around her bones had frayed in her fall, and sparks began to spit from her palm.

"Goodbye, Little Eva Root," said Mr. Magister, and the fingers of his flaming gloves squeezed above her in the empty air.

The white dress began to crumple, scorching and searing her; Eva could feel her skin beginning to bubble and burn, and she screamed, flaring flame pouring from the open wound in her left hand.

If it had been even a moment longer, Eva Root would've ended there on the floor.

But with a *bang*, Mr. Magister staggered back. The grip of her dress relaxed, the burning fire receding.

Five more now, in rapid succession: *bang-bang-bang-bang-bang!*

Mr. Magister was moaning on the ground, and before she knew what was happening, Eva was up on her feet.

There, far off, within the flicker of the fire, was a boy holding a smoking revolver. She could not distinguish his face, but on his nose he wore a pair of spectacles, the firelight gleaming strangely across all the facets of their shattered lenses.

Eva put her right hand into her pocket. It was empty— the spectacles weren't there.

Not three feet away, Mr. Magister twitched, groaned, rolled over.

Eva flew down the aisle toward the exit, bashing through the door, and just as it slammed shut behind her, it shook rhythmically with a hail of Mr. Magister's regurgitated bullets.

She was out.

She was out, but still, Mr. Magister was coming.

The sound of Eva's feet below her drumming against the frosty grass rose to Eva's ears as if from a distance.

Behind her, the largest structure ever raised had become a monumental inferno, the whipping wind flinging embers from its roof to consume the neighboring buildings.

The fairgrounds were still. Snow was falling, and it was terribly cold.

It had been September when last she left. How much time had passed since then?

The sky was glowing darkly, and the lurking lake seemed to toy with the reflected flames. Eva ran, ran, across bridges, beyond the sharp-cornered shoulders of building after building.

Where could she go? Mr. Magister's power was greatest on the fairgrounds, but he certainly was not limited to its bounds.

And like the flaring of a match, her mind filled with illumination. What had Henry said so long, long ago?

Of all the buildings on the fairgrounds, only one was built of real brick and stone.

Only one was fire resistant.

The Palace of Fine Arts, too, was in the process of being packed, its wide galleries strewn with dismounted paintings and crated statuary, and its hulking silence wrapped around Eva like still water.

Slowly, she wandered down the long nave of the building toward the rotunda.

Had it been Henry? Had he fired the revolver?

How?

And again, a memory stabbed through the thick blanket of obscurity that Mr. Magister had draped around his Pavilion:

The three of them, Mr. Magister and Henry and she, all sitting at dinner together.

The longer you practice the Impossible Art, Mr. Magister had said, *the more you may begin to suspect that our effects might well* precede *our causes, or, indeed, follow them long after they have passed out of memory.*

She had sat in his room in the farmhouse, and she had blown out the candle. *Come back, Henry,* she had said. *Please come back.*

If he had, Eva wished he'd lingered. She needed more help; she couldn't possibly escape Mr. Magister alone.

And the more she thought of it, the less likely it seemed that she could ever escape Mr. Magister. They were wired together, after all, she and Mr. Magister and Henry and the rest of the burnt apprentices. Aspects of a system, organs of a body, components of a circuit.

No wonder they had appeared to her—Cato and Meg.

She wished she could talk to them—all of them—just talk for a while, to hear what they knew and decide what to do.

And it was at precisely this moment that Eva passed a small sketch in a plain frame hanging on the gallery wall: a self-portrait of a young Italian artist peering around his easel.

It was not Henry, of course, but she could see the resemblance; his fingers were stained with charcoal.

"Better than nothing," she murmured. It took quite a bit of strength even to bend the fingers of her hurt left hand, but presently, she managed, and the sketch came away from the wall.

Unsure of where to put it, she carried it to the rotunda at the center of the palace. There she laid it on the floor.

In a nearby gallery, she found a large Swiss cuckoo clock that made her think of Cato—the gears in his machine shop, the great clockwork night. With the help of a packing trolley, she wheeled it back to the rotunda as well.

There—now she had Henry and Cato. Next, she turned her thoughts to Meg. Eva had thought of her in the farmhouse barn, imagined her responsible for the arrangement of the plants, and Meg had appeared to her just before she'd discovered the farmhouse's copper roots.

Greenery, then.

This was a good starting place; there were many artful landscapes and even a number of promising agricultural scenes on the walls, but none of the people in them felt even remotely like Meg.

It was in the Japanese gallery that Eva finally found her: a carving in wood of leaves and flowers and branches, so delicate and thin that she thought it might break the moment she laid hands on it.

There was a painting in the Austrian section depicting a grizzled old workman, flushed with effort and resting against a low stone wall. Though she had only ever met him briefly, Eva couldn't help but think of Vaclav when she looked at the fellow's unruly hair, and this painting, too, joined the emerging circle in the rotunda.

Iphigénie proved the hardest of them all to find. Even now, Eva was wearing the dress the girl had made, but still, she wasn't quite sure what to look for.

She was just about to turn back to the rotunda when, out of the corner of her eye, Eva saw a statuette in spotless white marble: a little fawn.

The label on its plinth read IPHIGENIA AT AULIS.

"Hello, old friend," Eva whispered.

By the time she'd completed the arrangement—the five artworks fixed in a wide circle, perfectly still in the darkness—Eva was exhausted, and she sat down heavily in the midst of them.

Time seemed to slow.

There they were, representations of Henry and Vaclav, Cato and Meg and Iphigénie.

She gave a shallow sigh. She couldn't flee, and she couldn't see how she could fight—her power was derived from Mr. Magister, and he was so very much stronger than she.

What was left, then? Surrender?

All around her, the others sat silent.

"Help," she said softly. "Come back and help me."

For a moment, the silence grew thicker, heavier, and Eva leaned forward expectantly, straining to hear.

The wire in her hand gave a sudden ragged buzz, and Eva jumped to her feet, shaking out the shock in quiet frustration.

She almost thought the answer might've been spoken aloud. But no. That was not how the dead communicated—not ever in her long experience.

And so, slowly, Eva walked around the broad circle, focusing, paying close attention to each one of them in their turn.

How can you help me?

What do you have left to say?

Vaclav was first. There sat the old workman with the unruly hair, leaning back against his low stone wall.

He was exhausted, cheeks flushed apple red behind his scruffy beard.

Eva could sympathize.

The workman's hands were filthy, his boots dusty and gray, and for the first time, Eva thought to wonder: Was he building the wall behind him, or knocking it down?

She leaned in to look closer, but what she saw only deepened the mystery: a heap of stone in the corner of the composition. Waiting to join the wall? Or just having come down from it?

And how different were they, really? Either way, he was building and dismantling—a wall and a cairn of stone.

Alternating current: *Solve et coagula.*

Eva couldn't see how she could overcome Mr. Magister by fighting him. What was the inverse, then? Could she somehow weaken him by cooperating?

The grizzled workman in the painting looked her straight in the eye, as if daring her to understand.

The next station in the circle was Iphigénie—the little marble fawn. There was something in its form, in the carving of its coiled muscles, that felt terribly real, as if it might jump down and flee at any moment. Eva's dress rustled lightly as she knelt, and for the first time, it occurred to her that the statuette was precisely the same shade of white.

Yes—two of a kind, Iphigénie and Eva. She wondered if they would've gotten along.

Eva reached out to give the fawn a gentle stroke and jumped back in shock. Her fingers had met not cold marble but warm flesh.

She blinked at the still statuette. Did it—somehow—live?

There was a tickling at her wrist; Eva seemed to have snagged her left cuff on the point of one of the fawn's ears, and now a loose white thread had been drawn out of the weave.

But how could that be? The dress had no seams and no closures—the weave was perfect, complete.

And yet, there it was.

Eva tugged at the thread gently, but it didn't move.

Now Eva's feet carried her around the edge of the fivefold circle toward Meg, and before her watching eyes, the loose thread in her cuff began to grow, sprouting tiny buds and leaves of white as it climbed up her wrist.

Only as the thread approached the open wound in Eva's palm did trepidation touch her heart, but too late—like a striking snake, the head of the growing thread dove into Eva's hand and began to wriggle into the fraying wire twined around her bones.

Eva winced and stumbled back, her heels clattering against the crates behind her.

The thread slowed and stilled; Eva peered into her hand and saw that the string was spliced, grafted like a root into the coiled, sputtering filament.

Someone—Iphigénie? Meg? all of them together?—had wired the dress *into her*.

And something she'd read in the Electricity Building lit up her memory:

More wire, more resistance.

Perhaps she was not as alone as she'd thought. Perhaps she could carry them all with her—together against Mr. Magister. And even if she was not strong enough to defeat him alone, perhaps together they might outlast him.

But it was so quick. She needed time, time to rest, to recover, to prepare. The graft in her hand didn't seem secure, and if she tugged on the string lightly, it threatened to unravel.

She just needed a little time.

And at the circuit's next station, it was given to her.

It began slowly at first, almost imperceptibly: the dial of Cato's clock stuttered and began to tick. Before long, its arms were spinning swiftly, like dancers in a round, on and on. The blossoms in Meg's carving wilted, fell, and bloomed again. Eva became dimly aware that things were shifting in the rotunda around her.

By the time the clock ticked to a stop, everything had changed.

Eva yawned and stretched. All the crates and carts around her had disappeared. Only the circuit of five dead Magicians remained.

Eva looked down at her hand and saw that the burn had healed, closing up entirely around the white thread from her cuff. When she pulled at it, she felt a strange tugging at the knucklebone within.

It was firmly rooted.

Outside the window, the sky was twilit. Eva felt odd; she didn't yet know it, but she had blinked and napped for half of the year.

What she did know was this: it was time.

Slowly, Eva turned to each of them in the circle. Henry was the last, the little self-portrait sitting alone and small on the floor.

Without him, she never would've known to come to the Palace of Fine Arts; without him, she would've burned beneath Mr. Magister in Manufactures and Liberal Arts.

Eva shut her eyes. "Thank you," she whispered.

When she opened them again, the self-portrait, the cuckoo clock, the painting, the carvings of marble and wood were all gone.

She was alone.

And she was ready.

The air outside was warm and fragrant, and the aroma of moist earth rose to Eva's nose. There was still a bit of fading sunlight in the sky.

She stopped and stood at the bottom of the stairs. The Palace of Fine Arts was behind her, whatever protection it had offered relinquished.

Would he come now?

Would it happen there?

But Eva wasn't content to wait.

She chose the lakeshore path, the waning summer light giving a last crystalline glitter to the rise and fall of the waves. The Fair was long closed now, and the buildings and structures showed their age like flimsy stage sets left to decay. Paint peeled; edges frayed. When the wind moved, Eva heard the clanking of cans and bottles, and newspapers skittered across the muddy ground like tumbleweed.

She passed the landing where, alongside the pier, the great battleship *Illinois* had been moored, complete with turrets, lifeboats, and main and secondary guns.

But she could see now that it was false: just a mock-up, a disguised jetty built on wooden pilings in the lake bed. Brick and cement peeked out at the waterline, where the lake had lapped away at the illusion.

It was not long until Eva's feet led her down to the massive Manufactures and Liberal Arts Building, which she had last seen under a cloud of consuming flame. Like many of its neighbors, it was badly damaged, scorched and burned, its walls and roofing eaten away, but it seemed that the worst had been averted: it still stood.

Only one edifice had been completely lost in her last meeting with Mr. Magister: the grand Peristyle, burned to the ground. All that remained of it was a vast field of gray rubble between the fairgrounds and the lake.

YE SHALL KNOW THE TRUTH, the arch had proclaimed, AND THE TRUTH SHALL MAKE YOU FREE.

The Magic Circle of the fairgrounds had been broken.

Across the burnt bog before her, the great gilded Statue of the Republic stood steadfast, gazing westward across the Grand Basin, and suddenly she was sure:

The Pavilion, so to speak, of Arrivals and Departures— it was there that the jaws of the serpent met its tail.

It was there that she would find him.

The Terminal Station.

It was dim inside, dank and smelly—nothing like the

bright locus of activity it had once been. The destitute had camped out here, nests of newspaper and cardboard crammed into corners, and under almost any other circumstance, Eva might've turned back quickly into the gathering night.

But there was no turning back now.

A mist like the memory of engine steam gathered near to the edge of the long train platforms.

Taking a deep breath, Eva strode in. "All right," she said. "I'm here."

The fog seemed to thicken around her, and the turnstiles whirred like the jaws of a trap.

"Eli?" she called out. "Jack?"

And from the far side of the fog, she heard the slow clacking of his heels.

"I believe you mean *Solway et Coagulo*," he said, snapping his watchcase shut. He was dressed for travel, as waxy and perfect as ever, except that six scorched bullet holes pocked the crisp linen of his shirt. "It speaks very highly of you, Eva, that you have chosen to return your power to the Machine willingly."

Eva shrugged. "We are who we are."

"I am afraid so," said Mr. Magister, and stepping back, he gestured to the slowly revolving turnstiles. "Shall we begin?"

13

E Pluribus Unum

The streets beyond the turnstiles were tidy and even, the houses of uniform red brick. Everything was in scrupulous order. Mr. Magister led Eva past a large building studded with awnings and porches where a painted sign read HOTEL FLORENCE.

"Is this Pullman?" she asked.

"I suppose," said Mr. Magister. "Incidentally."

Eva shook her head. "How can a place be incidentally somewhere?"

"Oh, it can't," said Mr. Magister. "But this place only looks like Pullman. That is how I prefer it to look."

"Then where are we, truly?"

Mr. Magister turned, scrutinizing Eva in the glare of the gas lamps. "Curious to the end, eh?"

Eva shrugged. "I want to understand."

"Would it surprise you, then, to learn that this, too, is the Pavilion of Magic? Insofar as there is such a thing. What I have called the Pavilion of Magic is, in essence, the internal temple: the sanctuary that every Magician must carve out of himself in order to manifest his operations. This is one of its more comfortable skins."

"Then was there ever really a Pavilion?"

"Why, of course there was. There still is, I imagine—just don't go looking for it on any map."

"It hardly seems fair," said Eva, "for things that aren't real to be of such terrible significance."

"Eva," said Mr. Magister. "In my experience, things that aren't real are the only things of any importance at all."

Presently, he turned aside at the front walk of one of the little brick houses. As far as Eva could see, they were all completely identical, each standing straight beneath its little gabled cap. "How can you tell them apart?"

Mr. Magister waggled his hands. "You might as well ask how I know the difference between my own fingers."

He climbed the front steps; Eva stayed on the sidewalk.

"Is that the end?" said Eva, nodding at the house. "In there?"

"That is my altar—yes."

It seemed like an ordinary brick house, just like all the rest.

Eva took a deep breath and let it out gently. "Then this is it."

Mr. Magister nodded.

Slowly, Eva climbed the steps. Mr. Magister turned toward the door.

"But wait," she said. "Before we go in: answer me one more question."

"Perhaps," said Mr. Magister.

"I want to know the reason. I want to know why."

Mr. Magister gave a sigh. "Yes," he said. "Yes."

He turned, paced to the edge of the porch, and sat down upon the top step.

"For purposes of my own, Eva, I spent quite some time gathering up the Great Fire of Chicago; I lost something within it that I hoped in vain to recover. In truth, I should have conceded the loss long before I did—as you have learned, death is rather an impenetrable barrier. But in any event, over the course of my search, I found myself swallowing the Great Fire many times over. And such a power, once admitted, is very difficult to evict.

"It took every ounce of my concentrated effort to keep the fire from consuming me. I could feel its potency, more than I could comprehend, within me all the time. And I couldn't stand not to have the use of it."

"The use of it?" said Eva. "For what?"

Mr. Magister frowned. "What is Mr. Rockefeller's

oil used for, or Mr. Carnegie's steel? The Vanderbilt railroads? The Morgan accounts? For power. For control.

"And that is what my Machine was meant to accomplish: the filtering of the raw power of the fire through the greatest force I have ever known—the glory and majesty of the Fair—in order to bring it back to me clean and cool and under control.

"That, at least, was the aim. But operations as complex and intricate as this one . . . these things are rarely simple. The power that has come back to me is not *cleansed* so much as *aged*: at least as strong as it was before, and no longer as sharp, but not *clean* by any means. And troublingly, it has brought certain things along with it—certain memories, and . . . and . . ."

Here Mr. Magister trailed off, floating for many breaths in the thought behind his eyes.

"And what?" said Eva finally.

But Mr. Magister smiled. "No," he said. "No, I am afraid that must be enough. Come." And he rose and turned toward the door.

There were many things that Eva didn't quite understand that night, and this was one of them: She could feel her will within her, awake and awaiting, buzzing with anticipation. But whether it was her desire to know or Mr. Magister's memory that brought the lady back, Eva could not say.

Mr. Magister pushed through the front door of the brick house. Eva followed him. Inside, there was no crucible, no scorched and fiery basement; inside, there was music.

Mr. Magister chuckled to himself. It was not a happy sound. "Clever," he said. "Very clever," and he took off his hat.

A woman in an ordinary white dress sat playing at an upright piano against the far wall. The window beside her was open, and despite the hour, Eva saw twinkling sunlight outside.

A gentle breath of breeze lifted the gauzy white curtain.

"Who is that?" said Eva.

"That is Kate," said Mr. Magister. "That Is The Reason. That was my wife."

Kate was not an expert pianist; she played slowly, deliberately, and the music meandered from chord to chord like a clear stream flowing across low, flat rocks. By and by, her hymn came to an end, and Kate lifted her fingers from the sun-splashed keys to fold them in her lap.

"Katie?" said Mr. Magister softly.

She did not turn.

And all of a sudden, Eva was filled with a feeling of strange familiarity. At the piano sat a dead woman, and behind her stood her husband, silent and grieving.

This was what Eva had done all her life.

This was a séance.

Eva took a step forward. "Would you like to speak with her?"

Mr. Magister cleared his throat. "If you could," he said, "please tell her to go."

Eva frowned in surprise. Never in her long experience had she been asked to simply dismiss a departed loved one. "Really?"

Mr. Magister nodded. "I can't have her seeing what's about to happen."

"Are you sure?" said Eva. "I don't mind."

Mr. Magister gave a little laugh, sad and fond and soft. "That is very kind of you, Eva. But, yes, I am sure."

"Is there anything you'd like to say before she leaves?"

"Tell her . . . ," he said, and Eva waited and waited until he shook his head. "No."

Eva went to the woman on the piano bench, laid a hand on her cold shoulder, and murmured, "He'd like you to go."

The woman rose and turned to face Mr. Magister, and as her eyes fell upon him, Eva was filled with sudden sorrow: a furious, squeezing regret so strong she could barely breathe.

"I think," Eva gasped, "I think she wants me to say that she's sorry."

"I know," said Mr. Magister.

But this was wrong—she could feel it in the heels of her hands, in her fingers, as if Kate wanted to reach out and wipe the mistake from the air.

"No," she said. "No, not to you. She was apologizing to me."

Mr. Magister's eyebrows fell. "To you? For what?"

Of this answer, Eva had no doubt. "For you."

Mr. Magister looked as if he had been slapped across the face. Kate strode past him, pulled the door open, and disappeared into the night.

"Kate," said Mr. Magister. "Katie, wait!"

Eva could see his will rising.

"Come back," he called. "Come back!"

But she did not.

For a long while, he stood by the open door, until, finally: "No," said Mr. Magister. "Let it be finished."

He turned and held out his right hand to Eva.

It began—as everything does—with a spark: a cracking electrical shock that flew between them. Eva flinched, but did not pull away.

Mr. Magister's cheeks were rosy red. Sweat beaded on his brow, and his extended hand trembled in the air.

Eva reached out and grasped it. His palm was far wider than her own, but still she held it firmly.

He was hot in her hand.

The sensation flowed steadily through Eva's fingers into her wrist, like warm water at first—almost pleasant. Mr. Magister was watching. His expression was disquieting: joy and anticipation, fear and hunger, anger and self-loathing. She wanted to avert her eyes, but Eva did not look away.

Then the fire spilled into her chest, and everything changed.

Eva was hot—so Impossibly hot.

Her heart began to pound, spreading the searing flame through every organ in her body. She could not possibly stay still, she needed to move, to run, to claw the heat out of her skin, but she could not: she had to hold firm.

A roaring filled her ears, her vision blurring with tears. Surely, she thought, surely, this had to be the limit—this was as much as she could take.

The saliva in her mouth began to steam.

She wanted to leap upon him, to batter him down and tear him with teeth. She hated him, could not possibly imagine who she was without him, and still the feeling grew, more and more, hotter and hotter, and her hands were shaking wildly, vibrating, sweat pouring down her neck. Eva opened her mouth to scream, but she found with surprise that she was speaking another language.

French.

She didn't know French.

Little by little, thread by thread, fuse- and filament-like, a bright glow was creeping into the weave of her dress.

Iphigénie had come back, and her words flew from Eva in a wild torrent. *"Crisse de câlisse de tabarnak d'osti de sacrament de trou viarge!"* Jack Coagulo stared at her, blown back by the explosive force of her fury. Her gown was shining so bright now that Eva could scarcely see the man beyond the glare. Eva pushed her voice to the very limit of its extremity; it began to splatter and break, and then, out of the corner of her eye, she saw it.

There's an odd thing as happens when the air gets real hot: narrow little cyclones kick up, and they draw the flame into the sky all thin, like a lightning storm in reverse. Fire devils, *they call 'em.*

There, in the corner: a growing pillar of flame.

Eva's dress flickered and seemed to go out, but as if in answer, the fiery pillar flared into full-fledged life like a lightbulb switched on in the dark.

Mr. Magister stumbled backward, and if Eva hadn't redoubled her grip, she might've lost hold of him.

Now the dress charged itself again, the electric energy traveling quickly down the thread grafted onto Eva's bones. The bricks of the house flew out of the wall, crashing and cracking all around them, the structure violently unbuilding itself.

Vaclav had come back, too.

Now Eva began to understand. As her dress reached the peak of its brightness, she felt her heart lifted by the appearance of a second pillar of flame at the edge of the room. The flood of angry French still flew from her mouth, and she poured all of her strength into the words.

"I—I—I . . . ," stammered Mr. Magister. "I do not understand."

The dress cycled, dimming down and beginning to glow once more. Now markings appeared on the floor, scrawling themselves out around their feet in charcoal: arcane glyphs and electrical symbols interwoven in a thick, thorny ouroboros that strengthened Eva and bound Mr. Magister in place.

Henry was there.

Eva's heart swelled; she took a step forward.

Before her, Elijah Solway's eyes swam with confusion and fear. He had miscalculated, misunderstood.

There were three pillars of fire surrounding them now, and Eva's dress was charging once more. Vaclav's furious demolition continued all around them, and as the brick walls fell away, it was not placid, orderly Pullman that they saw but rather the dilapidated Terminal Station on the fairgrounds, burning rapidly in angry flame. The roof above them had caved in, and the stars twinkled high in the sky like silvery pinpricks.

But they did not remain in the sky.

Cato had arrived.

Great orbs of flame began to crash all around them like molten cannonballs, tearing through the firmament, sending smithereens of Impossible glass glittering down like diamonds. It was a terrible cacophony now, the demolition, the falling clockwork stars, the screaming vitriol, and throughout it all, rubble on the floor flew aside to make room for more staves and runes and charcoal wards.

"No," said Solway. "No, I was wrong. This is wrong. Please."

But the pillars of fire numbered four now; her bright vestments were gathering light one final time, and as Solway tried to break away, twining green tendrils crept out of Eva's right-hand cuff, digging into his glove and skin, anchoring Solway to her:

Meg.

The light of the dress grew stronger and stronger, brighter and brighter. The little pressure gauge in Solway's waistcoat gave a glassy crack, and by the time the fifth pillar of fire was aflame, Eva felt invincible.

She was Potentate and She was Power: Mistress of the Machine, of the Fair, of the Country, of the World.

Things would be as She would make them.

Was this why he had done it? Was this what Mr. Magister had felt when he'd burned them all? Back when there had still been such a thing as Mr. Magister? Because there certainly was no longer: now there was only frantic little Eli Solway, down on his knees, begging softly.

"Please," he said. "Please. Just take it. Take it all—but let me go."

Eva's vestments thrummed gently with brilliant light. He seemed pathetic now—little and broken, the wax dripping from his mustache—and for a moment, she wondered what good it would do to snuff him out. But there was balance to be considered: the many murdered who called out within Her for justice.

And besides—Eva didn't want this sort of power.

"I'm sorry for you," she said. "Terribly sorry." The piano, bashed and burned and broken, began to play Kate's hymn. "But We are wired together. And We are who We are."

Solway's voice was soft and tremulous. "You gonna remember me?"

Eva nodded. "I'm afraid I must."

Solway sighed and shut his eyes.

There is no fire that burns forever. There is always

before, and there is always after, which is the same thing: the fuel and the fire, the flicker and the stillness.

Eva took a deeper breath than she had ever known, and it drew her down into Her True Pavilion. There she saw herself no longer surrounded by a Magic circuit of fiery pillars, no longer in Pullman or the flaming Terminal Station. There she was sitting at a séance before a vast and varied audience:

The dead. All of them.

In front of her, on his knees, sat a little burning candle of a man.

The hymn on the piano ended.

Eva pressed her eyes shut, leaned forward, and blew.

The candle guttered and died.

Darkness.

The smell of a blown-out candle is unmistakable— cooling wax, a trickle of feathery smoke—and on the morning of July 6, 1894, every single sleeper in Chicago woke with this aroma in their nose.

For those who remembered the smell long enough to investigate, the explanation was simple enough: overnight, the World's Columbian Exposition fairgrounds in Jackson Park had finally burned away. All the papers had the story, and though it was generally deplored as a waste of good architecture, it was not considered a very great tragedy. The public was now used to these fires—the Cold Storage disaster during the run of the Fair, the passing of the Peristyle last winter.

Besides—there was a group of well-to-do gentlemen interested in establishing a yacht club on the site. Perhaps it might come to some good in the end.

By lunchtime, the memory of the aroma had vanished from the city like a plume of smoke blown away on the wind.

And that, as they say, was that.

Time passes differently on trains. And that was just what Eva wanted: for things to be different.

And so she took to the rails—out of Chicago, on and away, switching directions at the drop of a hat in stations and depots all across the country. Before shelter or even food, she found herself wanting a new dress to put on; the one she wore was falling apart, brittle, ashy black, and there was a loose thread flopping from its left cuff that she couldn't bring herself to pull out.

She finally stopped, then, some days after setting out, in a little town deep in Pennsylvania to find work:

cleaning, cooking, whatever was offered, she didn't care. She did what was asked—quietly, efficiently, by the mundane strength of her hands, and afterward, in a hotel restaurant, she ate, slowly, deliberately—she'd almost forgotten how. That night, she took a bath before putting on her new dress, a plain workaday garment of no color and indifferent cut. She sat still in the tub staring at her toes until the water was cold.

She thought she might want to cry but never quite managed it.

The next day she traveled on.

And this became her way: on the move as much as possible, stopping when she needed money for food, or a bath, or a night off the rails. She gave no name, stayed silent, did her work, moved on.

At a certain point, she began to visit local newspaper offices, asking for stories of the Fair—just to be sure, just to know that it had truly been.

It was in this way that she learned the particulars of the fire that had taken the Peristyle the previous January. A short paragraph in the *Ann Arbor Argosy* cataloged the casualties suffered in combating the blaze. Police detective Charlton Webster, it seemed, had rushed to the scene in order to help and had died of his burns before he could reach the hospital.

Even Webster.

She thought of the Overstreets then—of Aunt Isabella and Uncle Jefferson—and she felt suddenly embarrassed ever to have called them that. They'd been kind hosts to her, very kind, but that was all. She wished that she could thank them somehow—perhaps a telegram?—but even this seemed too much of a risk, like stirring up the settled ash at the edges of an unfinished fire, and with some disappointment in herself, Eva discovered that she could not bear to do it.

Slowly, she felt the doors of Chicago shutting firmly behind her.

She was horribly, horribly tired.

In one little town, after a hard day's work, she was given a piece of fruit to eat as part of her evening meal—a little peach. She was hungry, hardly in a position to put it by, and so, with some misgiving, she ate it.

It wasn't remarkable in any way—neither particularly good, nor particularly bad—but when it came time to dispose of her scraps, she kept the pit.

On she traveled, station to station, depot to depot, state to state. All the while, the pit rode in her pocket. Weeks wore away, and months.

With the coming of cooler weather, the pain in Eva's left hand grew. There were certain days when she could not close her fingers with any force, and her work became more difficult. She got less done, earned less money, lived less comfortably.

It occurred to her, of course, that she might bridge the gap with Magic, but she found that she preferred the cold these days—the boring and ordinary, painstaking and reliable.

Magic, she just didn't trust.

Trains, hotel rooms. Silent sweaty work. October's breeze grew sharp teeth in November. Eva bought a coat. She had not slept in a room with any flame—hearth fire, candle, even gas jet—since Chicago, but as the winter loomed, this became more and more challenging. It was only the more expensive establishments that had radiators and electric lights, and one night in such a hotel cost as much as two in the sort of place to which she was accustomed.

She bought a scarf and two pairs of warm gloves and wore them all to bed.

Then, on a bright morning in December, Eva arrived in the tiny mountain town of St. Elmo, Colorado. There were several others disembarking from the train with her that morning, and as the little knot of arrivals dispersed into the street, an old, unwashed woman began to panhandle her way through the crowd.

"Please," she said. "Please. I'm only trying to get

down to Denver. Anything you can spare? It's almost Christmas."

A coin or two tinkled into the old woman's cup, but Eva could smell the gin on her from half a block away, and wasn't surprised that she'd had so little success.

When the old woman caught up with her, though, Eva found herself very surprised indeed.

It was Mrs. Blodgett; Mrs. Blodgett who had taken her from Fletcher's Gulch; Mrs. Blodgett who had chosen Eva; Mrs. Blodgett who had laid all the foundations.

Recognition flickered in the old woman's gaze, and immediately Eva felt her will rising. It was quiet Magic, to be sure, but Magic nonetheless: a sort of icy sheen that let Mrs. Blodgett's eyes slide across Eva's face without catching.

It was a strange feeling—terrifying at first, as if she'd transgressed a sacred boundary—but slowly, Eva brimmed with relief.

She had let her Magic slip, and nothing had happened.

Everything was fine.

Life lumbered on.

"Please, miss," said Mrs. Blodgett. "Please, anything you can spare."

Eva put her hand into her pocket in search of change; her fingers brought back the little peach pit.

She shut her eyes and wrapped it in her hands.

Come back, she thought. *Come back.* And it was not just of the fruit that she thought.

Eva opened her eyelids and then her fingers. In her cupped hands, there was a plump, ripe peach.

Mrs. Blodgett's gaze grew wide. Eva handed her the fruit, and the woman took a great hungry bite.

"Oh," said Mrs. Blodgett, her eyes fixed on the fruit. "Oh."

And when she looked up again, the girl was gone. It was just like Magic.

Of Truth and Falsehood

The following are matters of historical record:

I. On the evening of Friday, March 31, in the year 1848, two sisters—Maggie and Kate Fox, ages 14 and 11, respectively, of Hydesville, New York—began to demonstrate their ability to communicate, via rhythmic knocking, with an unseen spirit known as Mr. Splitfoot. This ability soon became well known, touching off an international Spiritualist craze. The phenomenon rose even as high as the White House, where President Abraham Lincoln was warned by medium Charles Colchester to be wary for his safety mere weeks before his assassination in April 1865.

In October 1888, Maggie Fox appeared before an audience of two thousand at the New York Academy of Music to reveal that the rhythmic tapping that had been attributed to Mr. Split-foot, a name for the devil, forty years earlier had been nothing more than the cracking of her toe joints. Roughly one year later, she recanted this confession, but she was unable to recover her career, and she died in poverty shortly before the opening of the World's Columbian Exposition in 1893.

2. On Sunday, October 8, 1871, at around 9 p.m., a fire started in the barn behind what is now 558 West DeKoven Street in Chicago, Illinois. The flames spread quickly and consumed over two thousand acres of the city, killing hundreds and

destroying millions of dollars' worth of property. Even before the flames had died out, a rumor—that Catherine O'Leary's cow had kicked over a lantern and ignited the blaze—was circulating. In 1893, the journalist who had initially reported the rumor admitted that it was fabricated, and the notion is now widely regarded as anti-Irish, anti-immigrant scapegoating.

3. Monday, May 1, 1893, marked the opening of the fabulous World's Columbian Exposition in Jackson Park, Chicago. The massive fair drew over 27 million visitors during its six-month run, and it is considered to be the grandest such undertaking ever mounted. With the exception of one particular pavilion— the existence of which is disputed by those uninitiated in the Impossible Art—every exhibit referenced in the preceding pages is attested to have been at the fair.

4. On Monday, July 10, 1893, the Cold Storage Building at the Columbian Exposition burned. Several lives were lost.

5. On Tuesday, October 10, 1893, the Chicago Fire Cyclorama was removed from view without explanation.

6. On Monday, January 8, 1894, fire broke out again on the grounds of the Columbian Exposition, which had been closed and derelict since the end of October. The grand Peristyle and the Manufactures and Liberal Arts Building, among others, were consumed.

7. On Friday, July 6, 1894, the remaining exposition buildings and pavilions—with the exception of the Palace of Fine Arts— were utterly destroyed by flames.

Readers wishing to verify these facts are advised to consult the following publications: Erik Larson's *The Devil in the White*

City; Donald L. Miller's *City of the Century;* and guides to the fair, including Rand, McNally & Co.'s *A Week at the Fair, Illustrating the Exhibits and Wonders of the World's Columbian Exposition, with Special Descriptive Articles and the Condensed Official Catalogue of the World's Columbian Exposition: Interesting Exhibits and Where to Find Them.* Other facts may be verified by recourse to contemporaneous newspaper coverage, now widely available in digitized form.

In reference to the truth or falsehood of the claims in these pages regarding the individual known as Mr. Magister and his involvement in these events, the publisher wishes to make no comment.

Acknowledgments

There have been Savits in Chicago for over one hundred years (though they came in as Savitskys), and my thanks and honor are due to the forebears who anchored my connection to that city and brought me back there time and again.

Anyone who writes about the World's Columbian Exposition these days does so in the shadow of Erik Larson, and there is no question that the fair in my imagination would have been much poorer without the gift of *The Devil in the White City*. Similarly, Donald L. Miller's *City of the Century* lit my way back into Chicago's sooty history, and I am very grateful for both.

If you find yourself looking for a little taste of the era of the fair, there are morsels hidden around Chicago waiting to be found. It's much smaller, but the reproduction of the gilded colossus of *The Republic* in Jackson Park offers a glimmer of the original's splendor. What was the Palace of Fine Arts is now the Museum of Science and Industry. The Glessner House on Prairie Avenue and the Driehaus Museum on East Erie Street provide excellent opportunities for immersion in the fabulous domestic settings of the era, and the sitting room at the Chicago Athletic Association Hotel is the most convenient and comfortable setting for time travel I have yet encountered.

My thanks, as always, to Catherine Drayton, Claire Friedman, and the whole Inkwell team, to Erin Clarke, and to everyone at Knopf BFYR. Mildred Hankinson's masterly illustrations have much deepened the world of the story, and I am very grateful for her contributions.

It was during the writing of this book that my darling Amalia Ósk joined our family, and her bright eyes and sweet soul have made every day richer since then. Nothing in the world could make me prouder than I am to be father to her and her sister, Lilja Meital. I love you both.

The process of welcoming Amalia into our family would've been almost insuperably difficult if not for the generous help of Nat Bernstein, who is a constant and beloved support to us.

Finally, this book was conceived before the global COVID-19 pandemic, but executed almost entirely under its cloud. No work at all would've gotten done in my house without a lot of careful cooperation and coordination, almost all of which belongs to the credit of my wonderful wife, my indefatigable partner, the backboard of my ideas: Livia. It's absurd that I haven't gotten around to dedicating a book to you yet, but none of them has felt perfect enough. You are the string to my kite, the spark to my kindling.

Thank you, thank you, thank you.